Dan Wells has a Bachelors in English from Brigham Young University where he was the editor of *The Leading Edge* magazine. He now runs www.timewastersguide.com.

DAN WELLS

headline

First published in Great Britain in 2009 by
HEADLINE PUBLISHING GROUP

10



Cataloguing in Publication Data is available from the British Library

ISBN 978 0 7553 4881 7

Typeset in Goudy by Ellipsis Books Limited, Glasgow

Printed and bound in Great Britain by
CPI Group (UK) Ltd, Croydon, CR0 4YY



HEADLINE PUBLISHING GROUP
An Hachette UK Company
338 Euston Road
London NW1 3BH

www.headline.co.uk
www.hachettelivre.co.uk

For Rob,
who gave me the best incentive a little brother can give:
he got published first

*I should have been a pair of ragged claws*
*Scuttling across the floors of silent seas.*

*The Love Song of J. Alfred Prufrock*
T.S. Eliot

# CHAPTER 1

Mrs Anderson was dead.

Nothing flashy, just old age – she went to bed one night and never woke up. The news said it was a peaceful, dignified way to die, which I suppose is technically true, but the three days it took for someone to realize they hadn't seen her in a while removed most of the dignity from the situation. Her daughter eventually dropped by to check on her and found her corpse three days rotted and stinking like roadkill. And the worst part isn't the rotting, it's the three days – three whole days before anyone cared enough to say, 'Wait, where's that old lady who lives down by the canal?' There's not a lot of dignity in that.

But peaceful? Certainly. She died quietly in her sleep on 30 August, according to the Coroner, which means she died two days before the demon tore Jeb Jolley's insides out and left him in a puddle behind the laundromat. We didn't know it at the time, but that made Mrs Anderson the last person in Clayton County to die of natural causes for almost six months. The demon got the rest.

Well, most of them. All but one.

We got Mrs Anderson's body on Saturday, 2 September, after the Coroner was done with it. Well, I guess I should say that my mom and Aunt Margaret got the body, not me. They're the ones who run the mortuary; I'm only fifteen. I'd been in town most of the day, watching the police clean up the mess with Jeb, and came back just as the sun was beginning to go down. I slipped in the back just in case my mom was up front; I didn't really want to see her.

No one was in the back yet, just me and Mrs Anderson's corpse. It was lying perfectly still on the table, draped in cloth. It smelled like rotten meat and bug spray, and the lone ventilator fan buzzing loudly overhead wasn't doing much to help. I washed my hands quietly in the sink, wondering how long I had, and gently touched the body. Old skin was my favourite – dry and wrinkled, with a texture like antique paper. The Coroner hadn't done much to clean up the body, probably because they were busy with Jeb, but the smell told me that at least they'd thought to kill the bugs. After three days in end-of-summer heat, there had probably been a lot of them.

A woman swung open the door to the front end of the mortuary and came in, green as a surgeon in her scrubs and mask. I froze, thinking it was my mother, but the woman just glanced at me and walked to a counter.

'Hi, John,' she said, collecting some sterile rags. It wasn't my mom at all, it was her sister Margaret – they were twins, and when their faces were masked I could barely tell the difference. Margaret's voice was a little lighter though, a little more . . . energetic. I figured it was because she'd never been married.

'Hi, Margaret.' I took a step back.

'Ron's getting lazier,' she said, picking up a squirt bottle of Dis-Spray. 'He didn't even clean her, just declared Natural Causes and shipped her over. Mrs Anderson deserves better than this.' She turned to look at me. 'You just gonna stand there, or are you gonna help me?'

'Sorry.'

'Wash up.'

I rolled up my sleeves eagerly and went back to the sink.

'Honestly,' she went on, 'I don't even know what they do over there at the Coroner's office. It's not like they're busy. We can barely stay in business here.'

'Jeb Jolley died,' I said, drying my hands. 'They found him this morning behind the Wash-n-Dry.'

'The mechanic?' asked Margaret, her voice dropping lower. 'That's terrible. He's younger than I am. What happened?'

'Murdered,' I said, and pulled a mask and apron from the wall. The demon had gotten him, but I didn't know that at the time. I didn't even know there *was* a demon until almost three months later. Back in August – which feels like a lifetime ago – nobody in Clayton County had any idea of the horror that was coming. 'They thought maybe it was a wild dog,' I told Margaret, 'but his guts were kind of in a pile.'

'That's terrible,' Margaret said again.

'Well, you're the one worried about going out of business,' I said. 'Two bodies in one weekend is money in the bank.'

'Don't even joke like that, John,' she said, looking at me sternly. 'Death is a sad thing, even when it pays your mortgage. You ready?'

'Yes.'

'Hold her arm out.'

I grabbed the body's right arm and pulled it straight. Rigor mortis makes a body so stiff you can barely move it, but it only lasts about a day and a half; this one had been dead so long the muscles had all relaxed again. Though the skin was papery the flesh underneath was soft, like dough. Margaret sprayed the arm with disinfectant and began wiping it gently with a cloth.

Even when the Coroner does his job and cleans the body, we always wash it ourselves before we start. Embalming's a long process, with a lot of very precise work, and you need a clean slate to start with.

'It stinks pretty bad,' I said.

'She.'

'*She* stinks pretty bad,' I said, correcting myself. Mom and Margaret were adamant that we stay respectful to the deceased, but it seemed a little late at this stage. It wasn't a person any more, it was just a body. A thing.

'She does smell,' said Margaret. 'Poor woman. I wish someone had found her sooner.' She looked up at the ventilator fan turning slowly above us. 'Let's hope the motor doesn't burn out on us tonight.' Margaret said the same thing before every embalming, like a sacred chant. The fan continued creaking overhead.

'Leg,' she said. I moved down to the body's foot and

pulled the leg straight while Margaret sprayed it. 'Turn your head.' I kept my gloved hands on the foot and turned to stare at the wall while Margaret lifted up the sheet to wash the upper thighs. 'One good thing that came of this though,' she said, 'is that you can bet every widow in the county got a visit today, or is going to get one tomorrow. Everyone who hears about Mrs Anderson is going to go straight to their own mother, just to make sure. Other leg.'

I wanted to say something about how everyone who heard about Jeb would go straight to their auto-mechanic, but Margaret never appreciated jokes like that.

We moved around the body, arm to leg, leg to arm, arm to torso, torso to head, until the whole thing was scrubbed and disinfected. The room smelled like death and soap. Margaret tossed the rags in the laundry bin and started gathering the real embalming supplies.

I'd been helping Mom and Margaret at the mortuary since I was a little boy, back before Dad left. My first job had been cleaning up the chapel: picking up programmes, dumping out ash-trays, vacuuming the floor, and other odd jobs that a six year old could do unassisted. I got bigger jobs as I grew older, but I didn't get to help with the really cool stuff – embalming – until I was ten. Embalming was like . . . I don't know how to describe it. It was like playing with a giant doll, dressing it and bathing it and opening it up to see what was inside. I watched Mom once when I was eight, peeking in through the door to see what the big secret was. When I cut open my teddy bear the next week I don't think she made the connection.

Margaret handed me a wad of cotton wool, and I held it at the ready while she packed small tufts carefully under the body's eyelids. The eyes were beginning to recede, deflating as they lost moisture, and cotton wool helped keep the right shape for the viewing. It helped keep the eyelids closed as well, but Margaret always added a bit of cream just in case, sealing the moisture in and keeping the lid closed.

'Get me the needle gun, will you, John?' she asked, and I hurried to put down the cotton wool and grab the gun from a metal table by the wall. It was a long metal tube with two finger holds on the side, like a hypodermic syringe.

'Can I do it this time?'

'Sure,' she said, pulling back the body's cheek and upper lip. 'Right here.'

I placed the gun gently up against the gums and squeezed, embedding a small needle into the bone. The teeth were long and yellow. We added one more needle to the lower jaw and threaded a wire through them both, then twisted it tight to keep the mouth closed. Margaret smeared sealing cream on a small plastic support, like the peel of an orange wedge, and placed it inside the mouth to hold everything closed.

Once the face was taken care of we arranged the body carefully, straightening the legs and folding the arms across the chest in the classic 'I'm dead' pose. Once the formaldehyde gets into the muscles it seizes up and goes rigid, so you have to set the features first thing so the family doesn't have a misshapen corpse at the viewing.

'Hold her head,' said Margaret, and I obediently put a hand on each side of the corpse's head to keep it steady.

Margaret probed with her fingers a bit, just above the right collarbone, and then sliced a long, shallow line in the hollow of the old woman's neck. It's almost bloodless when you cut a corpse, because the heart's not pumping so there's no blood pressure, and gravity pulls it all down into the body's back. Because this one had been dead longer than usual, the chest was limp and empty while the back was nearly purple, like a giant bruise.

Margaret reached into the hole with a small metal hook and pulled out two big veins – well, technically an artery and a vein – and looped a string around each one. They were purple and slick, two dark loops that pulled out of the body a few inches and then slipped back in. Margaret turned to prepare the pump.

Most people don't realize how many different chemicals embalmers use, but the first thing that catches your eye is not how many there are, but how many different colours they use. Each bottle – the formaldehyde, the anti-coagulants, the cauterants, the germicides, the conditioners, and more – has its own bright colour, like fruit juice, and the row of embalming fluids looks like the syrup flavours at a Sno-cone stand. Margaret chose her chemicals carefully, as if she was choosing ingredients for a soup. Not every body needed every chemical, and figuring out the right recipe for a given corpse was as much an art as a science.

While she worked on that I let go of the head and

picked up the scalpel. They didn't always let me make incisions, but if I did it while they weren't watching I could usually get away with it. I was good at it, too, which helped.

The artery Margaret had pulled out would be used to pump the body full of the chemical cocktail she was making; as they filled the body, the old fluids like blood and water would be pushed out of the exposed vein and into a drain tube – and from there into the floor drain. I was surprised to find out that it all just goes into the sewer system, but really – where else would it go? It's no worse than anything else down there.

I held the artery steadily and cut slowly across it, careful not to sever it completely. When the hole was ready I grabbed the canula – a curved metal tube – and slipped the narrow end into the opening. The artery was rubbery, like a thin hose, and covered with tiny fibres of muscle and capillary. I laid the metal tube gently on its chest and made a similar cut in the vein, this time inserting a drain pipe, which connected to a long coil of clear plastic tubing that snaked down into a drain in the floor. I then cinched tight the string Margaret had looped around each vein, sealing them shut.

'That looks good,' said Margaret, pushing the pump over to the table. It was on wheels to keep it out of the way, but now it took its place of honour in the centre of the room while my aunt connected the main hose to the canula I'd placed in the artery. She studied the seal briefly, nodded at me in approval, and poured the first chemical – a bright orange anti-coagulant to break up clots – into the tank on top of the pump. She pushed a button and the pump jerked sleepily to life, syncopated like a real heartbeat, and she watched it carefully while she fiddled with the knobs that controlled pressure and speed. The pressure in the body normalized quickly, and soon dark, thick blood was disappearing into the sewer.

'How's school?' Margaret asked, peeling off a rubber glove to scratch her head.

'It's only been a couple of days,' I said. 'Not a lot happens in the first week.'

'It's the first week of high school though,' said Margaret. 'That's pretty exciting, isn't it?'

'Not especially,' I said.

The anti-coagulant was almost gone, so Margaret poured a bright blue conditioner into the pump to help get the blood vessels ready for the formaldehyde. 'Meet any new friends?'

'Yeah,' I said, 'a whole new school moved into town over the summer, so miraculously I'm not stuck with the same people I've known since Kindergarten. And of course they all wanted to make friends with the weird kid. It was pretty sweet.'

'You shouldn't make fun of yourself like that,' she said.

'Actually I was making fun of *you*.'

'You shouldn't do that either,' said Margaret, grinning slightly. She stood back up to add more chemicals to the mixer. Now that the two pre-injection chemicals were on their way through the body she began mixing the true embalming fluid – a moisturizer and a water softener to keep the tissues from swelling, preservatives and germicides to keep the body in good condition (well, as good as it could be at this point), and dye to give it a rosy, lifelike glow. The key to it all, of course, is formaldehyde, a strong poison that kills everything in the body, hardens the muscles, pickles the organs, and does all of the actual 'embalming'. Margaret added a hefty dose of formaldehyde, followed by thick green perfume to cover the pungent aroma. The pump tank was a swirly pot of brightly-coloured gloop, like the slush machine at a gas station.

At this point, Margaret clamped down the lid and ushered me out the back door; the fan wasn't good enough to risk being in the room with that much formaldehyde. It was fully dark now, and the town had gone almost silent. I sat on the back step while Margaret leaned against the wall, watching through the open door in case anything went wrong.

'Do you have any homework yet?' she asked.

'I have to read the introductions of most of my textbooks over the weekend, which of course everybody always does, and I have to write an essay for my history class.'

Margaret looked at me, trying to be nonchalant, but her lips were pressed tightly together and she started blinking. I knew from long association that this meant something was bothering her.

'Did they assign a topic?' she asked.

I kept my face impassive. 'Major figures of American history.'

'So . . . George Washington? Or maybe Lincoln?'

'I already wrote it.'

'That's great,' she said, not really meaning it. She paused a moment longer, then dropped her pretence. 'Do I have to guess, or are you going to tell me which of your psychopaths you wrote it on?'

'They're not "my" psychopaths.'

'John . . .'

'Dennis Rader,' I said, looking out at the street. 'They just caught him a few years ago, so I thought it had a nice "current events" angle.'

'John, Dennis Rader is the BTK killer. He's a murderer. They asked for a great figure, not a—'

'The teacher asked for a major figure, not a great one, so bad guys count,' I said. 'He even suggested John Wilkes Booth as one of the options.'

'There's a big difference between a political assassin and a serial killer.'

'I know,' I said, looking back at her. 'That's why I wrote it.'

'You're a really smart kid,' said Margaret, 'and I mean that. You're probably the only student that's already finished with the essay. But you can't . . . it's not normal, John. I was really hoping you'd grow out of this obsession with murderers.'

'Not murderers,' I said. 'Serial killers.'

'That's the difference between you and the rest of the world, John. We don't see a difference.' And with that she went back inside to start work on the body cavity – sucking out all the bile and poison until the body was purified and clean.

Staying outside in the dark, I stared up at the sky and waited.

I don't know what I was waiting for.

# CHAPTER 2

We didn't get Jeb Jolley's body that night, or even soon after, and I spent the next week in breathless anticipation, running home from school every afternoon to see if it had arrived yet. It felt like Christmas. The Coroner was keeping the body much longer than normal in order to perform a full autopsy – that's where they cut a corpse open and study it to find out how it died, and when, and who killed it.

The *Clayton Daily* had articles on the death every day, finally confirming on Tuesday that the police suspected murder; their first impression had been that Jeb was killed by a wild animal, but there were apparently several clues that pointed to something more deliberate. The nature of those clues was not, of course, revealed. It was the most sensational thing to happen in Clayton County in my whole life.

On Thursday we got our history essays back. I got full points and *Interesting choice!* written in the margin. The kid I hung out with, Maxwell, missed two points for length and two more for spelling; he'd written half a page about Albert Einstein, and spelled Einstein a different way every time.

'It's not like there's a whole lot to say about Einstein,' said Max, sitting at the corner table of the school cafeteria. 'He discovered $e=mc^2$, and nuclear bombs, and that's it. I'm lucky I got a half-page at all.'

I didn't really like Max, which was one of the most socially normal things about me, as nobody liked Max. He was short, and kind of fat, with glasses and an inhaler and a closet full of secondhand clothes. More than that, he had a brash, grating attitude, speaking too loudly and too authoritatively on subjects that he really knew very little about. In other words, he acted like the bullies, but without any of the strength or charisma to back it up. This all suited me fine, because he had the one quality I most desired in a school acquaintance – he liked to talk, and didn't much care if I paid attention to him or not. It was part of my plan to remain inconspicuous: alone we were just one weird kid who talked to himself and one weird kid who never talked to anyone; together we were two weird kids having a semblance of a conversation. It wasn't much, but it made us look a little more normal. Two wrongs made a right.

Clayton High School was old and falling apart, like everything else in town. Kids bussed here from all over the county, and I guessed a good third of the students came from farms and townships outside the city limits. There were a couple of kids I didn't know – some of the outlying families home-schooled their kids up until high school – but for the most part they were the same old crowd I'd grown up with since Kindergarten. Nobody new ever came to Clayton, they just drove through on the interstate and glanced as they passed by. The city lay on the side of the highway and decayed, like a dead animal.

'Who did you write about?' said Max.

'What?' I hadn't been paying attention.

'I asked who you wrote about for your essay,' said Max. 'I'm guessing John Wayne.'

'Why would I do John Wayne?'

'Because you're named after him.'

He was right: my name is John Wayne Cleaver. My sister's name is Lauren Bacall Cleaver. My dad was a big fan of old movies.

'Being named after someone doesn't mean they're interesting,' I said, still watching the crowd. 'Why didn't you write about Maxwell House?'

'Is that a guy?' asked Max. 'I thought it was a coffee company.'

'I wrote about Dennis Rader,' I told him. 'He was BTK.'

'What's BTK?'

'Bind, Torture, Kill,' I said. 'BTK was how Dennis Rader signed his name in all the letters he wrote to the media.'

'That's sick, man,' said Max. 'How many people did he kill?' He obviously wasn't too disturbed by it.

'Maybe ten,' I said. 'The police aren't sure yet.'

'Only ten?' said Max. 'That's nothing. You could kill

more than that, robbing a bank. That guy in your project last year was way better at it than that.'

'It doesn't matter how many they kill,' I told him. 'And it's not cool – it's wrong.'

'Then why do you talk about them all the time?' asked Max.

'Because wrong is interesting.' I was only partially engaged in the conversation; on the inside I was thinking about how cool it would be to see a body that was all taken apart after an autopsy.

'You're weird, man,' said Max, taking another bite of his sandwich. 'That's all there is to say. Someday you're going to kill a whole bunch of people – probably more than ten, because you're such an over-achiever – and then they're going to have me on TV and ask if I saw this coming, and I'm going to say, "Hell, yes! That guy was seriously screwed up".'

'Then I guess I have to kill you first,' I said.

'Nice try,' said Max, laughing and pulling out his inhaler. 'I'm like your only friend in the world – you wouldn't kill me.' He took a puff from his inhaler and tucked it back into his pocket. 'Besides, my dad was in the Army, and you're a skinny emo. I'd like to see you try.'

'Jeffrey Dahmer,' I said, only half-listening to Max.

'What?'

'The project I did last year was on Jeffrey Dahmer,' I said. 'He was a cannibal who kept severed heads in his freezer.'

'I remember now,' said Max, his eyes darkening. 'Your posters gave me nightmares. That was boss.'

'Nightmares are nothing,' I said. 'Those posters gave me a therapist.'

I'd been fascinated – I tried not to use the word 'obsessed' – with serial killers for a long time, but it wasn't until my Jeffrey Dahmer report in the last week of middle school that Mom and my teachers got worried enough to put me into therapy. My therapist's name was Dr Ben Neblin, and over the summer I'd had an appointment with him every Wednesday morning. We talked about a lot of things, like my father being gone, and what a dead body looked like, and how pretty fire was, but mostly we talked about serial killers. He told me that he didn't like the subject, and that it made him uncomfortable, but that didn't stop me. My mom paid for the sessions, and I didn't really have anyone else to talk to, so Neblin got to hear it all.

After school started for the fall our appointments were moved to Thursday afternoons, so when my last class ended that day I loaded up my backpack with its way too many books and pedalled the six blocks over to his office. Halfway there I turned at the corner by the old theatre and took a detour. The Wash-n-Dry was only two blocks down, and I wanted to cycle by the place where Jeb got killed.

The police tape was down now, finally, and the laundromat was open but empty. The back wall only had one window, a small barred yellow one that I assume went into the restroom. The back lot was almost completely isolated, which the newspaper said was making the police investigation pretty hard. No one had seen or heard the attack, even though they guessed it had happened around ten o'clock at night, when most of the bars were still open. Jeb had probably been coming home from one when he died.

I half-expected to find some big chalk outlines on the asphalt, the body in one and the infamous pile of innards in a separate outline nearby. Instead, the whole area had been scoured with a high-pressure hose, and all the blood and gravel was washed away.

I dropped my bike by the wall and stooped down, walking around slowly to see what I could see, if anything. The asphalt was cool and shady, and almost smooth from the lack of loose stones. The wall had been scrubbed down as well, in a smaller area, and it wasn't hard to figure out where the body had been. I knelt down and peered at the ground, spotting here and there a purple smudge in the texture of the ground where dried blood had clung to the rock and resisted the water.

After a minute I found a darker stain on the ground nearby – a hand-sized splotch of something blacker and thicker than blood. I picked at it with my fingernail and it came up like greasy ash, as if someone had cleaned out a charcoal barbecue. I wiped my finger off on my pants and stood up.

It was strange, standing in a place where somebody had died. Cars buzzed slowly by on the street, muted by walls and distance. I tried to imagine what had happened here – where Jeb had been coming from, where he was going, why he cut through a back lot, and where he had been standing when the killer attacked. Perhaps he had been late for something, and rushed through to save time, or maybe he was drunk and weaving dangerously, uncertain where he was. In my mind I saw him red-faced and grinning, oblivious to the death that stalked him.

I pictured the attacker as well, wondering where I would hide if I were going to kill someone here. There were shadows in the lot, even by day; odd angles of fence and wall and ground. Perhaps the killer had lain in wait behind a cement block, or crouched in the shelter of a telephone pole. I imagined 'it' lurking in the dark, calculating eyes peering out as Jeb stumbled past, boozy and defenceless.

Was it hungry? Was it angry? The shifting theories of the police were ominous and tantalizing: what could attack so brutally, yet so carefully, that the evidence pointed to both man *and* beast? I imagined swift claws and bright teeth slashing through moonlight and flesh, sending arcs of blood high onto the wall behind. The part of the wall they had washed reached almost to the roof, a testament to the killer's ferocity.

I lingered a moment longer, guiltily taking it all in. Dr Neblin would wonder why I was late, and would chastise me when I told him where I had gone, but that's not what bothered me. In coming here I was digging at the foundations of something larger and deeper, scratching tiny lines in a wall I dared not breach. There was a monster behind that wall, and I had built it strong to keep the monster at bay; now it stirred and stretched, restless in its dreaming. There was a new monster in town, it seemed – would its presence awaken the one I kept hidden?

It was time to go. I got back on my bike and rode the last few blocks to Neblin's office.

'I broke one of my rules today,' I said, looking down through the blinds in Dr Neblin's office window to the street below. Bright cars rolled past in an unsteady parade. I could feel Neblin's eyes on the back of my head, studying.

'One of your rules?' he asked. His voice was even and steady. He was one of the calmest people I knew, but then again I spent most of my time with Mom and Margaret and Lauren. His calmness was one of the reasons I came here so willingly.

'I have rules,' I said, 'to keep myself from doing anything . . . wrong.'

'What kind of things?'

'What kind of wrong things?' I asked. 'Or what kind of rules?'

'I'd like to hear about both, but you can start with whatever you want.'

'Then we'd better start with the things I'm trying to avoid,' I said. 'The rules won't make any sense to you if you don't know those.'

'That's fine,' he said, and I turned back to face him. He was a short man, mostly bald on top and wearing small round glasses with thin black frames. He always carried a pad of paper, and occasionally made notes while we talked; that used to make me nervous, but he offered to let me see his notes any time I asked. He never wrote things like *what a freak* or *this kid is insane*, just simple notes to help him remember what we talked about. I'm sure he had a *what a freak* book somewhere, but he kept it hidden. And if he didn't have one yet, he was going to make one after this.

'I think,' I said, watching his face for a reaction, 'that fate wants me to become a serial killer.'

He raised an eyebrow; nothing more. I told you he was calm.

'Well,' he said, 'you're obviously fascinated by them – you've read more on the subject than probably anyone in town, including me. Do you want to become a serial killer?'

'Of course not,' I said. 'I specifically want to *avoid* becoming a serial killer. I just don't know how much chance I have.'

'So the things you want to avoid doing are, what – killing people?' He peered at me crookedly, a sign I had come to know meant he was joking. He always said something a little sarcastic when we started getting into the really heavy stuff. I think it was his way of coping with anxiety. When I told him about the time I dissected a dead gopher, layer by layer, he cracked three jokes in a row and almost giggled. 'If you've broken a rule that big,' he continued, 'I am obligated to go to the police, confidentiality or no.'

I'd learned the laws about patient confidentiality in one of our very first sessions, when I first talked about starting fires. If he thought that I had committed a crime, or that I was intending to, or if he thought that I was a legitimate danger to anyone, the law required him to tell the right authorities. He was also free under the law to discuss anything I said with my mother, whether he had a good reason or not. The two of them had held plenty of discussions over the summer, and she'd made my life hell because of them.

'The things I want to avoid are much lower on the ladder than killing,' I said. 'Serial killers are usually – virtually always, in fact – slaves to their own compulsions. They kill because they have to, and they can't stop themselves. I don't want to get to that point, so I set up rules about smaller things – like how I like to watch people, but I don't let myself watch one person for too long. If I do, I force myself to ignore that person for a whole week, and not even think about it.'

'So you have rules to stop yourself from small serial-killer behaviours,' said Neblin, 'in order to stay as far away from the big stuff as you can.'

'Exactly.'

'I think it's interesting,' he said, 'that you used the word "compulsions". That kind of removes the issue of responsibility.'

'But I'm *taking* responsibility,' I said. 'I'm trying to stop it.'

'You are,' he said, 'and that's very admirable, but you started this whole conversation by saying that "fate" wants you to be a serial killer. If you tell yourself that it's your destiny to become a serial killer, then aren't you really just dodging responsibility by passing the blame on to fate?'

'I say fate,' I explained, 'because this goes way beyond some simple behavioural quirks. There are some aspects of my life that I can't control, and they can only be explained by fate.'

'Such as?'

'I'm named after a serial killer,' I said. 'John Wayne Gacy killed thirty-three people in Chicago and buried most them in the crawlspace under his house.'

'Your parents didn't name you after John Wayne Gacy,' said Neblin. 'Believe it or not, I specifically asked your mom about it.'

'You did?'

'I'm smarter than I look,' he said. 'But you need to remember that one link to a serial killer is a coincidence, not a destiny.'

'My dad's name is Sam,' I said. 'That makes me the Son of Sam – a serial killer in New York who said his dog told him to kill.'

'So you have coincidental links to two serial killers,' he said. 'That's a little odd, I admit, but I'm still not seeing a cosmic conspiracy against you.'

'My last name is Cleaver,' I said. 'How many people do you know who are named after two serial killers and a murder weapon?'

Dr Neblin shifted in his chair, tapping his pen against his paper. This, I knew, meant that he was trying to think. 'John,' he said after a moment, 'I'd like to know what kind of things scare you, specifically, so let's pull back and look at what you said earlier. What are some of your rules?'

'I told you about watching people,' I said. 'That's a big one. I love watching people, but I know that if I watch one person for too long I'll start to get too interested in them – I'll want to follow them, watch where they go, see who they talk to, and find out what makes them tick. A few years ago I realized that I was actually stalking a girl at school – literally following her around everywhere. That kind of thing can go too far in a hurry, so I made a rule: if I watch one person for too long, I ignore them for a whole week.'

Neblin nodded, but didn't interrupt. I was glad he didn't ask me the girl's name, because even talking about her like this felt like breaking my rule again.

'Then I have a rule about animals,' I said. 'You remember what I did to the gopher.'

Neblin smiled nervously. 'The gopher certainly doesn't.' His nervous jokes were getting lamer.

'That wasn't the only time,' I said. 'My dad used to set traps in our garden for gophers and moles and stuff, and my job every morning was to go out and check them and bash anything that wasn't dead yet with a shovel. When I was seven I started to cut them open, to see what they looked like on the inside, but after I started studying serial killers I stopped doing that. Have you heard about the Macdonald triad?'

'Three traits shared by ninety-five per cent of serial killers,' said Dr Neblin. 'Bedwetting, pyromania, and animal cruelty. You do, I admit, have all three.'

'I discovered that when I was eight,' I said. 'What really got to me was not the fact that animal cruelty could predict violent behaviour – it's that up until I read about it, I never thought that it was wrong. I was killing animals and taking them apart, and I had all the emotional reaction of a kid playing with Lego. It's like they weren't real to me. They were just toys to play with. Things.'

'If you didn't feel that it was wrong,' asked Dr Neblin, 'why did you stop?'

'Because that's when I first realized that I was different from other people,' I said. 'Here was something that I did all the time, and thought nothing of it, and it turns out the rest of the world thinks it's completely reprehensible. That's when I knew I needed to change, so I started making rules. The first one was "don't mess with animals".'

'Don't kill them?'

'Don't do anything to them,' I said. 'I won't have a pet, I won't pet a dog on the street, and I don't even like to go into a house where someone has an animal. I avoid any situation that might lead me back to doing something I know I shouldn't do.'

Neblin looked at me for a moment. 'Any others?' he asked.

'If I ever feel like hurting someone,' I said, 'I give them a compliment. If someone's really bugging me, until I hate them so much I start to imagine myself killing them, I say something nice and smile really big. It forces me to think nice thoughts instead of bad ones, and it usually makes them go away.'

Neblin thought for a moment before speaking. 'That's why you read so much about serial killers,' he said. 'You don't feel right and wrong the way other people do, so you read about it to find out what you're supposed to avoid.'

I nodded. 'And of course it helps that they're pretty cool to read about.'

He made some notes on his pad.

'So which rule did you break today?' he asked.

'I went to the place where they found Jeb Jolley's body,' I said.

'I wondered why you hadn't mentioned him yet,' he said. 'Do you have a rule to stay away from violent crime scenes?'

'Not specifically,' I said. 'That's why I was able to justify it to myself. I wasn't really breaking a specific rule, even if I was breaking the spirit of them.'

'And why did you go?'

'Because someone was killed there,' I said. 'I . . . had to see it.'

'Were you a slave to your compulsion?' he asked.

'You're not supposed to turn that around on me.'

'I kind of am,' said Neblin. 'I'm a therapist.'

'I see dead bodies all the time in the mortuary,' I said, 'and I think that that's fine – Mom and Margaret have worked there for years, and they're not serial killers. So I see lots of live people, and I see lots of dead people, but I've never actually seen a live person turn into a dead one. I'm . . . curious.'

'And the scene of a crime is the closest you can get without committing a crime yourself.'

'Yes,' I said.

'Listen, John,' said Neblin, leaning forward. 'You have a

lot of predictors for serial-killer behaviour, I know. In fact, I think you have more predictors than I've ever seen in one person. But you have to remember that predictors are just that – they predict what *might* happen, they don't prophesy what *will* happen. Okay, ninety-five per cent of serial killers wet their beds and light fires and hurt animals, but that doesn't mean that ninety-five per cent of kids who do those things will become serial killers. You are always in control of your own destiny, and you are always the one who makes your own choices – no one else. The fact that you have those rules, and that you follow them so carefully, says a lot about you and your character. You're a good person, John.'

'I'm a good person,' I said, 'because I know what good people are supposed to act like, and I copy them.'

'If you're as thorough as you say you are,' said Neblin, 'nobody will ever know the difference.'

'But if I'm not thorough enough,' I said, looking out of the window, 'who knows what could happen?'

# CHAPTER 3

Mom and I ate dinner quietly in our small flat above the mortuary, letting the shared pizza box and the noise of the TV substitute for the companionship and conversation of a real relationship. *The Simpsons* was on. It was Saturday night, and we still didn't have Jeb's body; if the police kept it much longer we wouldn't be able to embalm it at all, just seal it in a bag and hold a closed-casket funeral.

Mom and I always disagreed on what kind of pizza to get, so we had the pizza place split it in half for us: my side had sausage and mushrooms, and her side had pepperoni. Even *The Simpsons* was a compromise – it came on after the news, and since changing the channel meant risking a fight, we just left it on.

On the first commercial break Mom put her hand on the remote, which usually meant she was going to mute the TV and talk about something – which usually meant we would get into an argument. She rested her finger on the mute button and waited, not pressing down. If she hesitated this long, whatever she wanted to talk about was probably pretty bad. After a moment she pulled back her hand, grabbed another piece of pizza, and took a bite.

We sat tensely through the next segment of the show, knowing what was coming and planning our attacks. I thought about getting up and leaving, escaping under the cover of non-commercial programming, but that would just antagonize her. I chewed slowly, watching numbly as Homer jumped and screamed and raced around on the screen.

Another commercial came on, and Mom's hand hovered over the remote again – just briefly this time – before punching the mute button. She chewed, swallowed, and spoke.

'I talked to Dr Neblin today,' she said.

I thought that might have something to do with this.

'He said that . . . well, he said some very interesting things, John.' She kept her eyes on the TV, and the wall, and the ceiling; anywhere but on me. 'Do you have anything to say for yourself?'

'Thank you for sending me to a therapist, and I'm sorry that I actually need a therapist?'

'Don't start snippy, John; we have a long way to go and I'd like to get through as much of it as we can before we get snippy.'

I took a deep breath, watching the TV. The Simpsons were back on, no less manic with the sound turned off. 'What did he say?'

'He told me that you . . .' She looked at me, black hair pulled back, green eyes lined with worry. She was about forty-five years old, which she claimed was actually quite young, but on a night like this, arguing in the sickly light of the TV, she looked beaten and weathered. 'He told me that you think you're going to kill somebody.' She shouldn't have looked at me; she couldn't say something like that and look at me at the same time without a flood of emotion rushing to the surface. I watched it redden her face and sour her eyes.

'That's interesting,' I said, 'since that's not what I told him. Are you sure those were the words he used?'

'The words aren't the issue here,' she said. 'This isn't a joke, John, this is serious stuff. The . . . I don't know. Is this how it's going to end for us? You're all I have left, John.'

'The actual words I used,' I said, 'were that I followed strict rules to make sure I didn't do anything wrong. It seems like you'd be pretty happy about that, but instead you're yelling at me. This is why I need therapy.'

'"Happy" is not a son who has to follow rules to keep himself from killing people,' she shot back. '"Happy" is not a psychologist telling me that my son is a sociopath. "Happy" is—'

'He said I was a sociopath?' That was kind of cool. I'd always suspected, but it was nice to have an official diagnosis.

'Antisocial Personality Disorder,' she said, her voice rising. 'I looked it up. It's a psychosis.' She turned away. 'My son's a psychotic.'

'APD is primarily defined as a lack of empathy,' I said. I'd looked it up too, a few months ago. Empathy is what allows people to interpret emotion, the same way ears interpret sound; without it you become emotionally deaf.

'It means I don't connect emotionally with other people. I wondered if he was going to pick that one.'

'How do you even know that?' she said. 'You're fifteen years old, for goodness' sake! You should be . . . I don't know, chasing girls or playing video games.'

'You're telling a sociopath to chase girls?'

'I'm telling you not to be a sociopath,' she snapped. 'Just because you mope around all the time doesn't mean you've got a mental disorder – it means you're a teenager. The thing is, John, you can't just have a doctor's note to get you out of life. You live in the same world as the rest of us, and you've got to deal with it the same way the rest of us do.'

She was right; I could see a lot of benefit in being officially sociopathic. No more annoying group projects at school, for one thing.

'I think this is all my fault,' she said. 'I dragged you into that mortuary when you were just a kid, and it messed you up for life. What was I thinking?'

'It's not the mortuary,' I said. I bristled at the mention of it – she couldn't take that away from me. 'You and Margaret have worked there for how long? And you haven't killed anybody yet.'

'We're not psychotic, either.'

'Then you're changing your story,' I said. 'You just said the mortuary messed me up, and now you say it messed me up because I was already messed up? If you're going to be like that then I can't win no matter what I do, can I?'

'There's plenty you could do, John, and you know it.

Stop writing homework assignments about serial killers, for one thing. Margaret told me you did it again.'

Margaret, you little snitch. 'I got full points on that paper,' I said. 'The teacher loved it.'

'Being really good at something you shouldn't be doing doesn't make it any better,' Mom said.

'It's a history class,' I said, 'and serial killers are a part of history. So are wars and racism and genocide. I guess I forgot to sign up for the "happy stuff only" history class – sorry about that.'

'I just wish I knew why,' she said.

'Why what?'

'Why you're so obsessed with serial killers.'

'Everybody's got to have a hobby,' I said.

'John, don't even joke about this.'

'Do you know who John Wayne Gacy is?' I asked.

'I do now,' she said, throwing up her hands. 'Thanks to Dr Neblin. I wish to God I'd named you something different.'

'John Wayne Gacy was the first serial killer I ever learned about,' I said. 'When I was eight years old I saw my name in a magazine next to a picture of a clown.'

'I just asked you ten seconds ago to stop obsessing about serial killers,' she said. 'Why are we talking about this?'

'Because you wanted to know why,' I said, 'and I'm trying to tell you. I saw that picture and I thought maybe it was a clown movie with the actor John Wayne – Dad used to show me his cowboy movies all the time. It turns out John Wayne Gacy was a serial killer who dressed up as a clown for neighbourhood parties.'

'I don't understand where you're going with this,' said Mom.

I struggled to explain what I meant. Sociopathy wasn't just being emotionally deaf; it was being emotionally mute, too. I felt like the characters on our muted TV, waving their hands and screaming and never saying a word out loud. It was like Mom and I spoke completely different languages, and communication was impossible.

'Think about a cowboy movie,' I said, grasping at straws. 'They're all the same – a cowboy in a white hat rides around shooting cowboys with black hats. You know who's good, you know who's bad, and you know exactly what's going to happen.'

'So?'

'So when a cowboy kills somebody you don't even blink, because it happens every day. But when a clown kills somebody, that's new – that's something you've never seen before. Here's someone you thought was good, and he's doing something so terrible that normal human emotion can't even deal with it – and then he turns around and does something good again. That's fascinating, Mom. It's not weird to be obsessed with that, it's weird not to be.'

Mom stared at me for a moment.

'So serial killers are some kind of movie hero?' she said.

'That's not what I'm saying at all,' I said. 'They're sick and twisted, and they do terrible things. I just don't think it's automatically sick and twisted to want to learn more about them.'

'There's a big difference between wanting to learn about

them and thinking you're going to turn into one,' said Mom. 'Now I'm not blaming you – I'm not the best mother, and goodness knows your father was an even worse parent. Dr Neblin said you make rules for yourself, to keep you away from bad influences.'

'Yes,' I said. Finally she was starting to listen – to see the good things instead of the bad.

'I want to support you,' she said, 'so here's a new rule: no more helping out in the mortuary.'

'What!'

'It's not a good environment for kids,' she said, 'and I should never have let you help in the back room in the first place.'

'But I—' But what? What could I say that wouldn't shock her even more? 'I need the mortuary because it connects me to death in a safe way'? 'I need the mortuary because I need to see the bodies open up like flowers and talk to me and tell me what they know'? She'd kick me out of the house altogether.

Before I could say anything else, Mom's cellphone rang. It was the tinny, electronic rendition of the *William Tell Overture* that Mom had designated as the special ring tone for the Coroner's office; a call to duty. There was only one thing the Coroner would be calling about at ten-thirty on a Saturday night, and we both knew it. She sighed and dug through her purse for the phone.

'Hi, Ron,' she said. Pause. 'No, that's okay, we were just finishing up anyway.' Pause. 'Yes, we know. We've been expecting it.' Pause. 'I'll be down in a minute, so whenever you can come by is fine. Seriously, don't worry about it – we both knew the hours when we signed up.' Pause. 'You, too. I'll talk to you later.'

She hung up the phone with a sigh. 'I suppose you know what that was about,' she said.

'The police are done with Jeb's remains.'

'They're delivering him in fifteen minutes,' she said. 'I need to get downstairs. I . . . we shall have to finish this discussion later. I'm sorry, John, about everything. This could have been a nice family dinner.'

I glanced back at the TV. Homer was strangling Bart.

'I want to help you,' I said. 'It's after ten – you'll be up all night if you try to do it alone.'

'Margaret will help,' she said.

'So it will take you five hours instead of eight – it's still too long. If I help we can be done in three.' I kept my voice calm and even; I couldn't allow her to take it all away, but I didn't dare let her know how important it was.

'The body is in very poor condition, John; he was torn apart. It's going to take a long time to put him back together, and it's going to be very disturbing, and you're a clinical psychopath.'

'Ouch, Mom.'

She gathered up her purse. 'Either it bothers you, in which case you shouldn't go, or doesn't bother you, in which case you should have stopped going a long time ago.'

'Do you really want to leave me here alone?'

'You'll find something constructive to do,' she said.

'We're going to go put a body together,' I said. 'What's

more constructive than that?' I winced immediately – dark humour wouldn't help my case at all. It had been a reflex, cutting the tension with a joke the way Dr Neblin did.

'And I don't like the way you joke about death,' she said. 'Morticians are surrounded by death – we breathe it every minute of every day. That much contact can make you lose your reverence for it. I've seen it in myself, and it bothers me. If death weren't so familiar to you, you might be a little better off.'

'I'm fine, Mom,' I said. What could I do to convince her? 'You know you need the help, and you know you don't want to leave me alone.' Even if I didn't have any empathy, Mom did, and that meant I could use it against her. Where logic failed, guilt might save the day.

She sighed and closed her eyes, squeezing them shut against some mental image I could only guess at. 'Fine. But let's finish the pizza first.'

My sister Lauren left home six years ago, two years after Dad did. She was only seventeen at the time, and goodness knows what she'd gotten into while she was gone. The house had a lot less screaming now, which was nice, but what screaming remained was usually focused on me. About six months ago Lauren came back to Clayton, hitchhiking in from who knows where, and contritely asked my mom for a job. They still barely spoke to each other, and she never visited us or invited us to visit her apartment, but she worked as the mortuary receptionist and got along well enough with Margaret.

We all got along well enough with Margaret. She was the rubber insulation that kept our family from sparking and shorting out.

Mom called Margaret while we finished our pizza, and apparently Margaret called Lauren because they were both there when we finally went downstairs to the mortuary – Margaret in her sweats and Lauren tarted up for a Saturday night on the town. I wondered if we'd interrupted anything in particular.

'Hey, John,' said Lauren, looking wildly out of place behind the classy desk in the front office. She wore a shiny black vinyl jacket over a brightly-coloured tank top, and her hair was up in an 80s-style fountain on top of her head. Maybe there was a theme night at the club.

'Hey, Lauren,' I said.

'Is that the paperwork?' Mom asked, looking over my shoulder at her.

'I'm almost done,' said Lauren, and Mom went into the back.

'Is it here already?' I asked.

'They just dropped him off,' she said, scanning the sheaf of papers one last time. 'Margaret has him in the back.'

I turned to go.

'You surviving?' she asked. I was anxious to see the body, but turned back to her.

'Well enough. You?'

'I'm not the one who lives with Mom,' she said. We stood in silence a moment longer. 'You heard from Dad?'

'Not since May,' I said. 'You?'

'Not since Christmas.' Silence. 'The first few years he sent me Valentines in February.'

'He knew where you were?'

'I asked him for money sometimes.' She put down her pen and stood up. Her skirt matched her jacket, shiny black vinyl. Mom would hate it, which was probably why Lauren bought it. She gathered the papers into a uniform stack and we walked into the back room.

A pale blue body bag filled the embalming table. It was all I could do not to run over and zip it open. Lauren handed the papers to Mom, who glanced at them briefly before signing a few sheets and handing the whole stack to the Coroner.

'Thanks, Ron. Have a good night.'

'I'm sorry to drop this on you this time of night,' he said, talking to Mom but looking at Lauren. He was tall, with black hair slicked back over his head.

'It's no problem,' said Mom. Ron took the papers and left out the back.

'That's all you need me for,' said Lauren, smiling at Margaret and me and nodding politely to Mom. 'Have fun.' She walked back to the front office, and a moment later I heard the front door swing shut and lock.

The suspense was killing me, but I didn't dare say anything. Mom was barely tolerating my presence here as it was, and to appear over-eager now would probably get me kicked out.

Mom looked at Margaret. Given time to prepare themselves they looked fairly different from each other, but on the spur of the moment like this, in drab housework clothes with their make-up left undone, you could barely tell them apart. 'Let's do it.'

Margaret switched on the ventilator. 'I hope this fan doesn't give out on us tonight.'

We put on our aprons and scrubbed up, and Mom unzipped the bag. Where Mrs Anderson had barely been handled, Jeb Jolley had been scrubbed and washed and picked over so many times by Ron and by the State forensic agents that he smelled almost entirely of disinfectant. The stench of rot seeped out more slowly as we rolled the body out of the bag and arranged it on the table. He had an enormous Y-incision cutting from shoulder to shoulder and down the centre of his chest; in most autopsies this line would continue down to the groin, but here it degenerated just below the ribs into a jagged web of rips and tears that took up most of his midsection. The edges were puckered and partially stitched, though many sections of skin were missing. The corners of a plastic bag peeked out through the holes in his abdomen.

I immediately thought about Jack the Ripper, one of the earliest recorded serial killers. He tore his victims apart so viciously that most of them were barely recognizable.

Had Jeb Jolley been attacked by a serial killer? It was certainly possible, but which kind? The FBI split serial killers into two categories: organized and disorganized. An organized killer was like Ted Bundy – suave, charming and intelligent – who planned his crimes and covered them up as well as he could afterwards. A disorganized killer was like the Son of Sam, who struggled to control his inner demons and then killed suddenly and brutally each time those demons broke free. He called himself Mr Monster. Which kind had killed Jeb – the sophisticate or the monster?

I sighed and forced myself to discard the thought. I'd always been obsessed with serial killers, and this wasn't the first time I'd been eager to find one in my home town. I needed to get my mind back onto the body itself, and appreciate it for what it was rather than what I wanted it to be.

Margaret folded the body open, revealing a large plastic bag containing most of its internal organs. These were normally removed during the course of an autopsy anyway, though of course in Jeb's case they were removed at or slightly before the time of death. Margaret set the bag on a cart and wheeled it over to the wall to work on the organs; they would be full of bile and other junk, stuff that the embalming fluid couldn't deal with, so it all had to be sucked out. In a normal embalming this is done after the formaldehyde gets pumped in, but the nice thing about an autopsy body was that you could do the embalming and the organ work at the same time. Mom and Margaret had been doing this together for so many years that they moved smoothly, without the need to talk.

'You help me, John,' said Mom, and reached for the disinfectant. She was too much of a perfectionist not to wash a body before she embalmed it, even one as clean as this. The body cavity was wide and empty, though the heart and lungs were mostly intact, and Jeb's midsection looked like a deflated, bloody balloon. Mom washed it first and covered it with a sheet.

A thought came unbidden to my mind: the organs had been piled up at the scene of the crime. Very few killers remained with the bodies after the fact, but serial killers did. Sometimes they posed it, or defaced it, or simply played with it like a doll. It was called ritualizing the kill, and it was a lot like what had happened to Jeb's organs.

Maybe it *had* been a serial killer. I shook my head to clear the thought away, and held the body while Mom sprayed it with Dis-Spray.

Jeb had not been a small man, and his limbs were even plumper now that they were filled with stagnant fluid. I pressed my finger against his foot and it held the shape for a few seconds, expanding back out slowly, like a marshmallow.

'Stop playing,' said Mom. We washed the body and then took the sheet back off of the main cavity. His insides were marbled with fat. There was still enough of his circulatory system in place to use the pump, but there were also a lot of open wounds and leaks that would make the pump lose fluid and pressure. We had to close them up.

'Get me string,' said Mom, 'about seven inches long.' I took off my plastic gloves and threw them in the trash, then began to cut lengths of string. She reached into the cavity and probed for severed major arteries, and each time she found one I handed her a piece of string to tie it off. While we worked Margaret turned on the vacuum and started sucking all the gunk out of the organs, one by one;

she used a tool called a trocar, which was basically just a vacuum nozzle with a blade on the end. She punched it into an organ, sucked out the gunk, then moved on to a new one.

Mom left one vein and one artery open in the chest cavity and began connecting them to the pump and the drain tube; there was no need to open the shoulder when the killer had already opened the chest for us. The first chemical in the pump this time was a coagulant, which seeped slowly through the body and helped close up all the holes. Some of it began to leak out into the empty torso, through tiny veins too small to close by hand, but this flow soon stopped as the coagulant did its work and sealed up the body.

While we waited I studied the slashes in its abdomen. They were certainly animalistic, and one spot on his left side showed what looked like a claw mark – four ragged slits, about an inch apart, that extended nearly a foot from its side toward its belly. This was the demon, of course, though we still didn't know that. How could we? Back then, none of us even knew that demons were real. I placed my own hand over it and guessed that whoever made the marks had a hand much bigger than mine. Mom frowned at me, and was about to say something when Margaret grumbled angrily.

'Dangit, Ron!' shouted Margaret. She didn't have much respect for the Coroner. I ignored her and looked back at the claw mark.

'What's wrong?' Mom asked, walking over to her.

'We're missing a kidney,' said Margaret, attracting my attention immediately. Serial killers often kept souvenirs of their kills, and body parts were a pretty famous choice. 'I've gone through the bag twice,' said Margaret. 'You'd think Ron would manage to send us all the organs, for crying out loud.'

'Maybe there wasn't one to send,' I said. They looked at me, and I tried to sound nonchalant. 'Maybe whoever killed him took it.'

Mom frowned. 'That's . . .'

'Entirely possible,' I said, interrupting her. How could I explain this without mentioning serial killers? 'You saw the size of that claw mark, Mom. If this was an animal going through his innards, it's no stretch to think that it ate something while it was in there.' It made sense, but I knew this was no animal. Some of the slashes were too precise, and of course there was the orderly pile of innards. Perhaps a serial killer who hunted with a dog?

'I'll check the papers,' said Mom, peeling off her gloves and tossing them in the trash as she went up front.

Margaret searched through the bag one more time, but shook her head; the kidney wasn't there. I could barely contain myself.

Mom returned with a copy of the papers Lauren had handed the Coroner. 'It's mentioned right here in the comments section: *Left kidney missing*. It doesn't say they're holding it for evidence and testing, it's just missing. Maybe he had it removed or something.'

Margaret held up the remaining kidney, pointing to the

severed tube that led to the missing one. 'This is a recent cut,' she said. 'There's no scarring or anything.'

'You'd think Lauren would have mentioned something,' said Mom irately, setting the papers down and pulling another pair of plastic gloves from the box. 'I'm going to have to talk to her.'

Mom and Margaret went back to work, but I stood still, a buzz of energy filling me up and emptying me out at the same time. This was not a murder, and it was not a wild animal.

Jeb Jolley had been the victim of a serial killer.

Maybe he'd come from another town, or maybe this was his first victim, but he was a serial killer just the same. The signs were obvious to me now. The victim had been defenceless, with no known enemies or close friends or relatives. His friends from the bar said he'd been peaceful and happy all night before he left, with no fights or arguments, so it wasn't a crime of passion or liquor. Someone with a need to kill had been waiting in the lot behind the Wash-n-Dry, and Jeb had been a target of opportunity, in the wrong place at the wrong time.

The newspaper and the crime scene itself had told a confusing story of fury blended with simplicity – of mindless animal violence giving way to calm, rational behaviour. The killer stacked the organs in a pile and, apparently, took the time after tearing the body apart to stop, slow down, and remove a very specific organ.

Jeb Jolley's death was practically a textbook example of a disorganized killer, lashing out ferociously and then staying, devoid of emotion or empathy, to ritualize the body – to arrange it, take a souvenir, and leave the rest for everyone to see.

It was no wonder the police hadn't mentioned the stolen kidney. If word got out that a serial killer was stealing body parts it would cause a huge panic. People barely felt safe as it was, and this was only the first death.

But it would not be the last. That was, after all, the defining trait of serial killers: they kept on killing.

# CHAPTER 4

It was early October – leaf-burning season. Fall was my favourite time of year, not because of school or harvest vegetables or anything mundane, but because the citizens of Clayton County would rake up their leaves and burn them, flames soaring high into the crisp autumn air. Our yard was small and virtually treeless, but the old couple across the street had a vast yard full of oaks and maples, and they had no children or grandchildren to take care of it for them. In the summer I mowed their lawn for five dollars a week; in the winter I shovelled their walks for cups of hot chocolate; and in the fall I raked their leaves for the pure thrill of watching them burn.

Fire is a brief, temporary thing – the very definition of impermanence. It appears suddenly, roaring into life when heat and fuel come together and ignite, and dances hungrily while all around it blackens and curls. When there is nothing left to consume it disappears, leaving only the ash of its unused fuel – those bits of wood and leaf and paper that were too impure to burn; too unworthy to join the fire in its dance.

It seems to me that fire leaves nothing behind at all – the ash, after all, isn't part of the flame, it's part of the fuel. Fire changes it from one thing to another, drawing off its energy and turning it into . . . well, into more fire.

Fire doesn't create anything new, it simply *is*. If other things must be destroyed in order for fire to exist, well, that's all right with fire. As far as fire is concerned, that's what those things are there for in the first place. When they're gone the fire goes too, and though you may find evidence of its passing you'll find nothing of the fire itself – no light, no heat, no tiny red fragments of cast-off flame. It disappears back to wherever it came from, and if it feels or remembers, we have no way of knowing if it feels or remembers us.

Sometimes, peering into the bright blue heart of a dancing flame, I ask if it remembers me. 'We've seen each other before,' I say. 'We know each other. Remember me when I'm gone.'

Mr Crowley, the old man whose leaves I burned, liked to sit on the porch and 'watch the world go by' as he called it, and if I happened to be raking his yard while he was out he would sit and tell me about his life. He had been a water-system engineer for the county for most of his life, until last year when his health got too bad and he retired. He was old anyway. Today he ambled out slowly and propped his leg up painfully on a stool when he sat down.

'Afternoon to you, John,' he said. 'Afternoon to you.' He was an old man but a large one, big-framed and powerful – his health was going, but he was far from feeble.

'Hi, Mr Crowley.'

'You can leave these be, you know,' he said, gesturing around at the leaf-covered lawn. 'There's plenty more to fall before we're done, and you'll just have to do it all over again.'

'It lasts longer this way,' I said, and he nodded in contentment.

'That it does, John, that it does.'

I raked for a while longer, pulling the leaves together with smooth, even strokes. The other reason I wanted to do his yard that afternoon, of course, was that it had been almost a month and the serial killer hadn't struck again. The tension was making me nervous, and I needed to burn something. I hadn't told anyone my suspicions that it was a serial killer, because who would believe me? I was obsessed with serial killers as it was, so they'd say, of course I'd think this would be one. I didn't mind. It doesn't matter what other people think when you're right.

'Hey John, come here for a second,' said Mr Crowley. He gestured me over to his chair. I grimaced at the interruption, but calmed myself and went over anyway. Talking was normal – it's what normal people do together. I needed the practice. 'What do you know about cellphones?' he asked, showing me his.

'I know a little,' I said.

'I want to send my wife a kiss.'

'You want to send a kiss?'

'Kay and I got these yesterday,' he said, fiddling awkwardly with the phone, 'and we're supposed to be able to take photos and send them to each other. So I want to send Kay a kiss.'

'You want to take a picture of yourself puckering up for a kiss and then send it to her?' Sometimes I didn't understand people at all. Watching Mr Crowley talk about love was like hearing him speak another language. I had no idea what was going on.

'Sounds like you've done this before,' he said, handing me the phone with a shaking hand. 'Show me how it's done.'

The camera button was pretty clearly labelled, so I showed him how to do it and he took a shaky picture of his lips. I showed him how to send the photo and went back to my raking.

The idea that I might be sociopathic was nothing new to me – I'd known for a long time that I didn't connect with other people. I didn't understand them, and they didn't understand me, and whatever emotional language they spoke seemed beyond my capacity to learn. Antisocial Personality Disorder could not be officially diagnosed until you were eighteen years old. Prior to that, it was just 'Conduct Disorder', but let's be honest: Conduct Disorder is just a nice way of telling parents their kids have Antisocial Personality Disorder. I saw no reason to dance around the issue. I was a sociopath, and it was better to deal with it now.

I raked the leafpile into a large fire-pit around the side of the house; the Crowleys used the pit for bonfires and hot-dog roasts in the summer, and invited the whole neighbourhood. I came every time, ignoring the people and tending solely to the fire. If fire was a drug, Mr Crowley was my best enabler.

'Johnny!' Mr Crowley shouted from the porch. 'She sent a kiss back! Come look!' I smiled at him, forcing myself to feign the absent emotional connection. I wanted to be a real boy.

The lack of emotional connection with other people has the odd effect of making you feel separate and alien – as if you are observing the human race from somewhere else, unattached and unwelcome. I've felt like that for years, long before I met Dr Neblin and long before Mr Crowley sent ridiculous love notes on his cellphone. People scurry around, doing their little jobs and raising their little families and shouting their meaningless emotions to the world, and all the while you just watch from the sidelines, bewildered. This drives some sociopaths to feel superior, as if the whole of humanity were simply animals to be hunted or put down; others feel a hot, jealous rage, desperate to have what they cannot. I simply felt alone, one leaf sitting miles away from a giant, communal pile.

I stacked some kindling carefully at the base of the leafpile and lit a match in its heart. Flames caught and grew, sucking in air, and a moment later the pile was roaring with heat, the bright fire dancing wickedly above it.

When the fire burned out, what would be left?

That night the killer struck again.

I saw it on TV during breakfast. The first death had

attracted a little exterior attention purely for its gory nature, but the second – just as gory as the first, and far more public – had caught the eye of a city reporter and his camera crew. They were there live, much to the consternation of the Clayton County Sheriff, broadcasting distant, blurred images of a disembowelled body all across the State.

There was no question now. It was a serial killer. My mom came in from the other room, her face half-covered in make-up; I looked at her, and she looked back. Neither of us said a word.

'This is Ted Rask coming to you live from Clayton, a normally peaceful town that is today the scene of a truly gruesome murder – the second of this nature in less than one month. This is a Five Live News exclusive report. I'm here with Sheriff Meier. Tell me, Sheriff, what do we know about the victim?'

Sheriff Meier was frowning under his wide grey moustache and glanced up testily as the reporter stepped towards him. Rask was famous for sensationalist melodrama, and from the Sheriff's scowl I could tell he wasn't pleased about the idea.

'At this time we do not wish to cause undue distress to the victim's family,' said the Sheriff, 'or unnecessary fear in the people of this county, and we appreciate the cooperation of everybody in remaining calm and not spreading rumours or misinformation about this incident.'

He had completely dodged the reporter's question. At least he wasn't rolling over to Rask without a fight.

'Do you know yet who the victim is?' asked the reporter.

'He was carrying ID, but we do not wish to release that information at this time.'

'And the killer,' said the reporter, 'do you have any leads about who that might be?'

'That information is not being released at this time.'

'With this incident coming so soon on the heels of the last one, and being so similar in nature, do you think the two might be connected?'

The Sheriff closed his eyes briefly, a visual sigh, and paused a moment before speaking. 'We do not wish to discuss the nature of this case at this time, to help preserve our investigation. As I said before, we appreciate everybody's discretion and calm attitudes in not spreading rumours about this incident.'

'Thank you, Sheriff,' said the reporter, and the camera swung back to a close-up of Rask. 'Again, if you're just joining us, we're in Clayton County, where a killer has just struck, possibly for the second time, leaving a dead body and a terrified town in his wake.'

'Stupid Ted Rask,' said Mom, stalking to the fridge. 'The last thing this town needs is a panic about a mass murderer.'

Mass murder and serial killing are completely different things, but I didn't especially want to start an argument about the distinction right then.

'I think the last thing we want are the killings,' I said carefully. 'Panic about the killings would be second to last.'

'In a small town like this a panic could be just as bad, or worse,' she said, pouring a glass of milk. 'People get scared and leave, or they stay at home nights with their doors locked, and suddenly businesses start to fail and tensions go even higher.' She took a swig of milk. 'All it takes then is one small-minded person to start looking for a scapegoat, and panic turns into murder pretty quick.'

'We can't show you the body,' said Rask on TV, 'because it truly is a gruesome, terrible sight, and the police won't let us get close enough, but we do have some details. Nobody seems to have witnessed the actual murder, but those who have seen the body up close report that the scene of death is much more bloody than the previous killing; if it is the same killer, it may be that he is becoming more violent, which could be an ominous sign of things to come.'

'I can't believe he's saying this,' said Mom, folding her arms angrily. 'I'm writing a letter to the Network today.'

'There is a patch of oil or something similar on the ground near the body,' Rask continued, 'possibly from a leaky engine in a getaway car. We'll bring you more details as they come in. This is Ted Rask with a Five Live News exclusive report: Death Stalks America's Heartland.'

I thought back to the stain I had seen behind the Wash-n-Dry – black and oily, like rancid mud. Was the patch of oil next to the new victim's body the same thing? There were deeper currents in this story, and I was determined to figure them all out.

'The central question of psychological profiling,' I said, staring intently at Max as he ate his lunch, 'is not "What is the killer doing?" but, "What is the killer doing that he doesn't have to do?"'

'Dude,' said Max, 'I think it's a werewolf.'

'It's not a werewolf,' I said.

'You saw the news today. The killer has "the intelligence of a man and the ferocity of a beast". What else is it going to be?'

'Werewolves aren't even real.'

'Tell that to Jeb Jolley and the dead guy on Route Twelve,' said Max, taking another bite and then continuing on with a mouth full of food. 'Something tore them up pretty good, and it wasn't some pansy serial killer.'

'The legends of werewolves were probably started because of serial killers,' I said. 'Vampires, too – they're men who hunt and kill other men, and that sounds like a serial killer to me. They didn't have psychology back then, so they just made up some crazy monster to explain it away.'

'Where do you get this stuff?'

'The Internet,' I said, 'but I'm trying to make a point here. If you want to get into the mind of a serial killer you have to ask, "What is he doing that he doesn't have to do?"'

'Why do I want to get into the mind of a serial killer?'

'What?' I asked. 'Why would you not? Okay, listen, we need to figure out why he does what he does.'

'No, we don't,' said Max. 'That's what the police are for. We're in high school, and what we need to figure out is what colour Marci's bra is.'

Why do I spend time with this kid?

'Think of it this way,' I said. 'Let's say that you are a big fan of . . . what are you a fan of?'

'Marci Jensen,' he said. 'And *Halo*, and *Green Lantern*, and—'

'*Green Lantern*,' I said. 'Comic-books. You're a big fan of comic-books, so let's say that a new comic-book author moves into town.'

'Cool,' said Max.

'Yeah,' I said, 'and he's working on a brand new comic-book, and you want to find out what it is. Would that be cool?'

'I just said it was cool,' said Max.

'You'd think about it all the time, and try to guess what he's doing, and compare your theories with other people's theories, and you'd love it.'

'Sure.'

'That's what this is like for me,' I said. 'A new serial killer is like a new author, working on a new project, and he's right here in town under our noses and I'm trying to figure him out.'

'You're crazy, man,' said Max. 'You're really, head-on collision, insane-asylum crazy.'

'My therapist actually thinks I'm doing pretty well,' I said.

'So whatever,' said Max. 'What's our big question?'

'*What is the killer doing that he doesn't have to do?*'

'How do we know what he has to do?'

'All he technically has to do,' I said, 'assuming he has a basic goal of killing people, is to shoot them. That's the easiest way.'

'But he's tearing them up,' said Max.

'Then that's our first thing: he approaches them in person and attacks them hand-to-hand.' I pulled out a notebook and wrote it down. 'That probably means that he wants to see his victims up close.'

'Why?'

'I don't know. What else?'

'He attacks them at night, in the dark,' said Max. He was getting into it now. 'And he grabs them when there's nobody else around.'

'That probably falls into the category of something he *has* to do,' I said, 'especially if he wants to attack them personally. He doesn't want anybody else to see him.'

'Doesn't that count for our list?'

'I guess, but nobody who kills really wants to be seen, so it's not a very unique trait.'

'Just put it on the list,' said Max. 'It doesn't always have to be just your ideas on the list.'

'Okay,' I said, writing it down, 'it's on the list. He doesn't want to be seen; he doesn't want anyone to know who he is.'

'Or what he is.'

'Or what he is,' I said. 'Whatever. Now let's move on.'

'He pulls out his victim's guts,' said Max, 'and he stacks them in a pile. That's pretty cool. We could call him the Gut Stacker.'

'Why would he stack their guts in a pile?' I asked. A girl walked by our table and gave us a curious look, so I lowered my voice. 'Maybe he wants to take time with his victims, and enjoy the kill.'

'You think he takes out their guts while they're still alive?' asked Max.

'I don't think that's possible,' I said. 'What I mean is, maybe he wants to enjoy the kill after the fact. There's a famous Ted Bundy quote—'

'Who?'

'Ted Bundy,' I said. 'He killed thirty or so people around the country in the seventies. He's the one they invented the term "serial killer" for.'

'You know some weird crap, John.'

'Anyway,' I went on, 'in an interview before he was executed he said that after you killed someone, if you had enough time, they could be whoever you wanted them to be.'

Max was silent for a moment.

'I don't know if I like talking about this any more,' he said.

'What do you mean? It didn't bother you a minute ago.'

'A minute ago we were talking about guts falling out,' said Max, 'and that's just gross, not scary. This stuff is kind of messed-up though.'

'But we just started,' I said. 'We're just getting into it. It's a serial-killer profile, so of course it's going to be messed-up!'

'It's just kind of freaking me out, okay?' said Max. 'I don't know. I gotta go to the bathroom.' He got up and walked away, but left his food behind. At least he wasn't leaving for good. Not that I cared if he did.

Why couldn't I just have a normal conversation with someone? About something I wanted to talk about? Was I really that screwed up?

Yeah, I was.

# CHAPTER 5

There is a lake outside of town, just a few miles past our house. Its real name is Clayton Lake, which should come as no surprise at this point since everything in the whole county is named Clayton, but I liked to call it Freak Lake. It is about a mile or so across, and a few miles long, but there isn't a marina or anything; the beaches are marshy and full of reeds, and the water fills up with algae every summer, so nobody really goes swimming, either. In the winter it freezes over, and people go skating and ice fishing there, but that's pretty much it. Every other season of the year there's no reason to go there at all, and nobody ever uses it for anything.

At least, that's what I thought before I found the freaks.

I honestly don't know if they're freaks or not, but I have to assume there's something wrong with them. I found them the year before, when I couldn't stand being home alone with Mom for another minute, and I hopped on my bike and pedalled down the road to nowhere. I wasn't going to the lake, I was just going, and the lake happened to be in the same direction. I passed a car with a guy in it, just sitting there, parked on the side of the road. Then I passed another. A half-mile later I passed an empty truck – I don't know where the driver was. A hundred yards down there was a woman outside of her car leaning on the hood – not looking at anything, not talking to anyone, just leaning there.

Why were they all here? The lake wasn't much to look at. There wasn't anything to do. My thoughts turned immediately to illicit activities – drug hand-offs, secret love affairs, people dumping bodies – but I don't think that was it. I think they were out there for the same reason I was out there: they needed to get away from everything else. They were freaks.

After that I went to Freak Lake whenever I wanted to be alone, which was more and more often. The freaks were there, sometimes different ones, sometimes the same, arrayed along the lakeside road like a string of rejected pearls. We never talked – we didn't fit anywhere else, so it was foolish to assume that we'd fit any better with each other. We just came, and stayed, and thought, and left.

After Max's outburst at lunchtime he steered clear of me the rest of the day, and after school I rode out to Freak Lake to think. The leaves had long passed the bright orange phase and had faded into brown, and the grass on the side of the road was stiff and dead.

'What did the killer do that he didn't have to do?' I said out loud, dropping my bike in the dirt and standing in a warm patch of sun. There were other cars visible, but none were near enough to hear. Freaks respected each other's privacy. 'He stole a kidney from the first one, but what did he take from the second?' The police weren't talking, but we'd get the body at the mortuary soon. I picked up a rock and threw it in the lake.

I looked down the road a few hundred yards to the nearest car; it was white and old, and the driver was staring out at the water.

'Are you the killer?' I asked softly. There were five or six people here today, at various points on the road. How long before Mom's prediction came true, and people in town started blaming each other? People feared what was different, and whoever was the most different would win the witch-hunt lottery. Would it be one of the freaks who escaped to the lake? What would they do to him?

Everyone knew I was a freak. Would they blame *me*?

The second body arrived at the mortuary eight days later. Mom and I had spoken little about my sociopathy, but I'd made sure to try harder in school as a way of throwing her off the scent – making her think about my good traits instead of my disturbing ones. Apparently it worked, for when I came home to the mortuary after school and found them working on the second victim's body, Mom didn't say a thing when I pulled on an apron and mask and started helping.

'What's missing?' I asked, holding bottles for Mom as she poured formaldehyde into the pump. Margaret had only a few organs on the side counter, and she was busily sticking them with the trocar and vacuuming them clean. I assumed the rest of the organs were already inside. Mom had covered the body with a sheet, and I didn't want to risk looking under it while she was standing right there.

'What?' asked Mom, watching the marks on the side of the pump tank as she poured.

'Last time there was a kidney missing,' I said. 'Which organ is it this time?'

'The organs are all there,' she said, laughing. 'Give Ron a break – he's not going to lose something every time. I talked to your sister about the paperwork though, and how she needs to read it a little more closely and tell me about any abnormalities she finds. Sometimes I don't know what to do with that girl.'

'But . . . are you sure?' I asked. The killer had to take something. 'Maybe it was the gall bladder, and Ron just thought this guy'd had it removed already, so he didn't notice.'

'John, Ron and the police – and the FBI, too, I should point out – have had this body for more than a week. Forensic experts have gone over it with a fine-toothed comb looking for everything they can find that will let them catch this sicko. If there was an organ missing, they would have noticed.'

'He's leaking,' I said, pointing at the body's left shoulder. A bright blue chemical was oozing out from under the sheet, mixed with swirls of clotted blood.

'I thought I patched it better than that,' she said, capping the formaldehyde and handing it to me. She pulled back the sheet to reveal the shoulder stump, tightly bandaged, the bottom half soaked through with blue and purple slime. The arm was gone. 'Bother,' she said, and started hunting for some more bandages.

'His arm is gone?' I looked up at my mom. 'I asked what was missing, and you didn't think to mention his arm?'

'What?' asked Margaret.

'The killer took the arm,' I said, stepping up to the corpse and pulling back the sheet. The abdomen was torn open, like before, but not nearly so grotesquely; the gashes were smaller, and there were fewer of them. The dead farmer – Dave Bird, according to his tag – hadn't been gutted. 'The eviscerating and the piling-up of the organs – he didn't do that this time.'

'What are you doing?' snapped Mom, snatching the sheet from my hand and covering the body back up. 'Show some respect!'

I was talking too much, and I knew I was talking too much, but I couldn't stop. It was like my brain had been cut open, and every thought inside was spilling out on the floor.

'I thought he was doing something with the organs,' I said, 'but he was just sifting through them to find what he wanted. He wasn't organizing them or playing with them or—'

'John Wayne Cleaver!' Mom said harshly. 'What on earth are you raving about?'

'This changes the whole profile,' I said, willing myself to shut up, but my mouth just kept going. My new discovery was too exciting. 'It's not what he's *doing* to the bodies, it's what he's *taking* from them. Pulling all the guts out was just an easy way to find a kidney, not a death ritual—'

'A death ritual?' Mom repeated. Margaret put down the trocar and looked at me; I could feel their eyes boring into me, and I knew I was in trouble. I'd said far too much. 'Would you like to explain yourself?' asked Mom.

I needed to play this off somehow, but I was too deep into it. 'I was just saying that the killer wasn't playing with the bodies,' I said. 'That's good, right?'

'You were excited,' Mom accused. 'You were tickled pink about this man's dead body and the way it was torn open.'

'But—'

'I saw joy in your face, John, and I don't think I've ever seen it before, and it was because of a dead body – a real person, with a real family and a real life, and you can't get enough of it.'

'No, that's not—'

'Out,' Mom said, her voice thick with finality.

'What?'

'Out,' she said. 'You're not allowed in here any more.'

'You can't do that!' I shouted.

'I'm the owner and your mother,' she said, 'and you're getting far too worked up about this, and I don't like the way you're acting or the things you're talking about.'

'But—'

'I should have done this a long time ago,' she said, putting a hand on her hip. 'You're restricted from the back room. Margaret won't let you in either, and I'll let Lauren know too. It's time for you to get some normal hobbies and some real friends, and I don't want to hear any backtalk about it.'

'Mom!'

'Not any,' she said. 'Go.'

I wanted to hit her. I wanted to hit the walls and the counters and the dead farmer on the table and pick up the trocar and jam it into Mom's stupid face and suck her brain right out—

No.

Calm down.

I closed my eyes. I was breaking too many rules. I couldn't think like that; I couldn't let that rage take over. I kept my eyes closed and slowly peeled off my gloves and mask.

'I'm sorry,' I said. 'I . . .' I couldn't just walk out of here and never come back. I had to fight, and . . .

No. Calm down.

'I'm sorry,' I said again. I took off my apron and walked through the back door. I could deal with this later. Right now my rules were more important.

I had to keep that monster behind its wall.

I hated Halloween. It was all so dumb – no one was really scared, and everyone walked around covered with fake blood or carrying rubber knives or, worst of all, wearing costumes that weren't even scary. Halloween was supposed to be the night when evil spirits walked the earth – the night when Druids burned children in wicker cages. What did that have to do with dressing up like Spider-man?

I stopped caring about Halloween when I was eight, about

the same time I started learning about serial killers. That doesn't mean I stopped dressing up, just that I stopped picking my own costumes. Each year my mom would choose something, and I'd wear it and ignore it and then forget about it until the next year. In fourth grade she actually sent me to school in a dress. I'd never lived it down. Someday I'd have to tell her about Ed Gein, whose mother dressed him as a girl for most of his childhood. He spent most of his adulthood killing women and making clothes out of their skin.

This year, you'd have thought that Halloween would be pretty cool. After all, we had a real demon in town, with fangs and claws and everything. That ought to count for something. But none of us knew about it yet, and it had only killed two people so far, so instead of cowering in our basements praying for salvation, we ended up in the High-School gym pretending to enjoy a Halloween dance. I'm actually not sure which is worse.

School dances in Middle School had been pretty terrible, and Mom made me go to all of them, and since she had no intention of changing that policy when I got to High School I hoped that at least the dances would get better. They didn't. The Halloween dance turned out to be especially stupid – a time for all the awkward, ungainly, half-developed mutants in High School to get together, in costume, and stand by the walls of the gym while coloured lights flashed anaemically and the Vice Principal played ten-year-old songs over the school PA. As part of Mom's 'make some real friends' initiative she was, as always, forcing me to go, though in a gesture of goodwill she allowed me to pick my own costume. Because I knew it would piss her off, I went as a clown.

Max was an Army Commando of some kind, wearing his dad's camouflage jacket and some blobby brown make-up on his face. He'd also brought a plastic gun, despite the school's repeated warning not to bring weapons, so of course the Principal had taken it at the door.

'This sucks,' said Max, punching his fist and glaring across the gym at the Principal. 'I'm going to go steal it back, dog, I really am. You think he's going to give it back?'

'Did you just call me "dog"?' I asked.

'Dude, I swear I'm going to get my gun back, and he won't even know it. My dad showed me some sweet moves – he'll never know I was even there.'

'You're wearing the wrong camouflage,' I said. We were in our regular position, lurking in the corner, and I was watching the flow of people to and from the refreshments and the walls.

'My dad got this jacket in Iraq,' said Max. 'It's as real as it gets.'

'Then it'll be awesome when Mr Layton hides your gun in Iraq,' I said, 'but we're at a school dance in North Dakota. If you don't want him to see you, you need to dress up as a car-crash victim. There's a lot of those tonight. Or you need a fake bullet-hole in your forehead.' Cheap prosthetic gore was the order of the day for at least half of the guys at the dance. You'd think that two gruesome murders in the community would make people a little more sensitive about that, but there you go. At least no one dressed up as an eviscerated auto-mechanic.

'That would have been sweet,' said Max, looking at a passing plastic bullet-hole. 'That's what I'm going to do tomorrow night for trick-or-treating – it'll scare the crap out of 'em.'

'You're going trick-or-treating?' laughed a voice. It was Rob Anders, walking past with a couple of his friends. They'd hated me since third grade. 'Couple of little babies going trick-or-treating – that's for kids!' They moved on, sniggering.

'I'm only going because of my little sister,' Max grumbled, glaring at their backs. 'I'm going to get my gun; this costume looks way cooler with a gun.' He stalked off towards the far door, leaving me alone in the dark. I decided to get a drink.

The refreshment table was pretty sparse – a tray of stale vegetables, a couple of half-doughnuts, and a bowl full of apple juice and Sprite. I poured myself a glass and immediately dropped it when somebody bumped me from behind. The juice fell back into the bowl, along with my cup, splashing up and soaking my wrist and arm. Rob Anders and his buddies snickered as they walked away.

I used to have a list of people I was going to kill one day. It was against my rules now, but sometimes I really missed that list.

'Are you it?' asked a girl's voice. I turned and saw Brooke Watson, a girl from my street. She was dressed a little like my sister had been the other night, in clothes from the eighties.

'Am I what?' I asked, fishing my cup out of the bowl.

'The clown from *It*, that Stephen King book,' said Brooke.

'Nope,' I said, wringing out my sleeve into the salvaged cup and sopping it with napkins. 'And I think that clown was named Pennywise.'

'I don't know, I've never read it,' she said, looking down. 'It's on my parents' bookshelf though, and I've seen the cover, so I thought that was maybe what you were dressed up as. I don't know.'

She was acting funny, like she was . . . I couldn't tell. I had trained myself to read visual cues from people I knew well, so that I could tell what they were feeling, but someone like Brooke was illegible to me.

I said the only thing I could think of. 'You're a punk?'

'What?'

'What do they call people from the eighties?' I asked.

'Oh,' she laughed. It was a beautiful laugh. 'I'm my mother, actually. I mean, these are her clothes from High School. I guess I should tell people I'm Cyndi Lauper though, or something, because dressing up as your mother is pretty lame.'

'I almost dressed up as my mother,' I said, 'but I was worried what my therapist would say.'

She laughed again, and I realized that she thought I was joking. It was probably for the best, since telling her the second half of my mom costume – a giant fake butcher knife through the head – would probably freak her out. She was really quite pretty – long blond hair, bright eyes, and a wide, dimpled smile. I smiled back.

'Hey, Brooke,' said Rob Anders, walking up with a malicious grin. 'Why are you talking to a little kid? He still goes trick-or-treating.'

'Really?' asked Brooke, looking at me. 'I was gonna go, too, but I wasn't sure – it still sounds fun, even if we are in High School now.'

I may not have understood whatever emotion Brooke was broadcasting, but embarrassment was one I was all too familiar with, and Rob Anders was shedding it now in waves.

'I . . . yeah,' said Rob. 'I think it does sound kind of fun. Maybe I'll see you out there.'

I felt a sudden urge to stab him.

'But what about this clown get-up, John?' he said, turning his attention to me. 'You gonna juggle for us, or cram a whole bunch of yourself into a car?' He laughed, and glanced behind him to see if his friends were laughing as well, but they'd wandered off to talk to Marci Jensen. She was dressed as a kitty, in a costume that made it very obvious why Max was obsessed with her bra. Rob stared for a moment, then turned back quickly. 'So what's it gonna be, clown? Why ya smiling so big?'

'You're a great guy, Rob,' I said. He looked at me oddly.

'What?' he asked.

'You're a great guy,' I said. 'That's a very good costume, and I especially like the bullet-hole in the forehead.' I hoped he would leave now. Saying nice things about people I got really mad at was one of my rules, to help keep things from escalating, but I didn't know how long I could keep it up.

'Are you making fun of me?' he asked, glaring.

I didn't have a rule for what happened if the person I complimented didn't leave.

'No,' I said. I tried to improvise, but I was already off-balance. I didn't know what to say.

'I think you're smiling because you're such a retard,' he said, stepping closer. '"Dur, I'm a happy clown".'

He was really making me mad. 'You're . . .' I needed a compliment. 'I heard you did well on that math test yesterday. Good job.' It was all I could think of. I should have walked away, but I wanted to talk to Brooke.

'Listen, you weirdo,' said Rob. 'This is the party for normal people. The freak party is down the hall, in the restroom with the Goths. Why don't you get out of here?'

He was acting tough, but it was still just acting – typical fifteen-year-old macho posturing. I was so mad I could have killed him right there, but I forced myself to calm down. I was better than this – and I was better than him. He wanted to act scary? I'd give him scary.

'I'm smiling because I'm thinking about what your insides look like.'

'What?' asked Rob, and then smirked. 'Oh, big man, trying to threaten me. You think you scare me, you little baby?'

'I've been clinically diagnosed with sociopathy,' I said. 'Do you know what that means?'

'It means you're a freak,' he said.

'It means that you're about as important to me as a cardboard box,' I said. 'You're just a thing – a piece of garbage that no one's thrown away yet. Is that what you want me to say?'

'Shut up,' said Rob. He was still acting tough, but I could see his bluster was starting to fail. He didn't know what to say.

'The thing about boxes,' I said, 'is that you can open them up. Even though they're completely boring on the outside, there might be something interesting inside. So while you're saying all of these stupid, boring things I'm imagining what it would be like to cut you open and see what you've got in there.'

I paused, staring at him, and he stared back. He was scared. I let him hang on to that fear for a moment longer, then spoke again.

'The thing is, Rob, I don't want to cut you open. That's not who I want to be. So I made a rule for myself: anytime I want to cut someone open I say something nice to them instead. That is why I say, Rob Anders of 232 Carnation Street, that you are a great guy.'

Rob's mouth hung open like he was about to talk, then he closed it and backed away. He sat down on a chair, still looking at me, then got up again and left the room. I watched him all the way out.

'I . . .' said Brooke. I'd forgotten she was there. 'That was an interesting way to get him off your back.'

I didn't know what to say – she shouldn't have heard that. Why was I such an idiot?

'Just stuff,' I said quickly. 'I heard that in a movie, I think. Who'd have thought it would scare him so much?'

'Yeah,' said Brooke. 'I have to . . . It was nice talking to you, John.' She smiled uncertainly and walked away.

'Dude, that was awesome,' said Max.

I turned around in surprise. 'When did you get here?'

'I was here for most of it,' he said, coming around the side of the refreshment table, 'and it was awesome. Anders practically crapped his pants.'

'So did Brooke,' I said, looking in the direction she had gone. All I saw was a mass of people in the darkness.

'That was hilarious!' said Max, scooping up some punch. 'And after she was so into you, too.'

'Into me?'

'You missed *that*? You're blind, man. She was so going to ask you to dance.'

'Why would she ask me to dance?'

'Because we're at a dance,' said Max, 'and because you're a raging hot furnace of clown lovin'. I'd be surprised if she ever talks to you again though; that was *awesome*.'

The next night Max and I went trick-or-treating with his little sister Audrey. We did his neighbourhood first, his mom following us nervously with a flashlight and a thing of pepper spray. When we finished there she drove us to my neighbourhood, and Mr Crowley shook his head when we visited their house.

'You shouldn't be out this late,' he said, frowning. 'It's not safe with that killer out there.'

'All the street lights are on,' I said, 'and the porch lights, and we've got an adult with us. They even said on the news that they put out some extra police. We're probably safer tonight than most others.'

Mr Crowley ducked behind his door to cough loudly, then turned back to us. 'Don't be out too long, you hear me?'

'We'll be careful,' I said, and Mr Crowley handed out the candy.

'I don't want this town to live in fear,' he said sadly. 'It used to be so happy here.' He coughed again and closed the door.

Things that had seemed silly in the light of day – fake blood and prosthetic limbs – seemed more ominous now in the darkness of night. More terrifying. The killer was back on everyone's mind, and they were nervous. All the store-bought goofy Halloween scares were replaced with true life-and-death terror. It was the best Halloween ever.

# CHAPTER 6

'This is Ted Rask with a Five Live News exclusive report from Clayton, a peaceful town in the grip of an escalating crisis thanks to what some are calling "the Clayton Killer", Many people here are afraid to leave their homes at night, and some are even afraid during the light of day. In spite of this pervading sense of fear, however, there is hope. The police and FBI have made an astonishing breakthrough in their investigation.'

It was six o'clock at night, and I was watching the news. Mom said it was weird for a fifteen year old to be so interested in the news, but since we didn't get Court TV the local news was usually the only thing that interested me. Besides, the serial killer was still a hot topic, and Ted Rask's ongoing coverage had become the most popular show in town, despite – or perhaps because of – its breathless sense of melodrama. Outside, a November snowstorm raged, but inside we warmed ourselves by the fire of a media frenzy.

'As you remember from my first report on the death of local farmer David Bird,' said Rask, 'there was an oily substance found near the site; we initially suspected it was left by some kind of getaway vehicle, but forensic tests have now shown it to be biological in nature. According to an unnamed source of mine inside the investigation, the FBI was able to find in that substance a very small sample of DNA in an advanced state of degeneration. Early this morning they identified that DNA as being human in origin – but that, unfortunately, is where the trail ends. The DNA does not match either of the victims, nor does it match any of the current suspects, local Missing Persons cases, or anyone in the state DNA records. I should stress here that the DNA database we're dealing with is very limited. The technology is new, and there are very few records in any city that date back more than five years. Without widespread DNA testing comparable to the National Fingerprint Database, this DNA signature may never be identified.'

He was so steely and serious, as if he could win a journalism award through sheer charisma. Mom still hated him, and refused to watch. It was only a matter of time, she said, before he started pointing fingers and somebody got lynched. Tensions were high in town, and the prospect of a third killing hung over us all like a cloud.

'While police have been testing the crime-scene evidence,' Rask went on, 'the Five Live News team has been doing an investigation of our own, and we've turned up something very interesting: an unsolved case from Arizona, more than forty years old, involving a black substance very similar to that found in this case. Could it help catch the killer? We'll have more on that story tonight at ten. This is Ted Rask, Five Live News. Back to you, Sarah.'

But Ted Rask did not come back at ten. The demon got him. His cameraman found him just after eight-thirty in the alley behind their motel, gutted and missing a leg. Smeared on his face and head was a huge blob of acrid black sludge. It must have been hot, because it blistered him red as a lobster.

'I hear you've been terrorizing the kids at school,' said Dr Neblin.

I ignored the doctor and stared out of the window, thinking about Rask's body. Something about it was . . . wrong.

'I don't want you to use my diagnosis as a weapon to scare people with,' said Neblin. 'We're doing this so you can improve yourself, not so you can throw your psychology in other people's faces.'

Faces. Rask's face had been smeared with the sludge – why? It seemed humiliating – something the killer had never been before. What was happening?

'You're ignoring me, John,' said Neblin. 'Are you thinking about the new murder last night?'

'It wasn't a murder,' I said. 'It was a serial killing.'

'Is there a difference?'

'Of course there's a difference,' I said, spinning around to stare at him. I felt almost . . . betrayed by his ignorance. 'You're a psychologist, you should know this. Murder is . . .

well, different. Murderers are people like drunks and jealous husbands – they have reasons for what they do.'

'Serial killers don't have reasons?'

'Killing is its own reason,' I said. 'There's something inside of a serial killer that's hungry, or empty, and killing is how they fill it. Calling it murder makes it sound cheap. Makes it sound stupid.'

'And you don't want serial killing to sound stupid.'

'It's not that, it's . . . I don't know how to say it.' I turned back towards the window. 'It feels wrong.'

'Maybe you're trying to make serial killers into something they're not,' said Neblin. 'You want them to have some kind of special significance.'

I ignored him, sullen. The cars outside drove slowly on the sheet of black ice that covered the street. I hoped one of them slid into a pedestrian.

'You saw the news last night?' asked Neblin. He was baiting me to talk by bringing up my favourite subject. I kept silent and stared out of the window.

'It seems a little suspicious,' he said. 'That reporter announced that he had a clue related to the killer, and then died just an hour and a half before he had the chance to reveal that clue to the world. It seems to me that he was on to something.'

Great thinking, *Sherlock*. The news at ten had made the same conclusion.

'I don't really want to talk about this,' I said.

'Then maybe we can talk about Rob Anders,' said Neblin.

I turned back to look at him. 'I wanted to ask who told you about that.'

'I got a call from the school counsellor yesterday,' said Neblin. 'As far as I know, she and I are the only ones he's talked to. You gave him nightmares though.'

I smiled.

'It's not funny, John, it's a sign of aggression.'

'Rob is a bully,' I said. 'He has been since third grade. If you want some signs of aggression, just follow him around for few hours.'

'Aggression is normal in a fifteen-year-old boy,' said Neblin. 'Bully or otherwise. Where I get concerned is when that aggression comes from a sociopathic fifteen year old who's obsessed with death – especially when, up until now, he's been a model of non-confrontational behaviour. What's changed for you recently, John?'

'Well, there's a serial killer in town stealing people's body parts. You may have heard; it's been in the news.'

'Has the presence of a killer in town affected you?'

The monster behind the wall stirred.

'It's very close,' I said. 'Closer than I've ever been to the killers I study. I'll check out books and go online and read about serial killers for – well, not for fun, but you know what I mean – but they're all so far away. They're real, and their realness is part of what's fascinating, but . . . this is Nowhere, USA. They're supposed to be real somewhere else, not here.'

'Are you afraid of the killer?'

'I'm not afraid of being killed,' I said. 'All three victims so far have been grown men, so I assume he's going to stick to that pattern. That means I'm safe, and Mom and Margaret and Lauren are safe.'

'What about your father?'

'My father's not here,' I said. 'I don't even know where he is.'

'But are you afraid for him?'

'No,' I said slowly. It was true, but there was something I wasn't telling him, and I could tell that he knew it.

'Is there anything else?'

'Should there be?' I asked.

'If you don't want to talk about it, we won't,' said Neblin.

'But what if we need to?' I asked.

'Then we will.'

Sometimes therapists could be so open-minded it was a miracle they kept anything in there at all. I stared at him for a while, weighing the pros and cons of the conversation I knew would come, and eventually decided it couldn't hurt.

'I had a dream last week that my dad was the killer,' I said.

Neblin didn't react. 'What did he do?'

'I don't know, he didn't even come to see me.'

'Did you want him to take you with him when he killed?' asked Neblin.

'No,' I said, uncomfortable in my chair. 'I . . . wanted to take him with me, where he couldn't kill any more.'

'What happened next?'

Suddenly I didn't want to talk about what happened

next, even though I was the one who brought it up. It was self-contradictory, I know, but dreams about killing your dad can do that to you. 'Can we talk about something else?'

'Sure we can,' he said, and made a note on his paper.

'Can I see that note?' I asked.

'Sure.' Neblin passed me his pad.

*First reason: Killer in town*
*Doesn't want to talk about father.*

'Why'd you write "first reason"?' I asked.

'The first reason why you scared Rob Anders. Are there more?'

'I don't know,' I said.

'If you don't want to talk about your father, how about your mother?'

The monster behind the wall stirred again. I'd come to think of it as a monster, but it wasn't anything like the demon that was killing everybody. That was a real thing, while this was just . . . well, me. Or the darker part of me, at least. You probably think it would be creepy to have a real monster hiding inside of you, but trust me – it's far, far worse when the monster is really just your own mind. Calling it a monster seemed to distance it a little, which made me feel better about it. Not much better, but I take what I can get.

'My mother is an idiot,' I said, 'and she won't let me into the back of the mortuary any more. It's been almost a month.'

'Until last night, nobody's died for almost a month,' he said. 'Why did you want to go in the back room if there was no work to do there?'

'I used to go there a lot – to think,' I said. 'I liked it.'

'Do you have anywhere else you can go and think?'

'I go to Freak Lake,' I said, 'but it's too cold now.'

'Freak Lake?'

'Clayton Lake,' I said. 'There's a lot of weird people there. But I practically grew up in that mortuary – she can't take that away.'

'You told me before that you'd only been helping in the back for a few years,' said Dr Neblin. 'Are there other parts of the mortuary you have an attachment to?'

'That reporter died last night,' I said, ignoring his question, 'and we might get him. They'll send him home for a funeral, of course, but they might send him to us first for embalming. I need to see that body and she's not going to let me.'

Neblin paused. 'Why do you need to see the body?' he asked.

'To know what he's thinking,' I said. Looking out the window again. 'I'm trying to understand him.'

'The killer?'

'There's something wrong about him and I can't figure it out.'

'Well,' said Neblin, 'we can talk about the killer, if that's what you want.'

'Really?'

'Really. But when we're done, you need to answer any question I ask.'

'What question?'

'You'll find out when I ask it,' said Neblin, smiling. 'So, what do you know about the killer?'

'Did you know he stole a kidney from the first body?'

Neblin cocked his head. 'I hadn't heard that.'

'Nobody has,' I said, 'so keep it quiet. When the body came to the mortuary the kidney was missing. Everything else looked like it had been shredded, but the kidney had been cut off pretty cleanly.'

'And what about the second body?'

'He took the arm,' I said, 'and the abdomen was slashed but not gutted; most of the innards were still inside.'

'And in the third he took a leg,' said Neblin. 'Interesting. So the piled-up organs in the first attack were incidental – he's not ritualizing the killings, he's just taking body parts.'

'That's *exactly* what I told Mom!' I said, pleased that he'd got it.

'Right before she threw you out of the back room?'

I shrugged. 'I guess it is a pretty creepy thing to say.'

'What's interesting to me,' said Neblin, 'is the way he leaves the bodies. He doesn't take them or hide them, he just leaves them out for people to find. That usually means the serial killer is trying to make a statement, so that we'll see the body and get whatever message he's trying to make. But if what you say is true then he's not displaying the bodies – he's just striking quickly and fading out, spending as little time with his kills as he can.'

'But what does that mean?' I asked.

'For one thing,' said Neblin, 'he probably hates what he's doing.'

'That makes a lot of sense,' I said, nodding. 'I hadn't thought of that.' I felt guilty for not having thought of it. Why hadn't it occurred to me that a killer wouldn't enjoy killing? 'But he defaced the reporter's body,' I said, 'so he had some kind of motive there beyond just ending his life.'

'With a serial killer,' said Neblin, 'the motive is very likely an emotional one: he was angry, or frustrated, or confused. Don't make the mistake of thinking that sociopaths can't feel. They do feel – very keenly – they just don't know what to do with their emotions.'

'You said he didn't like killing,' I said, 'but so far he's taken a souvenir from all three. That doesn't make sense. Why does he take things from an event he doesn't want to remember?'

'That's a good one to ponder,' said Neblin, jotting it down on his pad, 'but now it's time for my question.'

'All right,' I said, sighing and looking back out of the window. 'Let's get it over with.'

'Tell me what Rob Anders was doing right before you threatened to kill him.'

'I didn't threaten to kill him.'

'You talked about his death in a threatening manner,' said Neblin. 'Let's not split hairs.'

'We were in the gym at school for the Halloween dance,' I said, 'and he was kind of bugging me – teasing me and knocking over my drink and things like that. So then when I was talking to someone he came up and just really started making fun of me, and I knew the only two ways to get rid of him were to punch him or to scare him. I have a rule about not hurting people, so I scared him.'

'You don't have a rule about threatening to kill people?'

'It hadn't come up yet,' I said. 'I have one now.'

'Who were you talking to?'

'Why does that matter?'

'I'm just curious about who you were talking to.'

'Some girl.'

The monster behind the wall growled, low and rumbling.

Dr Neblin cocked his head. 'Does she have a name?'

'Brooke,' I said, suddenly uncomfortable. 'She's nobody; she's lived on my street for years.'

'Is she cute?'

'She's a little young for you, Doctor.'

'Let me rephrase that,' he said, smiling. 'Are you attracted to her?'

'I thought we were talking about Rob Anders,' I said.

'Just curious,' he said, making a note on his pad. 'We're about done for the day anyway. Is there anything else you want to talk about?'

'I don't think so.' Out of the window, cars passed carefully between the buildings, like beetles in a maze. The Five Live News van crept slowly past, headed east – out of town.

'Looks like he scared them off,' said Neblin, following my gaze.

He was probably right . . . Wait! That was it! That was the piece I'd been missing.

The killer scared them off.

'It's not a serial killer,' I said suddenly.

'It's not?' asked Neblin.

'It's all wrong,' I said. 'It can't be. He didn't run away after killing Rask: he displayed the corpse, just like you said, by smearing that sludge all over him. He wasn't just trying to cover up the news, he was trying to scare them away. Don't you see? He had a reason!'

'And you think serial killers don't have reasons.'

'They don't,' I said. 'Search through every criminal record you've got and you'll never find a serial killer who kills someone just because they're getting too close. Most of them go out of their way to get more media coverage, not less. They love it. Half of them write letters to the press.'

'Doesn't fame count as a reason?'

'It's not the same thing,' I said. 'They don't kill because they want attention, they want attention because they kill. They want people to see what they're doing. Killing is still the root reason – the basic need the killers are trying to fulfil. And this guy has something else; I don't know what it is, but it's there.'

'What about John Wayne Gacy?' asked Neblin. 'He killed gay men because he wanted to punish them. That's a reason.'

'Very few of the men he killed were actually gay,' I said. 'How much about him have you actually read? The gay thing wasn't a reason, it was an excuse – he needed to kill something, and claiming that he was punishing sinners let him feel less guilty about it.'

'You're getting a little overexcited, John,' said Neblin. 'Maybe we should stop now.'

'Serial killers don't have time to kill nosy reporters, because they're too busy killing people that fit their victim profile: old men, little kids, blonde college students, whatever,' I said. 'Why is this one different?'

'John,' said Neblin.

I could feel myself getting light-headed, like I was hyperventilating. Dr Neblin was right; it was time to stop. I took a deep breath and closed my eyes. There would be time for this later. Still, I felt a buzz of energy, like the sound of rushing water in my ears. This killer was something different, something new.

The monster behind the wall sniffed gruffly at the air. It smelled blood.

# CHAPTER 7

I first noticed the drifter by the movie theatre downtown. Clayton gets its fair share of drifters – people passing through looking for work, or food, or a bus fare to the next town over – but this one was different. He wasn't panhandling, and he wasn't talking to people, he was just looking. Watching. Nobody watched people that much, and for that long, except me, and I had serious emotional problems. I decided that anyone who reminded me of myself was worth keeping an eye on. He might be dangerous.

My rules wouldn't let me follow him, or even look for him, but I saw him a few more times over the next few days – sitting in the park watching kids slide down the ploughed-up snowbanks in the parking lot, or standing by the gas station, smoking, watching people fill up their tanks. It was like he was evaluating us, checking us all against some list in his head. I half-expected the police to come pick him up, but he wasn't doing anything illegal. He was just there. Most people – especially if they didn't read criminal profiling books for fun, like I did – would just pass right over him. He had some kind of strange ability to blend in, even in a pretty small place like Clayton County, and most people just didn't notice him.

When the news reported a burglary a few days later, he was the first person I thought of. He was alert, he was analytical, and he'd watched our town for long enough to know who was worth following home and robbing. The question was, was he only a burglar, or was he something more? I didn't know how long he'd been in town; if he'd been around for a while he might well be the Clayton Killer. Rules or no rules, I needed to see what he did next.

It was like standing on the edge of a cliff, trying to convince myself to jump off. I followed my rules for a reason – they helped keep me from doing things I didn't want to do – but this was a special case, right? He was dangerous, and if breaking this rule helped stop him – and it was really a pretty minor rule, after all – then it was good. It was a good thing to do. I wrestled with myself for a week, and finally rationalized the idea that it was better, in the long run, to break this one rule and follow the drifter. I might even save somebody's life.

The day before Thanksgiving I had no school, and though Ted Rask's body came into the mortuary that morning, Mom refused to let me help, so my day was free. I went downtown and rode around for an hour until I found him, sitting on the bus bench by Allman's hardware store. I went across the street to Friendly Burger and sat in a window booth to watch him.

He was the right size to be the Clayton Killer – not huge, but big, and he looked strong enough to take down a guy like Jeb Jolley. His hair was brown and long, about chin-length, and he wore it shaggy. It wasn't such a strange look in Clayton County, especially in the winter. It was freezing cold, and long hair helped keep your ears warm. He'd have done better if he had a hat, but then I suppose drifters can't be choosers.

His breath came out in short, hazy puffs – not the long, lazy clouds of the other people on the street. That meant he was breathing rapidly, which meant he was nervous. Was he looking for a victim?

The bus came and went, and he didn't get on. He was watching something across the street – across from him, which meant it was on the same side as me. I looked around. The Twain Station book store was on the left of the burger joint, and Earl's Hunting Supply store was on the right. The drifter was looking at the hunting store, which was a little ominous in itself. The street out front had a couple of cars, one of which looked familiar. Who did I know with a white Buick?

When Mr Crowley came out of the hunting store laden with fishing supplies, I knew why the car looked so familiar – it spent most of its time fifty feet from my house. Forcing yourself not to think about people made even simple details like that hard to remember.

When the drifter stood up and jogged across the street towards Mr Crowley, I knew the situation had become very important very suddenly. I wanted to hear this. I went outside, knelt down by my bike, and made a show of pretending to unlock the chain. I hadn't even chained it to anything, but it was next to some pipes and I figured neither Crowley nor the drifter was paying close attention. I was a good thirty feet away from them – if I was lucky, they wouldn't pay any attention to me at all.

'Fishing?' asked the drifter. He looked like he was about thirty-five or forty, weathered by wind and age. 'It's a little cold for that, this time of year.'

Mr Crowley looked up with a smile. 'Ice fishing,' he said, holding up a chisel. 'Lake froze over a week or two ago, and I figure it's safe to walk on by now.'

'You don't say,' said the drifter. 'I used to go ice fishing all the time back in the day. Good times.'

'A fellow fisherman?' asked Mr Crowley, perking up. 'Not too many people around here are into ice fishing. Earl here had to special order the new auger for me. As cold as it is today, and with the wind picking up, I bet there won't even be skaters. I'll have the whole lake to myself.'

'Is that so?' asked the drifter. I frowned. There was something in his voice that bothered me. Was he going to rob Crowley's house while he was out fishing?

*Was he going to follow Crowley to the lake and kill him?*

'You busy?' asked Mr Crowley. 'It gets awful lonely on that lake and I could do with the company. I've got an extra pole.'

*Crowley, you idiot.*

'That's very kind of you,' said the drifter, 'though I'd hate to impose.'

What was Mr Crowley thinking? I thought about jumping

up to warn him, but I stopped myself. I was probably just imagining things.

Though Mr Crowley was a perfect match for the victim profile – an older white male with a large build.

'Don't worry about it,' said Mr Crowley. 'Climb in. You have a hat?'

'I'm afraid not.'

'Then we'll swing by and get you one on our way out,' said Crowley, 'and a bit of extra lunch. A friend to fish with is worth five dollars, easy.'

They climbed into his car and drove away. I almost got up to warn him again, but I knew where they were going – and I knew that they'd delay for a while buying food and a hat. It would be a gamble, but I might be able to make it out there before them and hide. I wanted to see what happened.

I made it to the most well-used stretch of lake in just half an hour, where the slope down from the road to the shore was more gradual, and you could walk right out to the edge. There was no sign of Mr Crowley or his dangerous passenger, or of anybody else for that matter. We had the lake to ourselves. I hid my bike in a snow bank on the south side of the clearing, and crouched in a small stand of trees to the north. If Mr Crowley actually went through with it, this is where he would come. I sat down to wait.

The lake was frozen, as Crowley had expected, and dusted with grainy white snow. On the far side a low hill loomed up, tall only by contrast to the flat expanse of the lake.

Wind whipped across them both, spirals of air made visible by the snow within it, eddies and swirls and drill-bit tornadoes. I crouched in the shadows and froze as the wind made faces in the sky.

Exposure to nature – cold, heat, water – is the most dehumanizing way to die. Violence is passionate and real. The final moments as you struggle for your life, firing a gun or wrestling a mugger or screaming for help, your heart pumps loudly and your body tingles with energy; you are alert and awake and, for that brief moment, more alive and human than you've ever been before.

Not so with nature. At the mercy of the elements the opposite happens: your body slows, your thoughts grow sluggish, and you realize just how mechanical you really are. Your body is a machine, full of tubes and valves and motors, of electrical signals and hydraulic pumps, and they function properly only within a certain range of conditions. As temperatures drop, your machine breaks down: cells begin to freeze and shatter; muscles use more energy to do less; blood flows too slowly, and to the wrong places. Your senses fade, your core temperature plummets, and your brain fires random signals that your body is too weak to interpret or follow. In that state you are no longer a human being, you are a malfunction – an engine without oil, grinding itself to pieces in its last futile effort to complete its final, meaningless command.

I heard a car approach and turn off into the clearing. I watched from the corner of my eye, keeping myself hidden in the trees, and recognized Crowley's white Buick. The drifter got out first and stared darkly at the lake, until the other door opened and Crowley coughed.

'I haven't been ice fishing in an age,' said the stranger, glancing back at Mr Crowley. 'Thanks again for letting me tag along.'

'Not a problem at all,' said Mr Crowley, walking back to the trunk. He handed the stranger a fishing pole and a bucket full of tools, nets, an ice auger, and a pair of folding stools, then closed the trunk. He was carrying a pole of his own, and a small cooler. 'I keep two of everything, just in case,' he said, smiling. 'There's enough hot chocolate in here to keep us both warm and happy.'

'That lunch filled me right up,' said the drifter. 'Don't worry about it.'

'Out here we're partners,' said Crowley. 'What's mine is yours, and yours is mine.' He grinned.

'What's yours is mine,' repeated the stranger, and I felt the sense of danger rise. What was Mr Crowley doing? Picking up a drifter like this could be deadly, even if you didn't bring them out alone into the middle of nowhere – even if there wasn't a psycho killer on the loose.

I looked at the drifter's hands for any evidence of claw-like weapons, but they were empty and normal. Maybe he wasn't the killer, after all. Either way, I was dying of curiosity. If he was the killer, I wanted to see how he did it.

I frowned then, wondering at myself. Was I really more interested in watching the killer than in saving Crowley's life? I knew I shouldn't be. If I were a normal, empathic person, I'd jump up and save Crowley's life. But I wasn't.

So I watched.

Mr Crowley began walking carefully down the slope to the shore, and the stranger followed closely. I shrank back into my shelter of trees, trying to stay as small and as hidden as possible.

'Wait up a minute,' said the stranger. 'That coffee is finally catching up to me. I need to take a leak.' He set down his bucket and balanced the pole carefully across it. 'Won't be a minute.' He fled back up the slope and I cringed, terrified that he would come to my trees to pee, but he went to the other stand on the far side of the car.

My bike was right there. Surely he would see it.

The man delayed just long enough in choosing a good spot that I started to get suspicious. I glanced at Crowley and guessed that he was suspicious too; nervous lines creased his face, and he glanced back out at the ice as if it were a giant clock, and he was late for something. He coughed painfully.

I expected any minute for the drifter to see my bike and call out, or to pull a chainsaw out of the trees and leap down the bank with a howl, but nothing happened. He found a spot he liked, stood still, and after a long pause zipped up and turned around.

He must have been practically tripping over my bike. Why didn't he say anything? Maybe he'd seen it, and knew I was here, and was biding his time carefully until he could kill Crowley and me together.

'I gotta say again that this is awfully nice of you,' said the drifter. 'I'm mighty indebted to you, sir, and I don't know how I can ever repay you.' He laughed. 'Nicest thing I have is this hat, and you're the one that bought it.'

'We'll think of something,' said Crowley, and took off his glove to scratch the stubble of his beard. 'If nothing else, I'll just claim credit for all the good fish.' He smiled broadly, then coughed again.

'That cough sounds like it's getting worse,' said the stranger.

'Just a little problem with my lungs,' said Crowley, turning back to the frozen lake. 'It'll clear up soon.' He took a step onto the ice, probing it with one foot.

The drifter reached the bottom of the slope and stood for a moment by his bucket of tools. He went to pick it up, then stopped, glanced quickly back at the road, and slid his hand into his coat. When he pulled it back out he was holding a knife – not a switchblade or a hunting knife, just a long kitchen knife covered with dirt and rust. It looked like he'd stolen it from a junkyard.

'I'm thinking we ought to head out that way,' said Crowley, pointing north-east. 'Wind's just as bad everywhere, but that's the deepest part of the lake, and not too far from the head of the river. We'll get a little more current underneath us, and that makes for better fishing.'

The drifter stepped forward, his right hand tight around the knife and his left hand out to the side for balance. He was just an arm's length from Crowley's back; another step and he could strike a killing blow.

Crowley scratched his chin again. 'I'd like to thank you

for coming out here with me.' Cough. 'We'll make a good team, you and I.'

The drifter took a step closer.

'You have no family,' said Crowley, 'and I can barely breathe.' Cough. 'Between the two of us, I figure we make just about one whole person.'

'Wait . . . *what?*

The drifter paused, as perplexed as I was, and in that split second Crowley turned around and lashed out with his ungloved hand – longer now, somehow, and darker, his fingernails lengthening impossibly into sharp ivory claws.

The first swipe knocked the knife from the startled man's hand, spinning it straight past my stand of trees, and the second backhanded the stranger across the face, knocking him down into the cushion of snow. The drifter struggled to his feet, but Crowley dropped his cooler and pole and leaped on the man, roaring like a beast; another claw tore its way out of Crowley's other glove, shredding it as it grew, and both claws raked across the stranger's upraised arm, slicing flesh from bone. The man was hidden from my view now, deep in the snow, but I heard him cry out – a formless cry of pain and shock. Crowley roared back with a mouth full of gleaming, needlelike teeth. Two vicious strikes later and all was silent.

Mr Crowley crouched over the body in a cloud of steam, his arms too long and his unearthly talons bright with blood. His head had grown bulbous and dark; his ears were pointed like blades. His jaw was unnaturally low, and bristled with teeth. He panted heavily, and as I watched he slowly coalesced back into the form I knew. His arms and hands shortened, his claws shrank back to become regular fingernails, and his head deflated and reformed. A moment later it was plain old Mr Crowley again, as normal as could be. If not for the bloodstains on his clothes, no one would ever have guessed what he had become, or what he had done. He coughed and pulled the tattered glove from his left hand, dropping it wearily on the ground.

I sat in shock, my face bitten by the wind and my legs warm with my own urine. I didn't even remember peeing.

Mr Crowley was a monster.

Mr Crowley was *the* monster.

I was too scared to think about hiding – I simply sat and watched, freezing and nauseous. Crowley extended his right hand once more into a claw and began cutting away the stranger's layers of clothing.

'Try to kill me,' he muttered. 'I bought you a hat.'

He reached down with both hands and grimaced, and I heard a hideous cracking – one, two, three, four, five, six – a string of shattered ribs. He stooped lower, out of my sight, and stood up a moment later clutching a pair of shapeless, bloody bags.

Lungs.

Slowly, Mr Crowley began unbuttoning his coat . . . then his first flannel shirt . . . then his second . . . then his third. Soon his chest was bared to the cold and he gritted his teeth, breathing heavily and closing his eyes. He switched the ragged lungs into his human left hand, brought his demonic claw up to his belly, and sliced himself open just below the ribs. I gasped, just as a faint grunt escaped between Crowley's clenched teeth; it didn't look like he'd heard me. Blood poured from his open belly and he staggered one step, but quickly righted himself.

I felt past shock now – too numbed by what I had seen to do anything but stare.

Mr Crowley coughed again, wracked with pain, and shoved the lungs desperately into the gash in his abdomen. He fell to his knees, his face wrenched with agony, and I watched as the last bit of lung disappeared into him, as if drawn up by something inside. His eyes opened suddenly wide, wider, than I thought possible, and his mouth moved fearfully in a futile, noiseless gasp for air. Something dark oozed out of his wound and he reached for it quickly, pulling out another pair of lungs – similar to the first but black and sickly, like the lungs in a cancer commercial. The black lungs hissed as they slid from his open wound, and he dropped them on the stranger's dead body below. He paused there a moment, suspended in the utter silence of asphyxiation, motionless and airless, then gasped loudly and abruptly, like a diver emerging from a pool, desperate for air. He took three more breaths like that, huge and hungry, then began to breathe at a calmer, more measured pace. His right hand shrank back to normal, shifting somehow from monster to human, and he clutched his open wound with both hands. The hole sealed up, closing itself like a zipper. Half a minute later his chest was whole again, scarless and white.

The branches above me gave way suddenly, dropping a

clump of snow on the ground around my hiding-place. I bit my tongue to keep from screaming in alarm, and threw myself backward to lie prone in the hollow between the trunks. I could no longer see Crowley, but I heard him jump to his feet; I imagined him tensed and ready to fight – ready to kill anyone who'd witnessed even a part of his actions. I held my breath as he walked towards my trees, but he didn't stop or look in. He stepped past and stooped to look for something in the snow – the discarded knife, I assumed – and after a minute he straightened up and walked to his car. I heard the trunk click open, and a rustle of plastic, then the door slammed shut and he walked back to the corpse, his footsteps even and deliberate.

I'd just watched a man die. I'd just watched my next-door neighbour kill him. It was too much to process; I felt myself start to shiver uncontrollably, though whether it was from cold or from fear I couldn't tell. I tried to clamp down on my legs to keep them from shaking the undergrowth and giving me away.

I'm not sure how long I lay there in the snow, listening to him work and praying that he wouldn't find me. Snow was in my shoes, pants and shirt; it had crept down through my collar and up from my belt, all of it ice cold – so cold it burned. Outside, plastic rustled, bones thumped, and something squelched wetly, over and over. Eons later I heard Crowley dragging something heavy, followed by a grunt of effort and the click of his boots on the ice of the lake.

Two steps. Three steps. Four steps. When he reached ten steps I allowed myself to lean up – ever so slowly – and peer out of the trees. Crowley was out on the frozen water, a black plastic sack flung over his shoulders and the ice saw dangling from his belt. He walked slowly and carefully, testing his steps and trudging through the bitter wind. His silhouette grew smaller and smaller, and strong gusts heavy with shards of ice raced around him in fury, as if nature was angry at what he had done – or some darker power was pleased. Half a mile out, his lonely outline disappeared completely into the wind and snow, and he was gone.

I clambered awkwardly out of the trees, my legs like jelly and my mind racing. I knew I needed to cover my tracks somehow, and snapped off a low-hanging pine branch. I walked backwards toward my bike, brushing away my footprints as I went, as I'd seen an Indian do in one of those old John Wayne movies. It wasn't perfect, but it would have to do. When I reached my bike I pulled it up and raced around the far side of the trees, hoping Crowley wouldn't see my footprints that far away from the scene of the killing. I reached the road and jumped on, pedalling madly in order to reach town before he returned and passed me in his car.

Around me the pine trees were dark as demons' horns, and the setting sun on the oaks turned the bare branches red as bloody bones.

# CHAPTER 8

I slept very little that night, haunted by what I had seen at the lake. Mr Crowley had killed a man – killed him, just like that. One moment he was alive, screaming and fighting for his life, and the next moment he was nothing but a sack of meat. Life, whatever it was, had evaporated into nothing.

I longed to see it again, and I hated myself for it.

Mr Crowley was a monster of some kind – a beast in human form who seemed to have absorbed the lungs of the man he had killed. I thought about Ted Rask's missing leg, Jeb Jolley's kidney, and Dave Bird's arm: had Crowley absorbed those parts as well? I imagined him built entirely out of pieces of the dead: Dr Frankenstein and his monster rolled into one unholy killer. But where had it started? What had he been before the first piece was stolen? I saw again a vision of dark, leathery skin, a bulbous head and long, scythe-like claws. I was not religious, and knew next to nothing about the occult or the supernatural, but the word that leaped to mind was 'demon'. The Son of Sam had called the monsters in his life 'demons', and I figured if it was good enough for the Son of Sam it was good enough for me.

My mom was smart enough to leave me alone. I threw my pee-soaked clothes in the laundry when I got home and took a shower, and I suppose she saw the clothes, or smelled them, and assumed I'd had one of my accidents. It's rare for bedwetters to lose control while awake, but all of the reasons it might happen – intense anxiety, sadness, or fear – were sensitive enough that she avoided the subject that night and took out her frustration on the laundry instead of on me.

When I got out of the shower I locked myself in my room and stayed there until almost noon the next day, though I was tempted to stay longer. It was Thanksgiving, and Lauren had refused to come; the tension in the house would be overwhelming. After what I'd just been through, however, a tense dinner was nothing. I got dressed and went in the living room.

'Hi, John,' said Margaret. She was sitting on the couch and watching the end of the Macy's parade.

Mom looked up from the counter in the kitchen. 'Good morning, honey.' She never called me honey unless she was trying to make up for something. I grunted a vague response and poured a bowl of cereal.

'You must be starving,' said Mom. 'We're going to eat in just a couple of hours, but go ahead – you haven't eaten since lunch yesterday.'

I hated it when she was nice to me, because it seemed like she only did it in emergencies. It was like an open acknowledgement that something was wrong; I preferred to let things fester in silence.

I chewed my cereal slowly, wondering what Mom and Margaret would do if they knew the truth – that I had not been hiding because of fear or emotional turmoil, but because I was fascinated by the possibilities of a supernatural killer. I'd spent the night piecing together bits of the puzzle and the criminal profile, and I was delighted by how well it all worked. The killer was stealing body parts to replace ones that no longer worked. Crowley had bad lungs, so he got new ones, and it made sense that he'd killed the other victims for the same reason. His leg used to be so painful, but yesterday he had walked without limping or straining; he had replaced his bad leg with the one he stole from Rask. The black sludge found by each victim came from the degenerating parts he had discarded. The victims were old, large men because Crowley was an old, large man, and needed body parts that fitted him. The dual nature of the violent killings and the intellectual aftermath came from Crowley's own dual nature – a demon in a man's body.

Or, more correctly, a demon in a body made up of other men. The forty-year-old story Ted Rask had found in Arizona was probably the same thing – maybe even the same demon. Were there more demons like him? Had Crowley been in Arizona forty years ago? Rask was a showboating jerk, but he was on to something, and he'd died because of it.

But throughout my thinking I kept going back to the killing itself, and the blood and the sounds and the screams of a dying man. I knew, academically, that it should bother me more – that I should be throwing up, or crying, or blocking the memories out. Instead I simply ate a bowl of cereal and thought about what to do next. I could send the police to his house, but what evidence would they find? The last death had been a drifter that no one would even remember, let alone miss, and Crowley had sunk the body and all the evidence into the lake; he was getting smarter. Would they dredge a lake on an anonymous tip? Would they search a respected man's house on the word of a fifteen year old? I couldn't imagine that they would. If I wanted the police to believe me, I had to get them there at the scene of a murder. They had to catch him demon-handed. But how?

'John, can you help me with this stuffing?' Mom was standing by the table chopping celery, watching the parade in the other room.

'Sure,' I said, and got up. She handed me the knife and a couple of onions from the fridge. The knife was almost identical to the one the drifter had tried to kill Crowley with. I hefted it a bit, then chopped down through layers of onion.

'Time for the juice,' she said, and pulled the turkey out of the oven. She picked up a large syringe, poked it into the turkey, and squeezed the plunger. 'I saw this on TV yesterday,' she said. 'It's chicken broth, salt, basil, and rosemary. It's supposed to be really good.' By force of habit she'd poked in the syringe just above the turkey's collarbone, right where she would have inserted a pump tube in a corpse. I watched her inject the broth and imagined it swirling through the turkey, embalming it with salt and seasonings, filling it with an artificial perfection while a thick stream of blood and horror dripped out the bottom and fled underground. I peeled off the skin of the second onion, dry and papery, and chopped the bulb in half.

Mom covered the turkey and put it back into the oven.

'Don't we need to put the stuffing in?' I asked.

'You don't actually cook stuffing inside the turkey,' she said, rooting through the cupboard. 'That's a case of food poisoning waiting to happen.' She pulled out a small glass bottle with a tiny pool of brown at the bottom. 'Oh no, we're practically out. John, honey?'

There was that word again. 'Yeah?'

'Can you run over to the Watsons' and borrow some vanilla? Peg's sure to have some; at least someone on this street has her head on straight.'

That was Brooke's house. I hadn't allowed myself to think about her ever since Dr Neblin had asked me about her. I could feel myself fixating on her, thinking about her too much, so my rules stepped in to stop me. I wanted to say no, but I didn't want to have to explain why.

'Sure.'

'Take a coat, it snowed again.'

I pulled on my jacket and went down the stairs to the mortuary. It was dark and silent; I loved it like this. I'd have to come back later, if I could do it without making Mom suspicious. I pushed out through the side door and looked across the street at Mr Crowley's house. Snow had covered everything with a two-inch blanket of white.

Nothing was dirty after it snowed, at least not that you could see; the surface of every car and house and sewer grate was white and calm. I plodded through the snow to the Watsons', two houses over, and rang the doorbell.

'Brooke, can you get that?'

'I got it.' I heard footsteps, and soon Brooke Watson opened the door. She was wearing jeans and a sweatshirt, with her blond hair curled into a knot and held in place by a pencil. I'd avoided her since the dance, when she'd backed away so warily. Now she smiled – she actually smiled – when she saw me. 'Hey, John.'

'Hey. My mom needs some vanilla or something. Do you guys have any?'

'Like, ice cream?'

'No, it's brown, it's for cooking.'

'Mom,' she called, 'do we have any vanilla?' Brooke's mom stepped into the hall, wiping her hands on a towel, and waved me inside.

'Come in, come in. Don't leave him standing out there, Brooke, you'll freeze him to death.' She smiled as she said it, and Brooke laughed.

'You better come in,' she said with a smile. I kicked the snow off my shoes and stepped inside, and Brooke closed the door.

'It's your turn, Brooke, come on!' shouted a high voice, and I saw Brooke's little brother and father lying on the floor with a sprawling Monopoly game laid out in front of them. Brooke flopped down on the floor and rolled the dice, then counted out her move and groaned. Her little brother, Ethan, cackled with glee as she counted out a stack of play money.

'Pretty cold out there?' asked Brooke's father. He was still in his pyjamas, with thick wool socks on his feet to keep warm.

'It's your turn, Dad – go,' said Ethan.

'It's not bad,' I said, remembering last night. 'The wind's gone, at least.' *And I'm not hiding in the trees while my neighbour rips a man's lungs out, so that's good too.*

Brooke's mom bustled back into the room with a small Tupperware pot full of vanilla. 'That should be plenty to get you through,' she said. 'Would you like a cup of hot chocolate?'

'I would!' shouted Ethan, and jumped up and raced into the kitchen.

'No, thanks,' I said. 'Mom needs this for something, and I'd better get back with it soon.'

'If you need anything else, just let me know,' she said with a smile. 'Happy Thanksgiving!'

'Happy Thanksgiving, John,' said Brooke. I opened the door and she stood up to follow me. She looked as if she were about to say something, then wiggled her head and laughed. 'See you at school,' she said, and I nodded.

'See you at school.'

She waved as I walked down the steps, flashing her braces in a wide smile. It was achingly beautiful, and I forced myself to look away. My rules were too engrained. She was safer this way.

I trudged back home, the vanilla shoved deep into my

pocket and my hands curled into fists for warmth. Every house looked the same in the snow – a white lawn, a white driveway, a white roof, the corners rounded and the features dulled. No one would ever guess, driving by, that one home contained a joyful family, another contained a wretched half-family, and another hid the lair of a demon.

Thanksgiving dinner passed as well as could be expected at my house. Every channel was running either a family movie or a football game, and Mom and Margaret watched blandly as they ate; I arranged my chair to get a good view of the Crowleys' house, and stared out of the window all through the meal.

Mom flipped through the channels restlessly. Before Dad left, Thanksgiving was a football day, from start to finish, and Mom complained about it every year. Now she flipped through the games aggressively, pausing longer on the non-game channels as if to give them a higher status: they didn't remind her of Dad, so they were better than the rest.

My parents never got along super well, but it had grown worse in the last year before he left. Eventually he moved to an apartment on the other side of town, where he stayed for almost five months while the divorce wound its way through the intestinal tract of the county courts. I stayed with him every other week, but even the brief contact they made while making the switch was too much for my parents, and eventually they just stayed on opposite sides of the supermarket parking lot, late at night when it was empty, and I carried my pillow and backpack from one car to the other in the dark. I was seven years old.

One night, halfway to my mom's car, I heard my dad's engine roar; he turned on his headlights and pulled out onto the road, turning at the corner and disappearing in an angry rush of sound. It was the last time I ever saw him. He sent presents at Christmas, and sometimes on my birthday, but there was never a return address. He was as good as dead.

Our meal ended with a store-bought pumpkin pie and a can of spray-on cream. The turkey carcass crouched in the centre of the table like a bony spider; I thought about the dead man at the lake, and reached out and snapped a turkey rib with my fingers. The TV droned in the background. There was a marked absence of conflict; this was as close as my house got to happy.

'Good evening, and welcome to Five Live News. I'm Walt Daines.'

'And I'm Sarah Bello. Many people are choosing to celebrate their Thanksgiving holiday with deep fried turkey, but the deep fryers can be dangerous. More on that in a minute, but first an update on the Clayton County Killer who has thus far claimed three lives, including Five Live News reporter Ted Rask. Here's Carrie Walsh with a report.'

All three of us sat up straight, eyes glued to the TV.

'The town of Clayton is afraid,' said a young reporter standing by the Wash-n-Dry; she'd probably only come because she was too junior to pass the job on to anybody else. It was much brighter on TV than it was outside, and

I guessed that she'd probably filmed this segment around two in the afternoon. 'Police patrol the streets at all hours of the day, and even now, in full daylight, I am accompanied by an armed escort of police officers.' The camera pulled back to show that she was indeed flanked by an officer on each side.

'What is everyone so afraid of?' she went on. 'Three unsolved murders, in the space of just three months. The police have very few leads, but investigative reporter Ted Rask uncovered evidence so sensitive, the murderer killed him for it.' Her voice was even, but her eyes were bloodshot and her knuckles gripping the microphone were white as bone. She was terrified. 'Today, assisted by Agent Forman of the FBI, we bring that evidence to you, to help catch a killer.'

The scene cut away to some kind of records facility, as the FBI agent explained in voice-over the story of Emmet T. Openshaw, an Arizona man who disappeared from his home forty-two years ago. He was an adult, but not a very old one – forty, maybe? I'm no good at guessing ages. He looked vaguely familiar, in the way that old photos tend to do – that niggling impression in the back of your head that if the person had a modern haircut and clothes, it would be someone you saw every day. The police found blood and signs of violence, but no body; most importantly, and the reason the story was related to Clayton County, they also found a puddle of black sludge in the middle of the man's kitchen floor. The police had a few theories of their own, which the reporter nervously explained, but none of them matched what I had seen. How could they?

I stared at the TV screen and imagined the man in Arizona; he heard a knock on his door, opened it, and found Mr Crowley there with a story about a broken car or a lost map. Mr Crowley asked to come in, the man let him, and when his back was turned Crowley ripped his throat out and stole his . . . what? The police never found the body, so they never knew that the killer had stolen a piece of it.

But why would he hide his bodies back then, and not hide his first three now? It didn't make sense. Thinking back to the FBI classifications, it was as if he used to be an organized killer, and had become a disorganized one. And now his attack on the drifter had moved back to the organized side of the spectrum again. Why?

The news footage switched to show the FBI agent, sitting in a bland office for an interview that must have been filmed earlier. 'DNA testing has continued in the Clayton case,' said Agent Forman, 'and the sludge found next to the three Clayton victims is consistent. The FBI can't identify whose DNA it is, but we do know that it is definitely all from the same person.'

The same person? That didn't make any sense either. If the sludge came from the discarded organs, and each organ came from a different body, wouldn't the DNA be different each time? That kind of science was a little beyond the tenth-grade level, unfortunately, so I couldn't figure it out myself. And since I was basing my theories on information the FBI agent didn't have, he didn't offer any further explanation either.

'Emmet T. Openshaw died so long ago, unfortunately, that no DNA testing was possible,' said Agent Forman, 'and none of the sludge found in his home was saved as evidence. Quite frankly, we don't know why or even if this information is significant – only that the killer wanted to keep it quiet. If this information means anything to you, or if you have any leads at all, please talk to the police. Your identity will be kept confidential. Thank you.'

The screen switched back to the live reporter, who nodded curtly and looked at the camera. 'This is Carrie Walsh with Five Live News. Back to you, Sarah.'

Did they really want any leads at all? Even preposterous ones?

It was obvious that the demon was more than the sum of his parts. He could turn his hands – one of which had belonged to a farmer just two months ago – into demon claws. He needed body parts from humans, that much seemed certain, but when he absorbed them, they became a part of him. They took on his properties and strengths and, apparently, his DNA signature.

But if that were true, why was the DNA recognizably human? Did demons even have DNA?

Preposterous or not, I needed to go to the police. The only other choice was to try to stop him myself, and I had no idea where to begin. Could I shoot him? Stab him? He could heal back from some pretty serious wounds, so I doubted either of those would do any good. Besides that, I knew it would be wrong. I'd spent too much time protecting myself from thoughts of violence to stumble into it now.

The monster behind the wall strained and growled, awake and anxious to be set free. I didn't dare let it out – who knew what it would do?

My only dilemma, again, was how to get the police to believe me. I had to give them more than just my word; I had to offer some kind of evidence. If they came by and looked at Mr Crowley's house, they probably wouldn't find anything; he was being too careful now, and hiding his tracks too well. If I wanted them to know for sure, they had to see what I'd seen. They had to catch him in the act, save his victim, and see his demon claws for themselves.

The only way I could do that was to study him, and follow him, and call them when he made his move. I had to become Mr Crowley's shadow.

# CHAPTER 9

The hardest part was the first step: out of my door, across the street, and up Mr Crowley's path to his front porch. I hesitated before I knocked. If he had seen me at the lake – if he had any suspicion that I knew his secret – he might just kill me on sight. I knocked. It was several degrees below zero, but I kept my hands out of my pockets, ready to balance if I had to run.

Mrs Crowley opened the door. Was she a demon too?

'Hello, John. How are you today?'

'I'm fine, Mrs Crowley. How are you?' I heard a creak in the house behind her – Mr Crowley moving slowly from one room to another. *Did she know what he was?*

'I'm fine, dear. What brings you out here on such a cold evening?' Mrs Crowley was old and small, the most stereotypical 'little old lady' I'd ever seen. She wore wide glasses, and it occurred to me that Mr Crowley didn't. Did he steal new eyes every time his old ones wore out?

'It snowed last night,' I said. 'I want to shovel your walks.'

'On Thanksgiving?'

'Yes,' I said. 'I'm not really doing anything else.'

Mrs Crowley smiled slyly. 'I know why you're really here,' she said. 'You want some hot chocolate.'

I smiled – a careful, practised smile designed to look exactly like a fifteen-year-old boy caught in an innocent trap. I'd worked on it all night. Mrs Crowley gave me hot chocolate every time I shovelled their snow; it was the only time I was ever invited inside. I was here today because I needed to be invited inside. I had to see if Mr Crowley was healthy or sick, and how bad he was. Eventually he'd have to kill again, and I needed to know exactly when – if I wanted to send the police to catch him in the act.

'I'll put some on the stove right now,' she said. 'The shovel's in the shed.' She closed the door and I walked around the house, my feet crunching softly in the snow. It had begun.

Mr Crowley came on to the porch a few minutes later, the picture of health; he walked straight and tall, and never coughed once. His new limbs were working well for him. Mr Crowley walked to the edge of the railing and watched me; I tried to ignore him, but I was far too nervous to turn my back on him. I stood up and faced him.

'Good evening,' I said.

'Good evening, John,' he answered, as cheerful as I'd ever seen him. I couldn't tell if he suspected me or not.

'Did you have a nice Thanksgiving?' I asked.

'Just fine,' he said. 'Just fine. Kay cooks a mighty good turkey, I'll tell you – the best in the State.'

He wasn't just watching me, he was looking all around

– at the snow, the trees, the houses, everything. I'd almost say he was happy, and I guess that made sense. He had a brand new set of healthy lungs; he literally had a new lease on life. I wondered how long it would last.

He wasn't going to kill me; he didn't seem to suspect that I knew his secret at all. Satisfied that I was safe for now, I went back to my shovelling.

For the next two weeks I spent my days shovelling snow, and my nights praying for more. Every two or three days I found a new excuse to see them – shovelling another snowfall, or chopping firewood, or helping carry in the groceries. Mr Crowley was as nice as ever, talking and joking and kissing his wife. He seemed a paragon of good health, until one day I noticed a laxative while unloading a grocery bag.

'It's his tummy,' said Mrs Crowley with a mischievous grin. 'Us old folks can't eat like we used to. Things start to fall apart.'

'I thought he looked pretty healthy.'

'Just a little problem with his digestion,' she said. 'It's nothing to worry about.'

Well, not unless Mr Crowley has his eye on your digestive system.

But I wasn't afraid for her. Her seventy-year-old organs were probably not worth stealing, for one thing, but it was more than that. He treated her nicely; he kissed her hello every time he came into the room. Even if she was just his cover story, he wouldn't hurt her.

On 9 December, late one Saturday night, Mr Crowley slipped out of his house and removed his licence plates. I was watching from my window, fully dressed, just as I did every night, and as soon as he stowed the plates and drove away I sneaked downstairs and went out of the side door. The wind was blowing just enough to cut coldly through my scarf and into my face, and I had to cycle slowly to keep my balance on the icy roads. I'd taken the reflectors off of my bike, making me nearly invisible in the blackness, but I wasn't afraid of being hit. The roads were virtually empty.

Mr Crowley was also driving slowly, and I followed his tail-lights at a distance. The only things open this time of night were the hospital and the Flying J, both on the outskirts of town. I assumed he'd go to the latter to try to pick up another drifter, but instead he cruised slowly toward the tiny downtown area. It made sense – it would probably be empty this time of night, but if he did find anyone he could kill them with impunity. There were no open businesses, no homes, and no witnesses to hear the screaming.

Suddenly another car came around the corner, far ahead of me, and pulled up next to Mr Crowley at a stoplight. It was a police car. I imagined them asking him if everything was all right, if he needed anything, if he'd seen anything suspicious. The light turned green and the cars idled there a moment longer, then drove away. The cops went straight, and Crowley turned right. I pedalled hard to catch up, anticipating his route and turning down a side road to stay out of the street lights. I didn't want Crowley or the cops to see me.

When I found him again, Crowley was pulled over, talking to a man on the sidewalk. I watched them for several moments, seeing the man straighten up twice to look down the street; not searching for anything, simply looking. Would he be the one? He wore a dark parka and a baseball cap – not nearly warm enough for this weather, or this time of night. Crowley was almost certainly offering him a ride: *Come in out of the cold, we'll turn up the heat and take you where you need to go. Halfway there, I'll gut you like a fish.*

The man looked up again. I watched him without breathing. I honestly don't know if I wanted him to get in the car or not. I was going to call the cops, of course, but they might not make it in time. What would I do if this guy died? Should I abandon my plan and just run out now to warn him? If I saved him, Crowley would only look for somebody else. I couldn't follow him for the rest of my life, warning people. I had to take the risk and wait for the right moment.

The man opened the passenger door and got in Crowley's car. There was no turning back now.

There was a payphone outside of the gas station on Main, and if I could reach it in time I could call the police and tell them to find the car. They might arrest him, they might shoot him; either way it would be over.

Crowley's car turned right and I went left, keeping to the shadows until he was out of sight.

When I reached the payphone I covered the receiver

with my scarf, using gloves to keep everything free of fingerprints. I didn't want anyone to trace the call back to me.

'911,' said a voice. 'What is the address of the emergency?'

'The Clayton Killer has another victim, in his car, right now. Tell the police to look for a white Buick LeSabre, somewhere between downtown and the wood plant.'

'The . . .' The dispatcher paused. 'You say you saw the Clayton Killer?'

'I saw him pick up a new victim,' I said. 'Send someone now!'

'Do you have any evidence that this man is the killer?' asked the dispatcher.

'I saw him kill somebody else,' I said.

'Tonight?'

'Two weeks ago.'

'Did you report this incident to the police?' The dispatcher sounded almost . . . bored.

'You're not taking this seriously,' I said. 'He's going to kill somebody right now. Send the police!'

'A squad car has been advised to patrol the area between downtown Clayton and the Clayton wood plant, on the grounds of an anonymous tip,' said the bored dispatcher. 'The thirteenth anonymous tip of the week, I might add. Unless you'd like to give me a name?'

'You're going to feel really stupid in the morning,' I said. 'Send some cops now – I'll try to stall him.' I hung up and jumped on my bike. I had to find them.

They had turned towards the wood plant nearly ten

minutes ago; they could be anywhere by now, including Freak Lake. I drove back down Main Street to where he'd turned, to try to follow or guess his path, but halfway there I heard a car door slam, and went to investigate. A block and a half away, surrounded by quiet store-fronts and dimly lit by the light of the moon, Mr Crowley's car was parked behind another on the side of the road. Crowley was walking from his trunk towards a heap on the ground. As I got closer I could see that the heap was a body lying on a tarp. I was too late.

I dropped my bike in a shadow and crept closer to Crowley while his back was turned; I reached the corner of his block, just half a block away, and ducked into a store-front alcove. The second car was the victim's, I guessed, broken down in the worst possible place, on the worst possible night – in the dark, far from human ears, and close to Mr Crowley. Crowley had apparently found him looking for help and offered to take a look.

Next to the body on the tarp was a pile of steaming black sludge – he'd already made the switch, of stomach or intestines or whatever he needed from this one, and he'd had the foresight to lay out a groundcloth to catch the noxious evidence. He straightened the corners of the tarp and began to roll it up just as the police headlights came into view. I ducked down as they drove past, and watched through a corner of glass as Mr Crowley paused, hung his head, and slowly stood up.

One of the policemen stepped out of the car and drew his gun from behind the cover of his open doors; the other was silhouetted in the driver's seat, talking on a radio. The body was rolled up and hidden, but there was blood on the ground from the initial attack.

'Put your hands in the air,' said the cop. I knew some of the cops in town, but I couldn't recognize this one in the dark. 'Lie down on the ground, now!'

Mr Crowley slowly turned around.

'Sir! Do not turn around! Lie down immediately!'

Crowley faced them now, tall and broad in the brilliant headlights. His shadow stretched behind him for nearly a block, a giant made of darkness.

'Thank goodness you're here,' said Crowley. 'I just found him. I think that killer got to him.' Crowley's pants were soaked in the victim's blood; I was amazed he even attempted the lie.

'Turn back around and lie down on your stomach,' said the policeman. His gun was like an extension of his arms, black and straight. Crowley's claws were hidden now; he looked perfectly human, yet perfectly menacing. His eyes were thin and grim, his mouth closed tightly in a flat, emotionless line.

'Turn back around, and lie down on your stomach,' repeated the policeman. 'We will not ask you again.'

Crowley's eyes seemed to bore into them, and I wondered what he was feeling. Anger? Hate? I peered closer, seeing a glint of light on his cheek. Tears.

He was sad.

The policeman on the driver's side opened his door and stepped out. He was younger than his partner, and his hands trembled; when he spoke, his voice was shaky. 'Back-up's on its—' he said, but before he could even finish his sentence Crowley rushed them, still in full human form but snarling angrily. The older policeman shouted a warning and both men began firing, bullet after bullet slamming into Crowley's chest. He went down.

'Holy—' said the young cop.

The older cop lowered his weapon slowly and looked at his partner. 'Suspect down,' he said. 'I never would have guessed this tip was any good. What is this, the third one tonight?'

'Fourth,' said the young cop.

'Well, what are you waiting for?' asked the older one. 'Call for an ambulance!'

In a flash Crowley was up again, standing at the old cop's side – his face inhumanly elongated, his mouth a ragged quiver of fangs. The cop was dead almost instantly, bone-white claws slashing through his gut, and the demon Crowley leaped over the squad car towards the young cop. The man screamed and fired wildly, hitting the rear corner of Mr Crowley's car just before the demon jumped on him and pulled him down out of my view. The policeman screamed once more, then stopped.

As quickly as the violence had erupted, it ceased. The policemen, the demon, the guns, the street, the cold night sky . . . all were as silent as a tomb.

Crowley came around the side of the police car a moment later, dragging the two bodies with his right arm; his left hung uselessly at his side. He was fully human again. He unrolled the tarp and flopped the policemen's bodies next to that of the first victim, and stood for a moment, surveying the scene – three dead bodies, a sea of blood, two extra cars, and a bullet-hole in his own. He'd never be able to cover it all up before the police back-up arrived.

Crowley walked back to the police car and shut off the headlights; the carnage fell into grey silhouette. He rummaged around inside a while longer, and I heard nothing but cracks and scratches until at last he emerged and tossed a couple of black blocks onto the pile of bodies. I guessed it was the squad car's video camera, but there was no way to be sure from this distance.

There was still time. The police had called for back-up, but even if they hadn't, someone was bound to come and find him. He couldn't possibly hide all of this.

He pulled off his coat and flannel shirt, tossing them into the pile and standing pale and half-naked in the moonlight. His left arm was badly wounded from the bullet he'd taken, and he poked at it with a grunt. He reached up with his right hand – the fingers shifting fluidly into claws – and rested his fingers on his shoulder. He set his feet carefully on the sidewalk, bracing himself for something, and then nearly jumped as a cellphone chirped loudly at his waist. He grabbed it with his good hand and flipped it open, raising it to his ear.

'Hello, Kay. I'm sorry, dear, I couldn't sleep.' Pause. 'I didn't tell you because I didn't want to wake you. Don't worry, honey, it's nothing, just insomnia. I went for a drive.' Pause. 'No, it's not my stomach, I feel just fine.' He looked down at the pile of corpses at his feet. 'In fact, my stomach feels better than it has in weeks, dear.' Pause. 'Yes, I'll be home soon. You go back to sleep. I love you too, dear. I love you.'

So she wasn't a demon. She didn't know anything about it.

He turned off the cellphone and, fumbling with cold, clipped it back to his belt. Then he reached up and sliced into his left shoulder, cutting away the flesh and wrenching the bone free with a sickening pop. I fell back in surprise. He gasped, falling to his knees, and tossed the arm onto the first victim, where it began immediately to sizzle and collapse. Once separated from whatever dark energy kept the demon alive, the limb degenerated into sludge within seconds.

Awkwardly, with only one arm, Crowley did the same to the corpse of a policeman, removing first its coat and then its left arm. He held the limb up to his tattered shoulder and I watched in amazement as the flesh seemed to reach out to the new limb, pulling it close and knitting it into his body in one flowing movement. A moment later, the arm moved, rising up at the shoulder. Crowley swung it around in circles, first small ones, then wider and wider, feeling its weight and testing its motion. Satisfied, and shivering with cold, he pulled a handful of garbage bags from his trunk and began to pack up the bodies.

I found myself wondering, of all things, why he didn't just take the arm from his first victim. Why go to the trouble of undressing the policeman when there was a perfectly good body right next to it, prepped and ready to go?

I heard a car approaching, wheels ploughing heavily through the slush, and looked back. A pick-up passed a block and a half away, on Main Street, bright red in the street lights. There was no way they could have seen Mr Crowley's grisly work from so far away, and in the midst of such darkness. The truck drove on and its noise faded into the distance.

Crowley worked quickly and efficiently, stuffing the policemen into the trunk of the first victim's stalled car. The owner of the car, wrapped tightly in a garbage sack, went into the trunk of Crowley's own car, along with the bagged remnants of Crowley's clothes, his bloody tarp, and the stolen hardware from the police car. It was a smart plan. When investigators finally found the policemen they would appear to be the only victims, and the owner of the car would be the natural suspect. If Crowley hid the man's body well, they might never think that the man had also been a victim tonight. He'd be the prime suspect as the killer, throwing the police and the FBI off of Crowley's trail for weeks.

Crowley climbed into his own car, started the engine, and drove away. No one had come. He'd gotten away with it.

He'd faced two armed policemen and come away without a scratch – in better condition, in fact, than when he'd started. The evidence was gone, and what evidence was left behind all pointed at someone else. As soon as he was out of sight I ran back to my bike and pedalled as fast as I could in the opposite direction. The last thing I wanted was for someone to find me there and link me to the crime.

How could anyone stop this demon? He was virtually unkillable, and too strong and too clever even for the police. They'd done everything they could, used all of their training and skill – they'd riddled him with bullets, for goodness sake – and now they were dead. They were all dead.

All except me.

That was stupid. What could I do? Tip off more police, and lead them to their deaths like I'd led these two? They were dead because of me. Crowley had killed them, but only because I forced him into it. He'd only wanted to kill one man tonight, and because of my meddling two more were rotting in the trunk of a car. I couldn't do that again. It would have been better, perhaps, to leave him alone, to let him kill at his own pace – one per month instead of three in a single night. I would not be responsible for any more deaths.

Except he wasn't killing just one per month any more; his last victim had been less than three weeks ago. He was speeding up. His body, perhaps, was falling apart more quickly. How long before it became one per week? One per day? I didn't want to be responsible for those deaths either, not if I could stop them.

But how? I stopped pedalling and sat on my bike in the middle of the street, thinking. I couldn't attack him. Even if I had a gun, I'd seen how stupid that idea was. If two policemen, trained in combat, couldn't kill him, then I certainly couldn't do it. Not like that.

The monster behind the wall shifted, awake and hungry. *I can do it.*

No.

No?

Maybe I could. That was what I was afraid of, right? That I'd kill somebody? Well, what if the somebody I killed was a demon? Wouldn't that be okay?

No, it wouldn't. I controlled myself for a reason; the things I used to think about, the things I built that wall to prevent, were wrong. Killing was wrong. I wouldn't do it.

But if I didn't do it, Mr Crowley *would* kill – again and again.

'No!' I said aloud, angry at myself, angry at Crowley.

*Get angry! Let it out!*

No. I closed my eyes. I knew I had a dark side, and I knew what I was capable of – the same things that all the serial killers I'd read about and studied were capable of. Evil. Death. The same things that Crowley was capable of. I didn't want to be like him.

But if I stopped when I was done, I wouldn't be like him. If I stopped him, and then stopped myself, nobody else would have to die.

*Could* I stop myself? Once I tore that wall down, could I rebuild it?

Did I even have a choice? I might be the only one who could kill him. The alternative was to tell somebody, and if that led to any innocent deaths at all, even one, then it was a worse alternative. It would be better to kill him myself. No one need suffer at all except Crowley and me.

If I did it though, I'd have to be careful. Crowley was a creature of pure power – too powerful to confront head-on. The tactics I had studied, the killers I could emulate, specialized in crushing the weak – in overpowering those who could not defend themselves. This was completely different.

I threw up suddenly, turning my head and retching onto the road.

Seven people dead now. Seven people in three months. And he was speeding up. How many more would die if I didn't stop him?

I could stop him. Everyone had weaknesses, even demons. He killed because of a weakness, after all: his body was falling apart. If he had one weakness, he would have more; I could find them and exploit them, and I could stop him. I could save the town, and the county, and the world. I could stop the demon.

And I would.

No more questions, no more waiting. I made my decision. It was time to tear down the wall, to throw away all the rules I'd created for myself.

It was time to let the monster out.

I got back on my bike and rode home, a black hole in the night. Brick by brick the wall came down, and the monster stretched its legs, flexed its claws, licked its lips.

Tomorrow, we would hunt.

# CHAPTER 10

We woke the next morning to a fresh fall of snow – barely an inch, but all the excuse I needed. It was a lazy Sunday morning, but I crossed the street at eight o'clock, shovel in hand. Crowley's car was in the driveway, dusted with snow, and I stopped in surprise when I realized that the bullet-hole in the back corner had been replaced by a massive, crumpled dent. The lights had been shattered, and paint was chipping away in jagged flakes. It looked like he'd been in a car accident. I studied it a moment longer, wondering what had happened, then walked to the porch and rang the bell.

Mr Crowley himself answered the door – cheerful, human, and as unsuspicious as a man could be. I'd watched him kill four people over the last month, but even so I almost doubted – just for a second – that a man like him could hurt a fly.

'Mornin', John, what brings you— Well, I'll be! It did snow. Can't get one past you, can they?'

'No, they can't.'

'Well, there's hardly anything out there,' he said, 'and

we don't need to go anywhere today. Why don't you just leave it, and we'll give it a chance to drop some more before you go to all the trouble. No sense in shovelling twice.'

'It's no trouble, Mr Crowley,' I said.

'Who's that at the door?' called Mrs Crowley, bustling into view from elsewhere in the house. 'Oh, good morning, John. Bill, get away from the door, you'll catch your death!'

Mr Crowley laughed. 'I'm fine, Kay, I promise – not even a sniffle.'

'He was up all night,' said Mrs Crowley, wrapping a coat around his shoulders, 'goodness knows where doing goodness knows what, and then he tells me he crashed the car. We'd better have a look at the damage now that it's lighter out.'

I shot a glance at Mr Crowley, who winked and chuckled. 'I slid a bit on the ice last night, and she thinks it was a Communist plot.'

'Don't make fun, Bill, this is— Oh, my word, it's worse than I thought.'

'I was out driving last night,' said Mr Crowley, stepping out to join us on the porch, 'and slid on the ice out by the hospital – went right off the road and into a cement wall. Best place to do it though. A handful of nurses and doctors were right there in seconds to make sure I was okay. I keep telling her I'm fine, but she gets worried.' He put his arm around her shoulders, and she turned to hug him.

'I'm just glad you're all right,' she said.

Assuming he'd disposed of the body properly, the bullet in his car was the last bit of evidence that might have linked him to the killings, but he'd taken care of it admirably.

I had to give him credit, he was very good at covering his tracks. All he'd really had to do was pull out the bullet and slam that corner of the car into a wall hard enough to hide the previous damage. Doing it at the hospital had been especially smart. He now had a whole group of witnesses who thought they knew exactly what had happened to his car, and if push came to shove they could also testify that he'd been on the opposite side of town from the murders. He'd buried the evidence and given himself an alibi at the same time.

I turned to look at him with new respect. He was clever, all right – but why now, and not before? If he was so smart, why did he leave the first three bodies out where anyone could find them? It occurred to me that maybe he was new at this, and only just now learning how to do it well. Maybe he hadn't killed that man in Arizona, after all – or maybe there had been something different about that killing that hadn't prepared him for these.

'John,' said Mrs Crowley, 'I want you to know that we appreciate everything you do for us. We can't turn around these past few weeks without finding you there to help.'

'It's nothing,' I said.

'Nonsense,' she said. 'This is one of the worst winters in years, and we're too old to get through it alone – you've seen how Bill's health comes and goes. And now something like this . . . well, it's good to know our neighbours are watching out for us.'

'We don't have any children of our own,' said Mr Crowley, 'but you're practically like a grandson to us. Thanks.'

I stared at them both, studying the signs of gratitude I'd come to recognize in them – smiles, clasped hands, a few tears in the corners of Mrs Crowley's eyes. I expected sincerity from her, but even Mr Crowley seemed touched. I hefted the shovel and started clearing off the steps.

'It's nothing,' I said again.

'You're a sweet boy,' said Mrs Crowley, and they both went inside.

Somehow it felt appropriate that the only person who thought I was sweet was a woman who lived with a demon.

I spent the rest of the morning clearing their walks and their driveway, and thinking about how to kill Mr Crowley. My rules kept popping into my mind, unbidden – they were too ingrained to leave without a fight. I thought about different ways of killing him, and immediately found myself saying nice things about him; I ran over his daily schedule in my head, and immediately felt myself straying to other topics. Twice I actually stopped shovelling and turned to go home, subconsciously trying to distract myself from becoming fixated. My old rules would have told me to ignore Mr Crowley for a full week, as I had forced myself to ignore Brooke, but things were different now and the rules had to go. I'd been training myself for years to stay away from people, to root out any attachments that tried to form, but all of those barriers needed to come down; all of those mechanisms needed to be turned off, or stowed away, or destroyed.

It was creepy at first – like sitting very still while a

cockroach climbs onto your shoe, up your leg, and under your shirt, and you never brush it away. I imagined myself covered with roaches, spiders, leeches, and more, all wriggling, probing and tasting, and I had to stay motionless and let myself become completely accustomed to them. I needed to kill Mr Crowley (a maggot crawling onto my face), I wanted to kill Mr Crowley (a maggot crawling into my mouth), I wanted to cut him open (a swarm of maggots crawling all over me, burrowing into me . . .).

I spat them out and shivered, coming back to reality, standing on the sidewalk and pushing away the snow. This would take a while.

'John, come in and have some hot chocolate!' It was Mr Crowley, calling from the open door. I finished the last few feet of sidewalk and went in, sitting at their kitchen table and smiling politely and wondering if cutting him open would even work. I remembered the gash in his belly when he'd stolen the drifter's lungs, sealing itself closed like a Ziploc bag. He could heal himself back from a barrage of gunshots. I smiled again, took another sip of chocolate, and wondered if he could regrow his head.

Dark thoughts filled the rest of my day, and one by one I tore my rules apart. When I went to school the next morning I felt haggard and terrified – like a new person in an old body that barely fitted. People ignored me just as they always had, but it was a new pair of eyes that looked back, a new mind that watched the world through this alien shell. I walked through the halls, sat through my classes, and stared at the people around me as if seeing them for the first time. Someone shoved me between classes and I followed him the length of the hall, imagining what it would be like to take my revenge slowly, piece by piece, while he hung from a hook in the basement.

I shook my head and sat down on the stairs, breathing heavily. This wasn't right; this was what I'd fought against all my life. Children streamed by like cattle in a slaughterhouse; like blood in a web of arteries. The bell rang loudly and they disappeared like roaches, scattering and swarming into their holes. I closed my eyes and thought about Mr Crowley. *That's why you're doing this*, I reminded myself. *That's who you want; leave the rest alone*. I took another deep breath and stood up, wiping clammy sweat from my forehead. I had to go to class. I had to be normal.

Halfway through class the Principal summoned all teachers to a special meeting, and my English teacher, Ms Parker, returned fifteen minutes later paler than I'd ever seen a live body. The room fell silent as she came in, and we watched her walk slowly to her desk and sit down heavily, as if the weight of the entire world was on her shoulders. It had to have something to do with the killer, and I worried for a moment that Crowley had already killed again, and I'd missed it, but no. It was too soon. They must have found the policemen's bodies.

After a minute of deathly silence, no one daring to speak, Ms Parker looked up.

'Let's get back to work.'

'Wait,' said Rachel, one of Marci Jensen's best friends. 'Aren't you going to tell us what's going on?'

'I'm sorry,' said Ms Parker, 'it's just that I got some very bad news. It's nothing.' She squinted as soon as she said it, her eyes red, and I wondered if she would start crying.

'It sounds like all the teachers got very bad news,' said Marci. 'I think we deserve to know what it was.'

Ms Parker rubbed her eyes and shook her head. 'I should be handling this better. That's why they told the teachers first – so we could make it easier for the rest of you. I'm obviously not doing a very good job.' She dried her eyes and looked up. 'Principal Layton just informed us that two more bodies have been found.' There was a collective gasp from the students. 'The bodies of two policemen were found in the trunk of a car downtown.'

Brooke wasn't in my class this period, and I wondered if her teacher was sharing the same news. How would Brooke react to it?

'Is it the same guy?' asked a kid named Ryan, two rows behind me.

'They think it is,' said Ms Parker. 'The . . . wounds on the victims seem like the first three. And it had the same . . . stuff, the black stuff.'

'Do they know the policemen's names?' asked Marci. She was as white as a sheet. Her dad was a cop.

'It wasn't your father, honey. He's the one who found the car and called in the report.'

Marci burst into tears, and Rachel got up to hug her.

'Did the killer take anything from the bodies?' asked Max.

'I really don't think that's an appropriate question, Maxwell,' said the teacher.

'I bet he did,' said Max, grumbling.

'I know this is hard,' said Ms Parker. 'Believe me, I . . . well, I'm as shaken up as you are. We only have one school counsellor, and anyone is free to go see her if they want, but if you prefer to talk to me, or go to the restroom, or sit quietly, then do so – or we can talk about it as a class.' She hid her face in her hands. 'They said that we shouldn't worry – that the pattern is consistent, or something. I don't know how that's supposed to comfort you, and I'm so sorry. I wish I knew what to say.'

'It means that his methods haven't changed,' I said. 'They're worried that we'll think he's getting worse, because two bodies were found this time instead of one.'

'Thank you, John,' said Ms Parker, 'but we don't need to dwell on the . . . criminal's methods.'

'I'm just explaining what the cops meant,' I said. 'They obviously thought it would make us feel better.'

'Thank you,' she said, nodding.

'But he *did* kill two this time,' said Brad. He and I used to be friends when we were little, but it had been years since we'd done anything together. 'How can they say his methods haven't changed?'

Ms Parker thought for a moment about what to say, but stared back blankly. After a moment she turned to me. I was the expert.

'The point they're trying to make,' I said, 'is that the killer still has himself under control. If he were killing a different type of victim, or if he were killing more viciously or more frequently, it would mean that something has changed.' All eyes were on me, and for once they weren't scowling or sneering – they were listening. I liked it.

'See, serial killers don't attack randomly,' I went on. 'They have specific needs and mental problems that shape everything they do. For whatever reason, this guy needs to kill adult males, and that need builds up and up until he can't control it, and he lets loose. That process takes about a month, in his case, which is why we've had one victim per month.'

It was all lies – he *was* killing more frequently, and he *wasn't* a regular serial killer, and his need was physical instead of mental – but it was what the police were thinking, and it was what the class wanted to hear. 'The good news is, this means he won't kill anyone in this room.' *Until he gets desperate and you happen to be in the wrong place at the wrong time*.

'But there were two victims,' said Brad again. 'That's twice as many people this time. That seems like a pretty big difference to me.'

'He didn't kill two people because he's getting worse,' I said. 'He killed two because he was stupid.' I didn't want to stop talking – I was still too delighted that people were actually listening. I was talking about what I loved, and nobody shut me up or said I was a freak; they wanted to hear it. It was like a rush of power.

'You've seen the way he just leaves his bodies there for anyone to find. He probably just jumps them at random, grabbing the first guy to pass by, killing him, and running off. This time, that guy happened to be a cop, and cops have partners, and he realized too late that he couldn't kill one without killing them both, if he wanted to get away with it.'

'Shut up!' yelled Marci, standing up. 'Shut up shut up shut up!' She threw a book at me, but it went wide and clattered against the wall. Ms Parker leaped up to stop her.

'Everybody calm down,' said Ms Parker. 'Marci, come with me – get her bag, Rachel. That's right, let's go.' She put her arms around Marci and led her carefully to the door. 'The rest of you stay here; and stay quiet. I'll be back as soon as I can.' They left the room and we sat there for several minutes, first in silence, then in low murmurs of private conversation. Someone kicked my chair and told me to stop being a jerk, but Brad leaned closer to ask me a question.

'Do you really think his methods are staying the same?' asked Brad.

'Of course not,' I said. With Ms Parker gone I could get a little more vivid in my discussion. 'He used to kill one defenceless person in each attack, and this time he killed two armed policemen. That's escalation, whether they want to tell us it is or not.'

'Crap, man,' he said. The guys around him shook their heads.

'This happens all the time with serial killers,' I said. 'Whatever his need is, one kill a month isn't satisfying it any more. It's like an addiction – after a while, one cigarette isn't enough, so you need two, then three, then a whole pack, or whatever. He's losing control, and he's going to start killing a lot more often.'

'No, he's not,' said Brad, leaning closer. 'They found these bodies in a car, which means they can find this bastard by tracking his plates. And then I'm going to go to his house and kill him myself.' The other guys nodded grimly. The witch hunt had begun.

Brad wasn't the only one who wanted revenge. The cops didn't release the name of the car's owner, but a neighbour recognized it on the six o'clock news and by the ten o'clock news there was a mob outside the guy's house, throwing rocks and shouting for blood. Carrie Walsh, the terrified news intern, was still stuck with this story, and the camera showed her crouched next to the news van while a crowd behind her shouted angry slogans at the house.

'This is Carrie Walsh with Five Live News, coming to you live from Clayton County, where tempers, as you can see, are flaring dangerously.'

I recognized Max's dad in the mob, shouting and shaking his fist. He still wore his hair shaved short, infantry style, from his time in Iraq, and his face was red with anger.

'The police are here,' said Carrie, 'and have been since before the mob formed. This is the home of Greg and Susan Olson, and their two-year-old son. Mr Olson is a construction worker and the owner of the car in which two police officers were found dead earlier today. Mr Olson's whereabouts are still unknown, but the police are looking for him in connection with the murders. They are here today both to question his family, and to protect them.'

At that moment the mob started shouting more loudly, and the camera swung around and focused on a man – the FBI agent from before, Agent Forman – leading a woman and child out of the house. A local cop followed them out with a suitcase, and several more worked to keep the crowd back. Carrie and her cameraman pushed forward through the mob and called out questions to the police. The cops helped Mrs Olson and her son into the back of a squad car, and Agent Forman approached the camera. On every side, angry people shouted and chanted, 'Married to a murderer!'

'Excuse me,' said Carrie, 'can you tell us what's going on here?'

'Susan Olson is being placed in protective custody, for the safety of herself and her child.' The man spoke quickly, as if he'd prepared the statement before leaving the house. 'At this time we do not know if Mr Greg Olson is a suspect or a victim, but he is certainly a person of interest in this case and we are working around the clock to find him. Thank you.' He got into the car and it drove away, leaving several police behind to quell the mob and restore order.

Carrie looked as if she wanted to stay as close to the police as possible, and her hands were shaking, but she found a member of the mob and started to interview him. With shock I realized that it was Mr Layton, my Principal.

'Excuse me, sir, may I ask you a few questions?'

Mr Layton was not ranting like many in the crowd, and

looked embarrassed to be suddenly on camera; I imagined he'd get a good talking-to from the school board the next morning. 'Um, sure,' he said, squinting into the camera light.

'What can you tell us about the feelings in your town today?'

'Well, look around you,' he said. 'People are angry – they're very angry. In fact, they are getting carried away. Mobs are always stupid, I know, except for that brief moment where you're in one, and they make perfect sense. I already feel stupid just for being here,' he said, glancing up at the camera again.

'Do you think that this kind of thing will happen again with the next death?'

'It could happen again tomorrow,' said Mr Layton, throwing up his hands. 'It could happen again whenever something gets the people riled up. Clayton is a very small community – probably everyone in town knew one of the victims, or lived in one of their neighbourhoods. This killer, whoever it is, is not just killing nobodies, he's killing *us*; he's killing people with faces and names and families. I honestly don't know how long this community can contain that kind of violence without exploding.' He squinted into the camera again and slunk off into the shadows.

Around them the mob was dispersing, but for how long?

It only took a few days for new DNA evidence to come through, all but exonerating Greg Olson, and the police plastered it across the news in an attempt to give Mrs Olson and her child a bit of their life back. The police had, of course, cleared away the snow at the scene of the attack and found the sidewalk covered with blood, much of it almost certainly from Olson himself, in quantities that made him almost certainly another victim.

Rumours started to spread about a third set of tyre-tracks, phantom bullets that had been fired but not found and, most telling of all, a DNA signature that matched the mysterious black substance – only this time the DNA hadn't come from the sludge but from a bloody smear inside the police car. This meant that there were four people at the scene of the killings, not three, and FBI forensic people were sure that the fourth – *not* Greg Olson – was the murderer.

Of course, some people began to suspect there was a fifth.

'You seem different today,' said Dr Neblin. It was Thursday, and time for our weekly session. I'd been tearing down my system of rules for five days now.

'What do you mean?' I asked.

'Nothing,' he said. 'You're just . . . different. Anything new?'

'You always ask that right after somebody dies,' I said.

'You're always a little different after somebody dies,' said Neblin. 'What did you think of it this time?'

'I try not to,' I said. 'You know, rules and all. What did *you* think of it?'

Neblin paused only a moment before responding.

'Your rules have never stopped you from thinking about

the killings before,' he said. 'We've talked about them quite a bit.'

That was a stupid mistake. I was trying to act as if I were still following my rules, but apparently I wasn't very good at it. 'I know, I just . . . it seems different now, don't you think?'

'It certainly does,' said Dr Neblin. He waited for me to say something, but I couldn't think of anything that didn't sound suspicious. I'd never tried to hide anything from Neblin before – it was hard.

'How's school?' he asked.

'Fine,' I said. 'Everyone's afraid, but that's pretty normal, I guess.'

'Are you afraid?'

'Not really,' I said. I was more afraid than I'd ever been, but not for any reason he knew about. 'Fear is a weird thing, when you think about it. People are only afraid of other things, they're never afraid of themselves.'

'Should people be afraid of themselves?'

'Fear is about things that you can't control,' I said, 'the future, or the dark, or someone trying to kill you. You don't get scared of yourself because you always know what you're going to do.'

'Are you afraid of yourself?'

I looked out of the window and saw a woman down on the sidewalk, standing in a beaten snowdrift and watching the traffic. 'It's like that woman,' I said, pointing at her. 'She could be afraid that a car might hit her, or that the ice might make her slip, or that the other side of the street won't have anywhere to stand, but she's not afraid of crossing the street. Crossing is her own decision, and she's already made it, and she knows how to do it, and it should be pretty easy. She's going to wait until there are no cars, and step carefully on the ice, and do everything she can control to keep herself safe. But it's the things she can't control that scare her. Things that could happen to her, not things that she does. She doesn't lie in bed in the morning and say "I hope I don't come to any streets today, because I'm afraid I might try to cross them". Here she goes.'

The woman saw a break in the traffic and hurried across the street. She reached the other side.

'Safe,' I said. 'Nothing happened at all. Now she's going back to work, where she's going to think about other things she's afraid of, like "I hope my boss doesn't fire me", "I hope the letter makes it there on time", "I hope the cheque doesn't bounce".'

'You know her?' asked Neblin.

'No,' I said, 'but she's on foot in this part of town at four in the afternoon, so there's only a couple of things she could be doing – the bank or the post office seem like the most obvious destinations.'

I stopped suddenly, and looked back at Neblin. I'd never theorized about people in front of him before – my rules had never let me think that much about a random stranger. I wanted to accuse him of tricking me, but he hadn't done anything – just let me talk. I watched his eyes, looking for some sign that he knew the significance of what I'd been doing. He was staring straight back, thinking. Analyzing.

'Good guesses,' said Neblin. 'I don't know her either, but I'd bet you're right about most of those things.' He was waiting for something – for me to admit what I'd done maybe, or tell him why my rules were so different today. I said nothing.

'The latest news on the killing last weekend was a 911 call,' he said.

Uh oh.

'Apparently somebody called in from a payphone – one just up on Main Street – and reported an attack from the Clayton Killer. The theory right now is that the killer got to Greg Olson, then some witness called it in, and when the dispatcher sent the police to the crime scene, the killer got them, too.'

'I hadn't heard about that,' I said. 'Makes sense though. Do they know who the caller was?'

'He wouldn't identify himself,' said Neblin, 'or *she* wouldn't. The voice was kind of high, so they think it was either a woman or a child.'

'I hope it was a woman,' I said.

Neblin raised an eyebrow.

'Whatever happened that night,' I said, 'I'm sure it's not the kind of thing a child should ever have to see. It could really mess him up.'

# CHAPTER 11

Mr Crowley woke up every morning around six-thirty. He didn't use an alarm, he just woke up. Decades of working at the same job, day after day, had conditioned him until it was second nature, and now, long after retirement, he couldn't help himself. I knew this because I watched from my window across the street for a few days, seeing which lights turned on when, and once I knew where to go I crouched and listened outside of his house. Normally I couldn't have done that without leaving incriminating footprints in the snow but, as luck would have it, someone kept Mr Crowley's paths remarkably clean. I could come and go as I pleased.

At six-thirty in the morning Mr Crowley woke up and swore. It was like clockwork – he was an old, vulgar cuckoo you could practically set your watch to. It was the only time he swore all day, as far as I could tell. I suppose it helped him cleanse his mind and start the day fresh, gathering the night's dark thoughts into a plug of mental mucus and spitting it out in a single word. His bedroom was in the back right corner of the house, and after his daily cuss he walked in the dark to the bathroom and washed, I guess his face, in the sink. The light came on, the toilet flushed, and he ran himself a hot shower that steamed the outer window. By 7 a.m. he was dressed and in the kitchen.

His breakfast I determined primarily by smell. First the bitter charcoal stench of an uncleaned stovetop burner, then the bland heat of boiling water, and at last the rich aroma of cracked wheat and maple sugar. It made me hungry every time. From my spot by the kitchen window I could climb onto the narrow ledge of the house's foundation, fully out of view from the street, and look through a gap in the curtains to watch his arm as he ate. It moved up and down slowly and rhythmically, bringing the spoon to his mouth and then dropping back to wait while he chewed. I could move farther if I wanted, to see more of him as he ate, but only at the risk of being discovered. I was content to stay out of sight and fill in the gaps with my mind.

He scraped his chair across the floor, took six steps to the sink and rinsed out his bowl with a burst of water that sounded like popping static on a radio. That's usually when Kay woke up and wandered in, and he kissed her good morning.

I spied on him like that for a week, once even skipping school to find out what he did during the day. What I was looking for, and couldn't find, was fear. If I could find out what, if anything, he was afraid of, I'd be able to use it to stop him. I knew I wasn't heading for a straight fight. The only way I could beat this demon was to out-think it, get it into a position of weakness, and crush it like a bug. That was easy for most serial killers, because they attacked people weaker than themselves. I was attacking something far stronger. Knowing there was no chance he'd be afraid of me, I had to find something else he was afraid of. Once I'd found it, I could poke him with it and see how he reacted. If he reacted strongly enough, I might even be able to trick him into a stupid mistake, and give myself an opening.

When I couldn't find any indications of fear in his behaviour, I decided to go back to basics – to the psychological profile I'd started building back when I first suspected it was a serial killer. I dug out my notebook late one night and read through my list: *He approaches his victims in person and attacks them up close*. I used to think that said something important about his psychology, and why he did what he did, but now I knew better. He did what he did because he needed new organs, and he attacked the victims in person because his demon claws were simply the best weapon he had.

The next item on the list was exactly what I was looking for. *He doesn't want anyone to know who he is*. Max had made me write it down, but I had thought it was too obvious. The trouble was, it was so obvious I hadn't even considered it. It was the perfect fear: he didn't want anyone to know what he really was. I smiled to myself.

'Not a werewolf, Max, but pretty close.'

Mr Crowley was a demon, and he didn't want anyone to know it. Even a normal killer wouldn't want anyone to know their secrets. What Mr Crowley feared – the first bit of pressure I could start exerting on him – was discovery.

It was time to send him a note.

Writing the note was more complicated than I'd expected. Just like with the 911 call, I didn't want anyone to be able to trace it back to me. I couldn't use my own handwriting, obviously, so I needed a computer to print it out on. Even that had a hitch. I'd read about a murder case once where they called in an expert to prove which typewriter the fake suicide letter was written on, and I assumed you could do the same with printers. That meant I couldn't use our printer at home. The printer at school was a possibility, but we had to log in to use those, which would leave a clear electronic record of exactly who had written the note.

I decided to use the printer at the library, during their busiest time of day, when no one had the time to pay attention to a fifteen-year-old kid. I could slip in, write it up, print it out and be gone without a trace. Since the weather was still ice cold, I could even wear gloves without making anyone suspicious, and thus avoid any fingerprints. I buried the note in the middle of lines of meaningless text, just in case someone got to the printer first and read what I was writing.

When I got it home I cut out the phrase I wanted and pasted it onto a clean sheet.

My first note was simple:

I KNOW WHAT YOU ARE

Delivering the note was just as difficult as making it. It had to be somewhere Kay wouldn't find it, because she'd probably go right to the police, or at the very least tell a neighbour. Any normal person would. Mr Crowley, on the other hand, would almost certainly keep it to himself; he wouldn't want to show anything that would cast suspicion on him. If he took the note to the police they'd want to know more about him – any enemies he might have, things he might have done, anything that might make someone want revenge. Those were questions he didn't want the police to even ask, let alone learn the answers to. He would keep it quiet, yes.

The other problem was finding a way to deliver the note without making it obvious that I had done it. It would be easy to hide it in the shed, for example, because Kay would never find it there, but I was in the shed all the time. I'd be the first person who came to mind when he tried to guess who'd left it. Nor did I want to hide it somewhere that would focus his attention on my various watching spots around the house. If I slipped it through, say, the kitchen window, I'd never be able to hide outside and watch him eat breakfast again. I had to choose my delivery system very carefully.

Eventually I settled on his car. Crowley and his wife both drove it about half the time, but there were specific instances where one would drive without the other – Kay buying groceries, for example, which she did every Wednesday morning, and always alone. For Mr Crowley it was football games, which he watched at the bar downtown. I began studying his evening schedule and comparing it to the *TV Guide*, and discovered that he went to the bar every time there was a Seattle Seahawks game on ESPN; I guess he didn't get that channel at home. The next time there was a Seahawks game I sneaked over before it started and placed the folded note under his windshield wiper.

I watched his driveway from my window, peering out between a crack in the shades so small that he could never have known I was there. He left his house, smiling cheerfully about something, and noticed the note while he was unlocking the car door. He picked it up, unfolded and read it, then surveyed the street with dark eyes. His cheer was gone. I shrank back, vanishing into the darkness of my room. Mr Crowley crumpled up the note and stuffed it into his pocket, then got into his car and drove away.

That night we had a Neighbourhood Watch party, which is where everyone on the street gets together in the Crowleys' yard and talks and laughs and pretends that nothing is wrong, and meanwhile all our empty houses are ripe for burglary. This particular party was not about burglary, however, but serial killing. We were all gathered in a large, 'safe' group, watching out for each other. There was even a little speech about safety, and locking your doors and that kind of thing. I wanted to tell them that the safest thing they could do was to not bring everyone into Mr Crowley's back yard, but he seemed tame enough that night. If he was capable of flipping out and murdering fifty people at once, he was at least not inclined to do it right then. I wasn't ready to attack him yet, either. I was still trying to learn more about him. How could I kill something that had already regenerated from a hail of bullet wounds? This kind of thing takes planning, and planning takes time.

More so than to talk about safety, the real purpose of the party was to send a message to ourselves that we hadn't been beaten – that even with a killer in town, we weren't afraid, and we weren't going to collapse into a mob. Whatever. More important than any hollow declaration of bravery was the fact that we were roasting hot dogs, which meant I got to stoke a fire in the Crowleys' fire-pit.

I started with a massive blaze, burning huge blocks of wood from a dead tree the Watsons had cut out of their back yard over the summer. The fire was bright and warm, perfect for starting the party, and then as the safety talk dragged on I went to work with the poker and a long pair of tongs, shaping and cultivating the fire to produce thick beds of bright-red coals. Cooking fires are different from normal fires, because you're looking for steady, even heat instead of simple light and warmth. Flames give way to low flares and the brilliant red glow of wood burning from the inside out. I arranged the fire carefully, routing oxygen through miniature chimneys to create wide roasting ovens. Just in time, the meeting ended and the crowd turned to begin cooking.

Brooke was there with her family, of course, and without making it obvious I watched her and her brother as they skewered a pair of hot dogs and approached the pit; Brooke smiled as she came, and crouched down next to me. They were holding their sticks out over the centre of the blaze, where the flames still danced, and I wrestled with myself for almost thirty seconds before daring to talk to her.

'Try down here,' I said, pointing with my tongs to one of the beds of coals. 'They'll cook better.'

'Thanks,' said Brooke, and eagerly pointed it out to Ethan. They moved their hot dogs, which immediately began to darken and cook. 'Wow,' she said, 'that's great. You know a lot about fire.'

'Four years of Cub Scouts,' I said. 'It's the only organization I know that actually teaches little boys how to light things on fire.'

Brooke laughed. 'You must have done great on your Arson merit badge.'

I wanted to keep talking, but I didn't know what to say. I'd said way too much at the Halloween party, and probably terrified her, and I didn't want to do that again. On the other hand, I loved her laugh, and I wanted to hear it again. Anyway, I figured, if she made an arson joke, I could probably make one too without looking too creepy.

'They said I was the best student they'd ever had,' I said. 'Most Scouts only burn down a cabin, but I burned down three cabins and an abandoned warehouse.'

'Not bad,' she said, smiling.

'They sent me to compete at the national level,' I added. 'You remember that forest fire in California last summer?'

Brooke smiled again. 'Oh, that was you? Nice work.'

'Yeah, I won a prize for that one. It's a statue, like an Oscar, but it's shaped like Smokey the Bear and filled with gasoline. My mom thought it was a honey bottle and tried to make a sandwich.'

Brooke laughed out loud, almost dropped her hot-dog skewer, and then laughed at that, too.

'Are they done yet?' asked Ethan, examining his hot dog. It was the fifth time he'd pulled it out, and it had barely had time to brown.

'Looks like it,' said Brooke, looking at her own hot dog and standing up. 'Thanks, John.'

I nodded, and watched as they ran back to the card table for buns and mustard. I saw her accept a ketchup bottle from Mr Crowley, and the monster in my mind reared up and bared its fangs, growling angrily. How dare he touch her? It looked like I needed to keep an eye on Brooke, to keep her safe. I felt myself starting to snarl, and forced my mouth into a smile instead. I turned back to the fire and saw my mom grin at me mischievously from the other side. I growled inside – I didn't want to deal with whatever stupid reference she was sure to make about Brooke when we got home. I determined to stay at the party as late as possible.

Brooke and Ethan didn't come back to the fire to eat, and I didn't get another chance to talk to her that night; I saw her handing out styrofoam cups of hot chocolate, and hoped she would bring one to me, but Mrs Crowley beat her to it. I waited until she was gone and threw it in the fire, watching the chocolate blacken on the wood and the styrofoam curl and bubble and disappear into the coals. Brooke's family left soon after.

Soon the hot dogs were all roasted, and as people began to drift away I fed the fire several large logs, stoking it into a blinding column of roaring flame. It was beautiful: so hot that the reds and oranges accelerated into blinding yellows and whites; so hot that the crowd drew back and I shed my coat. It was as bright and warm as a summer day next to that fire, though it was night-time in late December everywhere else, and I walked around the edges poking it, talking to it – laughing with it as it devastated the wood and annihilated the paper plates. Most fires crackle and pop, but that's not really the fire talking, it's the wood. To hear the fire itself you need a huge blaze like this one, a furnace so powerful it roars with its own wind. I crouched as close as I dared and listened to its voice, a whispered howl of joy and rage.

In my biology class we'd talked about the definition of life. To be classified as a living creature, a thing needs to eat, breathe, reproduce and grow. Dogs do, rocks don't; trees do, plastic doesn't. Fire, by that definition, is vibrantly alive. It eats everything from wood to flesh, and it breathes air just like a human, converting oxygen to carbon. Fire grows, and as it spreads it creates new fires that spread out and make new fires of their own. Fire drinks gasoline and excretes cinders; it fights for territory; it loves and hates. Sometimes when I watch people trudging through their daily routines I think that fire is more alive than we are – brighter, hotter, more sure of itself and where it wants to go. Fire doesn't settle; fire doesn't tolerate; fire doesn't 'get by'. Fire *does.*

Fire *is*.

'On what wings dare he aspire?' said a voice. I spun around and saw Mr Crowley, sitting a few feet behind me in a camp chair, staring deeply into the fire. Everyone else had left, and I'd been too absorbed in the fire to notice.

Mr Crowley seemed distant and preoccupied. He was not talking to me, as I had at first assumed, but to himself. Or maybe to the fire. Never shifting his gaze, he spoke again. 'What the hand, dare seize the fire?'

'What?' I asked.

'What?' he echoed, as if shaken from a dream. 'Oh John, you're still here. It was nothing, just a poem.'

'Never heard it before,' I said, turning back to the fire. It was smaller now, still strong but no longer raging. I should have been terrified, alone in the night with a demon – I thought immediately that he must have found me out somehow, must have known that I knew his secrets and had left him the note. But it was obvious that his mind was somewhere else. Something had obviously disturbed him, to put him into such a melancholy frame of mind. He was thinking about the note perhaps, but he was not thinking about me.

More than that, his thoughts were absorbed in the fire, drawn to it and soaked into it like water in a sponge. Watching the way he watched the fire, I knew that he loved it like I did. That's why he spoke – not because he suspected me, but because we were both connected to the fire and so, in a way, to each other.

'You've never heard it?' he asked. 'What do they teach

you in school these days? That's William Blake!' I shrugged, and after a moment he spoke again. 'I memorized it once.' He drifted into reverie again. '"Tyger, Tyger, burning bright In the forests of the night, What immortal hand or eye Could frame thy fearful symmetry?"'

'It sounds kind of familiar,' I said. I never paid much attention in English, but I figured I'd remember a poem about fire.

'The poet is asking the tiger who made him, and how,' said Crowley, his chin buried deep under his collar. '"What the hammer? what the chain? In what furnace was thy brain?"' Only his eyes were visible, black pits reflecting the dancing fire. 'He wrote two poems like that, you know – "The Lamb" and "The T'ger". One was made of sweetness and love, and one was forged from terror and death.' Crowley looked at me, his eyes dark and heavy. '"When the stars threw down their spears And water'd heaven with their tears; Did he smile his work to see? Did he who made the Lamb make thee?"'

The fire rustled and cracked. Our shadows danced on the wall of the house behind us. Mr Crowley turned back to the fire.

'I'd like to think the same one made them both,' he said. 'I'd like to think it.'

The trees beyond the fire glowed white, and the trees beyond those were lost in blackness. The air was still and dark, and smoke hung like fog. Firelight caught the haze and lit it up, blotting out the stars.

'It's late,' said Mr Crowley, still unmoving. 'You run on home; I'll sit up with the fire till the coals die out.'

I stood and reached in with the poker, preparing to spread the coals around, but he put out a shaky hand to stop me.

'Let it be,' he said. 'I never like to kill a fire. Just let it be.'

I set down the poker and walked across the street to my house. When I reached my room I looked out of the window and saw him, still sitting, still staring.

I'd watched that man kill four people. I'd watched him tear out organs, rip off his own arm and transform before my eyes into something grotesquely inhuman. Somehow, despite all of that, his words by the fire that night disturbed me more than anything he had ever done.

I wondered again if he knew about me – and if he did, how long I had before he silenced me the way he had silenced Ted Rask. I was safe at the party, and afterwards, because there were too many witnesses – if I'd disappeared from his yard, after fifty or more people had seen me there, it would raise too much suspicion. I decided there was nothing I could do. If he didn't know, I needed to keep going with my plan, and if he did, then there wasn't much I could do about it. Either way, I knew that my plan was working: my note had bothered him, maybe very deeply. I had to keep up the pressure, building more and more fear until he was terrified, because that's when I could control him.

The next day I sent another note, to make my intentions clear:

I AM GOING TO KILL YOU

# CHAPTER 12

Brooke woke up every morning around seven o'clock. Her dad got up at six-thirty, showered and dressed, and then woke up the kids while their mom made breakfast. He went into Ethan's room and flipped on the light, sometimes yanking the covers away playfully, sometimes singing loudly, and once actually tossing a bag of frozen broccoli into his bed when he refused to get up. Brooke, on the other hand, was more privileged – her dad simply knocked on her door and told her to wake up, leaving only when he heard her answer back. She was a young woman, after all, both more responsible than her brother and more deserving of privacy. Nobody barged in, nobody peeked in, nobody saw her at all until she wanted them to.

Nobody but me.

Brooke's room was on the first floor of their house, in the back left corner, which meant that she had two windows – one on the side facing the Petermans' house, which she always kept tightly curtained; and one on the back, facing the woods, which she kept uncovered. We lived on the edge of town, so there were no rear neighbours, no other houses, and no people at all for miles. She thought no one could see her. I thought she was beautiful.

She slept in thick grey sweats, which seemed like an oddly dull colour for her. I watched her sit up into view, pushing aside the bedspread and stretching luxuriously before combing out her hair with her fingers. Sometimes she scratched her armpits or her butt – something no girl would ever do if she knew she were being watched. She made faces in her mirror; sometimes she danced a little. After a minute or two she gathered up her clothes and left the room, headed for the shower.

I wondered if I could offer to shovel their snow, like I did with Mr Crowley, so I could put the ladder where I wanted it and grant myself more access to the yard. It would probably be suspicious though, unless I did the whole street, and I didn't have time for that. I was far too busy as it was.

Each day I found a way to give Mr Crowley a new note, leaving some on his car, like before, others taped to his windows or shoved into doorways higher than Kay could reach. After the second one, none of the notes were direct threats. Instead, I sent him evidence that I knew what he was doing.

JEB JOLLEY – KIDNEY
DAVE BIRD – ARM

As I left him notes about the victims, I made sure to leave out the drifter he'd killed by the lake – partly because I didn't know his name, and partly because I was still afraid that Mr Crowley had seen my bike tracks in the snow, and I didn't want him to put two and two together.

On the last day of school I sent him a note that said:

GREG OLSON – STOMACH

This was the biggie, because Greg Olson's body hadn't been found yet. As far as Crowley knew, nobody knew about the stomach. After he read it he locked himself in the house, brooding; the next morning he went to the hardware store and bought a couple of padlocks, adding extra security to his shed and cellar door. I was a little worried that he'd become too paranoid, and that I'd start to lose track of him, but no sooner was he finished locking up than he came to our house and gave me a new key to the shed.

'I've locked up the shed, John. Can't be too careful these days.' He handed me the key. 'You know where the tools are, so just keep it clean like you always do, and thanks again for all your help.'

'Thanks,' I said. He still trusted me – I felt like whooping for joy. I gave him my best 'surrogate grandson' smile. 'I'll keep the snow shovelled.'

My mom came down the stairs behind me. 'Hello, Mr Crowley. Is everything okay?'

'I've added some new locks,' he said. 'I'd recommend you do the same. That killer's still out there.'

'We keep the mortuary locked up pretty tightly,' said Mom, 'and there's a good alarm system in the back where we store the chemicals. I think we're okay.'

'You got a good boy,' he said, smiling, then trouble clouded his face and he glanced down the street suspiciously. 'This town's not as safe as it used to be. I'm not trying to scare you, I just . . .' He looked back at us. 'Just be careful.' He turned and trudged back across the street, his shoulders heavy. I closed the door and smiled.

I'd tricked him.

'Doing anything fun today?' asked Mom. I looked at her and she put up her hands innocently. 'Just asking.'

I brushed past her and climbed the stairs. 'I'm going to read for a while.' It was my standard excuse for spending hours at a time in my room, watching the Crowleys' house from my window. This time of day I couldn't get up close, so watching through the window was all I had.

'You've been spending too much time in your room,' she said, following me up the stairs. 'It's the first day of Christmas vacation – you should go out and do something enjoyable.'

This was new – what was she up to? I'd been out of the house almost as much as I was in it, creeping around outside Mr Crowley's house – and Brooke's. Mom didn't know where I went or what I was doing, but she couldn't possibly think that I was spending too much time in my room. She had something else on her mind.

'There's that movie we keep seeing ads for,' she said. 'It finally made it to town yesterday; you could go see that.'

I turned and stared at her again. What was she up to?

'I'm just saying it might be fun,' she said, ducking into the kitchen to avoid my gaze. She was nervous. 'If you want to go,' she called out, 'I've got some money for tickets.'

'Tickets' is plural – was that her game? There's no way I was seeing a movie with my mom. 'You can see it if you like,' I said. 'I want to finish this book.'

'Oh, I'm too busy right now,' she said, emerging from the kitchen with a handful of bills. She held them out with an anxious smile. 'You can go with Max. Or Brooke.'

Aha. This was about Brooke. I felt my face go red, then I turned and stalked into my room. 'I said no!' I slammed the door and closed my eyes. I was angry, but I didn't know why. 'Stupid Mom trying to send me to a stupid movie with stupid . . .' I couldn't say her name out loud. No one was supposed to know about Brooke – Brooke didn't even know about Brooke. I kicked my backpack and it slumped over, too full of books to fly across the room like I wanted it to.

Sitting in the dark with Brooke wouldn't be so bad, I thought, no matter what movie it was. I heard her laugh in my head, and thought about witty things I could say to make her laugh again. 'This movie sucks – the director should be strangled with his own film.' But Brooke wouldn't laugh at that; her eyes would go wide and she'd back away, just like at the Halloween dance.

'You're a freak,' she'd say. 'You're a sick, psycho freak.'

'No, I'm not – you know I'm not!' I'd reply. 'You know me better than anyone in the world, because I know you better than anyone in the world. I see things nobody else does. We've done homework together, we've watched TV together, we've talked on the phone to—'

Yeah – who *had* she been talking to on the phone? I'd find out and I'd kill him.

I cursed at the window and I pulled myself together.

I was in my room, breathing heavily. None of it was true. Brooke didn't know me, because we hadn't shared anything, because everything we'd ever done together was really only stuff she'd done alone, while I spied on her through her window. I'd watched her do her homework a few nights ago, and knew that we had the same assignment, but it didn't count as doing it together because she didn't even know I was there. And then when the phone rang and she picked it up and said hello to someone else it was like a wedge between us, and she smiled at the invader and not at me, and I wanted to scream but I knew that no one was interrupting anything because I was the only one in the world who knew that anything was going on.

I pressed my palms into my eyes. 'I'm stalking her,' I muttered. It wasn't supposed to be like this; I was supposed to be watching Mr Crowley, not Brooke. I broke my rules for him, not for anyone else, but the monster had shattered the wall and taken over before I even knew what it was doing. I barely even thought of the monster any more, because we'd merged so completely into one. I looked up and paced across my room to the window, staring out at Mr Crowley's house. 'I can't do this.' I paced back to my bed and kicked my backpack harder this time, skidding it across the floor. 'I need to see Max.'

I picked up my coat and rushed out without saying anything to Mom. She'd left the money on the edge of the kitchen counter and I grabbed it as I passed, shoving it into my pocket and slamming the door behind me.

Max's house was just a few miles away, and I could get there pretty quickly on my bike. I looked away as I passed Brooke's house, and flew down the road too fast, not caring about ice or watching for cars. I saw myself putting my hands around Brooke's neck, first caressing it, then squeezing it until she screamed and kicked and choked and every thought in her entire head was focused on me, and nothing but me, and I was her whole world and—

'No!'

My back wheel caught a patch of black ice and swerved out from under me, spinning me to the side. I managed to stay upright, but as soon as I was steady again I leaped off the bike and picked it up and swung it like a club into a telephone pole. It clanged and vibrated in my hands, solid and real. I dropped it and leaned against the pole, gritting my teeth.

*I should be crying. I can't even cry like a human.*

I looked around quickly to see who was watching. A few cars were driving by, but no one was paying me any attention. 'I need to see Max,' I muttered again, and picked up my bike. I hadn't seen him outside of school in weeks – I spent all of my time alone, hiding in the shadows and sending notes to Mr Crowley. That wasn't safe, even without my rules. Especially without my rules. My bike looked okay – scratched, maybe, but not dented. The handlebars were skewed to the side, but I was able to compensate for it by holding them crooked. I rode straight for Max's house and forced myself to think about nothing but him. He was my friend. Friends were normal. I couldn't be a psycho if I had a friend.

Max lived in a duplex on Redwood Street, by the wood plant, in a neighbourhood that always smelled like sawdust and smoke. Most of the people in town worked at the plant, including Max's mom; his dad drove a truck, usually hauling wood from the plant, and was gone as often as he was home. I didn't like Max's dad, and anytime I went to his house the big diesel cab was the first thing I looked for. Today it was gone, so Max was probably home alone.

I dropped my bike in their front yard and rang the bell. I rang a second time. Max opened it with a dull expression, but his eyes lit up when he saw me.

'Check it out, man – come see what my dad got me!' He threw himself onto the couch, picking up an Xbox 360 controller and holding it up like a prize. 'He can't be here for Christmas so he gave it to me early. It's awesome.'

I closed the door and took off my jacket. 'Cool.' He was playing some racing game, and I breathed a sigh of relief. This was exactly the kind of mindless time sink I needed. 'Do you have two controllers?'

'You can use Dad's,' he said, pointing at the TV. A second controller was sitting next to it. 'Just make sure you don't wreck it, because when he comes back he's going to bring Madden, and we're going to play a whole football season together. He'll be pissed if you wreck his controller.'

'I'm not going to hit it with a hammer,' I said, turning it on and retreating to the couch. 'Let's play.'

'In a minute,' he said. 'I've got to finish this first.' He unpaused the game and did a couple of races, assuring me between each one that it was just a tourney thing and it would be over soon and he didn't know how to save until he got to the end. Eventually he set up a head-to-head race and we played for an hour or two. He beat me every time, but I didn't care. I was acting like a normal kid, and I didn't have to kill anybody.

'You suck,' he said eventually. 'And I'm hungry. You want some chicken?'

'Sure.'

'We have some left over from last night. It was our early Christmas party for Dad.' He went into the kitchen and brought back a bucket of fried chicken, half-empty, and we sat on the couch watching TV and throwing back the bones as we finished each piece. His little sister wandered out, took a piece, and quietly wandered back into her room.

'You going anywhere for Christmas?' he asked.

'Nowhere to go,' I said.

'Us neither.' He wiped his hands on the couch and rooted through the bones for another drumstick. 'What you been doing?'

'Nothing,' I said. 'Stuff. You?'

'You've been doing something,' he said, eyeing me. 'I've barely seen you in two weeks, which means you've been doing something on your own. But what could it be? What does the psychotic young John Wayne Cleaver do in his spare time?'

'You caught me,' I said. 'I'm the Clayton Killer.'

'That was my first guess too,' he said, 'but he's only killed, what, six people? You'd do way better than that.'

'More isn't automatically better,' I said, turning back to the TV. 'Quality's got to count for something.'

'I bet I know what you've been doing,' he said, pointing at me with his drumstick. 'You've been mackin' on Brooke.'

'"Mackin'?"' I asked.

'Making out,' said Max, puckering his lips. 'Getting it on. Busting a move.'

'I think "busting a move" means dancing,' I said.

'And I think you are a fat liar,' said Max.

'Do you mean phat with a P-H or fat with an F?' I asked. 'I can never tell with you.'

'You are so totally into Brooke,' he said, taking a bite of chicken and laughing with his mouth wide open. 'You haven't even said no yet.'

'I didn't think I had to deny something that nobody could possibly believe,' I said.

'Still haven't said no.'

'Why would I be after Brooke?' I asked. 'It doesn't even know I'm— dammit!'

'Whoa,' said Max. 'What's going on?'

I had called Brooke 'it'. That was stupid. That was . . . horrifying. I was better than that.

'Did I hit a little too close to the target?' asked Max, relaxing again.

I ignored him, staring straight ahead. Calling human beings 'it' was a common trait of a serial killer – they didn't think of other people as human, only as objects, because that made them easier to torture and kill. It was hard to hurt 'him' or 'her', but easy to hurt 'it'. 'It' didn't have any feelings. 'It' didn't have any rights. 'It' was just a thing, and you could do whatever you wanted with it.

'Hello?' said Max. 'Earth to John.'

I'd always called corpses 'it', even though Mom and Margaret made me stop if they heard me. But I'd never called a person 'it', ever. I was losing control. That was why I had come to see Max, to get in control again, and it wasn't working.

'You want to see a movie?' I asked.

'You want to tell me what the crap is going on?' asked Max.

'I need to see a movie,' I said, 'or something. I need to be normal – we need to do normal stuff.'

'Like sitting on the couch and talking about how normal we are?' asked Max. 'Us normal people do that all the time.'

'Come on, Max, I'm serious! This whole thing is serious! Why do you think I even came here?'

His eyes narrowed. 'I don't know,' he said. 'Why did you come here?'

'Because I'm . . . something's happening,' I said. 'I'm not . . . I don't know! I'm losing it.'

'Losing what?'

'Everything,' I said. 'I'm losing it all. I broke all the rules, and now the monster's out, and I'm not even me any more. Can't you see?'

'What rules?' asked Max. 'You're freakin' me out, man.'

'I have rules to keep me normal,' I said. 'To keep me . . . safe. To keep everyone safe. One of them is that I have to hang out with you because you help me stay normal, and

I haven't been doing it. Serial killers don't have friends, and they don't have partners, they're just alone, so if I'm with you I'm safe and I'm not going to do anything. Don't you get it?'

Max's face grew clouded. I'd known him long enough to learn his moods – what he did when he was happy, what he did when he was mad. Right now he was squinting, and kind of frowning, and that meant he was sad. It caught me by surprise, and I stared back in shock.

'Is that why you came here?' he asked.

I nodded, desperate for some kind of connection. I felt like I was drowning.

'And that's why we've been friends for three years? Because you force yourself to be, because you think it makes you normal?'

*See who I am. Please.*

'Well, congratulations, John,' he said. 'You're normal. You're the big freakin' king of normal, with your stupid rules and your fake friends. Is anything you do real?'

'Yeah,' I said. 'I . . .' But right there, with him staring at me, I couldn't think of a thing.

'If you're just pretending to be my friend, then you don't actually need me at all,' he said, standing up. 'You can do that all by yourself. I'll see you around.'

'Come on, Max,'

'Get out of here,' he said.

I didn't move.

'Get out!' he repeated.

'You don't know what you're doing,' I said. 'I need to—'

'Don't you dare blame me for you being a freak,' he shouted. 'Nothing you do is my fault. Now get out of my house!'

I stood up and grabbed my coat.

'Put it on outside,' said Max, throwing open the door. 'Dangit, John, everyone in school hates me. Now I don't even have my freak friend any more.' I walked out into the cold and he slammed the door behind me.

That night Crowley killed again, and I missed it. His car was gone when I got back from Max's, and Mrs Crowley said he'd gone to watch the game. There wasn't a game that night for any of his teams, but I cycled downtown anyway to see if I could find him. His car wasn't at his favourite sports bar, nor at any of the others, and I even drove out to the Flying J to see if I could find him there. He was nowhere. I got home long past dark and he still hadn't come back, and I was so mad I wanted to scream. I sat down on the doorstep to think.

I wanted to go and see what Brooke was doing – in fact, I was desperate to see what she was doing – but I didn't. I bit my tongue, daring myself to draw blood, but instead I stood up and punched the wall.

I couldn't let the monster take over. I had a job to do, and a demon to kill. I couldn't let myself lose control before I did what I needed to do – no, that wasn't right. I couldn't let myself lose control at all. I had to stay focused. I had to get Crowley.

If I couldn't find him, at least I could send him a note.

I'd gotten so distracted today I hadn't prepared one yet, and I needed to let him know that even though I couldn't see it, I knew what he was doing. I racked my brain for something I could write on without incriminating myself; the mortuary stationery was out, of course, and I didn't dare go upstairs looking for paper in case Mom was still awake. I ran over to Mr Crowley's yard, nearly invisible in the darkness, and looked for something else. Eventually I found a bag of snow salt on his porch; he kept it there to salt his steps and sidewalks for ice. It gave me an idea, and I came up with a plan.

At 1 a.m. when Crowley pulled in, his car swung around and stopped suddenly, half in and half out of his driveway. There in the headlights was a word written in salt crystals, each letter three feet long on the asphalt and shining brilliantly in the headlights:

DEMON

After a moment Mr Crowley drove forward and smeared the words with his car, then got out and swept away the remnants with his foot. I watched him from the darkness of my bedroom, pricking myself with a pin and grimacing at the pain.

# CHAPTER 13

'Merry Christmas!'

Margaret bustled in the door with an armful of presents, and Mom kissed her on the cheek.

'Merry Christmas to you,' said Mom, taking a few of the presents and stacking them by the tree. 'Do you have anything else in the car?'

'Just the salad, but Lauren's bringing it up.'

Mom went white, and Margaret grinned deviously.

'She's really here?' asked Mom quietly, poking her head out to look down the steps. Margaret nodded. 'How did you do it?' asked Mom. 'I've invited her five times and couldn't get a yes out of her.'

'We had a really good talk last night,' said Margaret. 'Also, I think her boyfriend dumped her.'

Mom looked around the room frantically. 'We're not ready for four. John, run down and get another chair for the table; I'll set another place. Margaret, you're wonderful.'

'I know,' said Margaret, pulling off her coat. 'What would you do without me?'

I was sitting by the window, staring intently at Mr

Crowley's house across the street. Mom asked me two more times for a chair before I stood up, took her key, and headed out the door. It was only in the past few days that she'd let me touch the key again, and then only because she'd bought too much food for Christmas, and we'd had to store the extra in the mortuary freezer. I passed Lauren on the stairs.

'Hey, John,' she said.

'Hey, Lauren.'

Lauren glanced up at the door. 'Is she in a good mood?'

'She almost blew streamers out her ears when Margaret said you were here,' I said. 'She's probably killing a goat in your honour right now.'

Lauren rolled her eyes. 'We'll see how long that lasts.' She glanced up the stairs. 'Stick close, okay? I might need back-up.'

'Yeah, me too.' I took another step downstairs, then stopped and looked back up at her. 'You got something from Dad.'

'No way.'

'They got here yesterday – one box for each of us.' I'd shaken mine, poked it, and held it up to the light, but I still couldn't tell what it was. All I really wanted was a card. It would be the first news we'd had from him since last Christmas.

I got an extra chair from the mortuary chapel and brought it back upstairs. Mom was flitting from room to room, talking out loud to herself as she took coats and set the table and checked the food. It was her trademarked style of indirect attention – not talking to Lauren or giving her any special treatment, but showing that she cared by making herself busy on Lauren's account. It was sweet, I guess, but it was also the embryonic stage of an 'I do so much for you and you don't even care' yelling match. I gave it three hours before Lauren stormed out. At least we'd have time to eat first.

Christmas lunch was ham and potatoes, though Mom had learned her lesson from Thanksgiving and did not attempt to cook it herself. We bought the ham pre-cooked, stored it in the embalming-room freezer for a few days, and then heated it up Christmas morning. We ate in silence for nearly thirty minutes.

'This place needs some Christmas cheer,' said Margaret abruptly, setting down her fork. 'Carols?'

We stared at her.

'Didn't think so,' she said. 'Jokes then. We'll each tell one, and the best wins a prize. I'll start. Have you done geometry yet, John?'

'Yeah, why?'

'Nothing,' said Margaret. 'So there once was an Indian chief with three daughters, or squaws. All the braves in the tribe wanted to marry them, so he decided to hold a contest. All the braves would go out hunting, and the three who brought back the best hides would get to marry his squaws.'

'Everyone knows this one,' said Lauren, rolling her eyes.

'I don't,' said Mom. I didn't either.

'Then I'll keep going,' said Margaret, smiling, 'and don't you dare give it away, Lauren. So anyway, all the braves went out, and after a long time they started to come back with wolf hides and rabbit hides and things like that. The chief was unimpressed. Then one day a brave came back with a hide from a grizzly bear, which is pretty amazing, so the chief let him marry his youngest daughter. Then the next guy came back with a hide from a polar bear, which is even more amazing, so the chief let him marry his middle daughter. They waited and waited, and finally the last brave came back with the hide from a hippopotamus.'

'A hippopotamus?' asked Mom. 'I thought this was in North America.'

'It is,' said Margaret, 'that's why a hippopotamus hide was so great. It was the most amazing hide the tribe had ever seen, and the chief let that brave marry his oldest and most beautiful daughter.'

'She's two minutes older than I am,' said Mom, glancing at me with a mock sneer. 'Never lets me forget it.'

'Stop interrupting,' said Margaret. 'This is the best part. The squaws and the braves got married, and a year later they all had children – the youngest had one son, the middle squaw had one son, and the oldest squaw had two sons.'

She paused dramatically, and we stared at her for a moment, waiting. Lauren laughed.

'Is there a punchline?' I asked.

Lauren and Margaret said it in unison: 'The sons of the squaw of the hippopotamus are equal to the sons of the squaws of the other two hides.'

I smiled. Mom laughed, shaking her head. 'That's the punchline?' she asked. 'Why is that even funny?'

'It's the Pythagorean theorem,' said Lauren. 'It's a math formula for . . . something.'

'Right-angled triangles,' I said, and looked pointedly at Margaret. 'I told you I'd already done geometry.'

Mom thought a bit and then laughed again when she finally got it. 'That's the dumbest joke I've ever heard.'

'Then you'd better think of something better,' said Margaret. 'Lauren's turn.'

'I helped with yours,' she said, stabbing a bite of salad. 'That counts.'

'You then,' said Margaret to Mom. 'I know you've got something funny in that head of yours.'

'Oh boy,' said Mom, leaning on her fist. 'Joke, joke, joke. Oh, I've got one.'

'Let's hear it,' said Margaret.

'Two women walked into a bar,' said Mom. 'The first one looked at the other one and said, "I didn't see it either".' Mom and Margaret burst out laughing, and Lauren groaned.

'A little short,' said Margaret, 'but I'll let it slide. All right then, John, it's up to you. What have you got?'

'I don't really know any jokes,' I said.

'You've got to have something,' said Lauren. 'Where's that old joke book we used to have?'

'I realy don't know one,' I said. I pictured Brooke laughing when we talked about the Arson merit badge, but I couldn't really turn that into a joke. Did I know any jokes at all?

'Wait, um, Max told me a joke once, but you're going to hate it.'

'No matter, said Margaret, 'lay it on us.'

'You're really going to hate it,' I said.

'Get on with it,' said Lauren.

'As long as it's clean,' said Mom.

'That's funny,' I said, 'because it's about cleaning.'

'I'm intrigued,' said Margaret, leaning on the table.

'What do you do when your dishwasher stops working?' Nobody offered an answer. I took a deep breath. 'You slap her.'

'You're right,' said Mom with a frown. 'I hate it. But the good news is, you just volunteered to clear the table. Let's head into the living room, ladies.'

'I say I won,' said Margaret, standing up. 'My joke was funniest.'

'I think I won,' said Lauren, 'because I got away without telling one.'

They shuffled into the other room and I gathered up the dishes. Usually I hated clearing the table, but I didn't mind today – everyone was happy, and no one was fighting. We might last longer than three hours after all.

When I finished stacking dishes in the sink I joined them in the living room, and we handed out presents. I think I gave everyone hand lotion. Mom gave me a reading lamp.

'You spend so much time reading,' she said, 'and sometimes so late at night, I figured you could use it.'

'Thanks, Mom,' I said. *Thanks for believing my lies.*

Margaret got me a new backpack – one of those big mountaineer packs with a water bottle and a drinking tube built into it. I always laughed at the kids who wore them.

'The pack you've got is falling apart,' said Margaret. 'I'm amazed those straps are still attached.'

'There's a couple of threads still hanging on,' I said.

'This one will carry all your books without breaking.'

'Thanks, Margaret.' I put it to the side with a resolve to try to remove that dopey water tube later.

'I've never read this, so it might suck,' said Lauren, handing me a book-shaped present, 'but I know there was a movie, and the title seemed kind of appropriate, if nothing else.'

I opened it up and found a thick comic book – a graphic novel, or whatever the big ones are called. The title was *Hellboy*. I held it out and pointed at the title, and Lauren grinned.

'It's two presents in one,' she laughed. 'A comic book and a nickname.'

'Yay,' I said flatly.

'The first person to call him Hellboy has to open her presents outside,' said Mom, shaking her head.

'Thanks though,' I said to Lauren, and she smiled.

'Time to open your father's,' said Mom, and Lauren and I each took our box. They were simple brown shipping boxes – we'd left them that way just in case the gift inside wasn't wrapped. You could never tell with Dad. Mine was small, about the size of a textbook but considerably lighter. I used my house key to cut open the packing tape. Inside was a card and an iPod. I tore open the card, slowly and deliberately, trying not to look excited. It had a goofy cartoon cat and one of those horrible poems about what a great son I was. Dad had written a note at the bottom, and I read it silently.

*Hey, Tiger – Merry Christmas! Hope you had a great year. Enjoy ninth grade while you can, because next year is High School and it's a whole new ballgame. The girls are going to be all over you! You're gonna love this iPod – I filled it up with all of my favourite music, all the stuff we used to sing together. It's like having your dad in your pocket. See you around.*

*Sam Cleaver*

I'd already started High School, so he was a year off, but I was too intrigued by the music thing to care. I didn't even know where Dad was living – he hadn't put a return address on the package – but I could remember riding in the car and singing along to his favourite bands: the Eagles, Journey, Fleetwood Mac and others. It surprised me, for some reason, that he remembered that too. Now I could pull out my iPod, pick a song, and be closer to my father than I'd been in five years.

The iPod box was still in shrinkwrap. I tore the plastic off, confused, and ripped open the box; the iPod was untouched, and the library was completely empty. He'd forgotten.

'Dammit, Sam,' said Mom. I turned and saw that she had read the card – she'd seen the screwed-up school year and the promise he immediately broke, and she was hanging her head wearily, rubbing her temples. 'I'm so sorry, John.'

'That looks cool,' said Lauren, glancing over. 'I got a portable DVD player and a DVD of the Apple Dumpling Gang – apparently we used to watch it together, and he thought it was special or something. I don't remember it.'

'He makes me so mad,' said Mom, standing up and walking into the kitchen. 'He can't even buy your love without screwing it up.'

'An iPod seems pretty cool to me, too,' said Margaret. 'is there something wrong with it?' She read the card and sighed. 'I'm sure he just forgot, John.'

'That's the whole problem!' shouted Mom from the kitchen. She was banging dishes around noisily, venting her anger on them as she clattered them through the sink and into the dishwasher.

'Still though,' said Margaret, 'it's better to have an empty one anyway – you can fill it with whatever you want. Can I look at it?'

'Go ahead,' I said, standing up. 'I'm going out.'

'Wait, John,' said Mom, rushing in from the kitchen, 'let's have dessert now. I bought two different pies, and some whipped cream, and—'

I ignored her, taking my coat from the hall closet and walking to the door. She called me back again and I slammed the door shut, stomping down the steps and slamming the outside door as well. I got on my bike and rode away, never looking back to see if they had followed me out; never looking up to see if they were watching through the window. I didn't look at Mr Crowley's house, I didn't look at Brooke's house, I just pedalled my bike and watched the sidewalk lines fly by and hoped to God on every street I crossed that a truck would slam into me and wipe me across the pavement.

Twenty minutes later I was downtown, and I realized that I'd driven almost directly to Dr Neblin's office. It was closed, naturally – locked and hollow and dark. I stopped pedalling and sat there, maybe for ten minutes, watching the wind whip banks of snow into the air and twirl them around and smash them into brick walls. I didn't have anything to do, or anywhere to go, or anyone to talk to. I didn't have one single reason to exist.

All I had was Mr Crowley.

There was a payphone at the end of the street; the same one I'd used to call 911 a month ago. I didn't know why, but I propped my bike against it, dropped in a quarter, and dialled Mr Crowley's cellphone. While it rang I pulled up the tail of my T-shirt and wrapped it over the end of the phone to hide my voice, praying that it would actually work. After three rings he answered.

'Hello?'

'Hello,' I said. I didn't know what to say.

'Who is this?'

I paused. 'I'm the one who's been sending you notes.'

He hung up. I swore, pulled out another quarter, and dialled again.

'Hello?'

'Don't hang up.'

Click.

I only had two quarters left. I dialled again.

'Leave me alone,' he said. 'If you know so much about me then you know what I'll do if I find you.' Click.

I had to think of something to keep him on the line; I needed to talk to someone, to anyone, demon or not. I dropped in my last quarter and dialled again.

'I said—'

'Does it hurt?' I asked, interrupting him. I could hear him breathing heavily, hot and angry, but he didn't hang up. 'You ripped off your own arm,' I said, 'and cut open your own stomach. I just want to know if it hurts.'

He waited, saying nothing.

'Nothing you do makes sense,' I said. 'You hide some bodies and you don't hide others. You smile at a guy one minute and rip his heart out the next. I don't even know what you—'

'It hurts like hell.' He stayed silent a moment. 'It hurts every time.'

He answered me. There was something in his voice – some emotion I couldn't identify. Not quite happiness, not quite fatigue; it was something in the middle.

Relief?

Months of curiosity poured out in a flood. 'Do you have to wait for something to break down before you replace it?' I asked. 'Do you have to steal parts from people? And what about that guy in Arizona – Emmet T. Openshaw. What did you steal from him?'

Silence.

'I stole his life.'

'You killed him,' I said.

'I didn't just kill him,' said Crowley. 'I stole his life. He would have had a long one, I think; as long as this, at least. He would have gotten married and had kids.'

That didn't sound right.

'How old was he?' I asked.

'Thirty, I think. I tell people I'm seventy-two.'

I had assumed Openshaw was older, like the recent victims. 'You hid his body well enough that no one ever found it – so why didn't you hide Jeb Jolley's? Or the two after that?'

Silence. A door closed.

'You still don't know, do you?'

'You're acting like a first-time killer,' I said, trying to puzzle through it. 'You've gotten better with each one, and you've started hiding the bodies, which makes sense if you've never done this before, but you have – is it all an act? But why would you pretend to be inexperienced if you could just keep it completely quiet instead?'

'Hang on,' he said, and coughed loudly. He muffled the phone, but I could still hear loud coughs. Fake coughs, it sounded like, and something else behind them. A rumble. He unmuffled the phone, but it was harder to hear than before – there was static on the line, or white noise.

What was he doing?

'I acted inexperienced because I was,' he said. 'I've taken

more lives than you can guess, but Jeb was the first one I . . . didn't keep.'

'You didn't *keep*? But . . .' Could he keep souls? Could he absorb lives as well as body parts?

Or could he take lives *instead* of body parts?

'You took Emmet's whole body,' I said, 'and his shape. And you took someone else's body before that, and someone else's before that. It makes sense. You never had to hide the bodies before because you took everything, and left your old body behind. That's why there was so much sludge in Emmet's house. You discarded an entire body there, not just a part, and you—'

Ding . . . ding . . . ding . . .

'What's that?' I asked.

'What's what?' he said.

'That noise. It sounded like a—' I slammed down the phone and grabbed my bike, looking wildly down the road.

It was a turn signal. Crowley was in his car, and he was looking for me.

There was no one on Main Street. I jumped on my bike and shot down to the corner, swerving around it too quickly and sliding on the ice. He wasn't on this street either. I righted myself and pedalled as hard as I could to the next corner and spun around that as well, in the other direction, away from his house and the route he was probably coming from.

That's why he said so much. Mr Crowley was on a cellphone, and he had caller ID. He must have figured out I was on a payphone, and kept me talking while he went outside, started his car and came to look for me. There were only two or three payphones in town, and he was probably checking them all – the Flying J, the gas station by the wood plant, and the gas station where I'd been on Main. The gas station where I'd been talking had been closed for Christmas, thank goodness, so there would be no clerks to describe me when kindly old Mr Crowley showed up asking questions. But Christmas was also a problem. Every building downtown was closed, every door locked, and every store empty. There was nowhere for me to hide.

What would be open at Christmas in a tiny town like Clayton? The hospital – but no, there was probably a payphone there as well, and Crowley might drop by to check it. Just then, I heard a car and turned straight off the sidewalk onto a snow-covered lawn, forcing my way along the side of an apartment building. There was a gap between two buildings, and halfway down a gas meter; I squeezed around it and crouched down on the other side, eyeing the street at the end of a long, brick canyon. The car I heard didn't pass by – I didn't know who it had been, or where it had been going, only that I needed to hide.

I spent the rest of the afternoon there, and into the evening, shivering in the snow. I could feel my body reacting, shutting down from cold, but I didn't dare move. I imagined a fire-eyed Mr Crowley driving back and forth across the town, weaving a net tighter and tighter around me.

When it had been dark for nearly an hour I dragged my

bike back out, my limbs stiff and my hands and feet burning with cold. I made my way home, saw that Crowley's car was parked neatly in his driveway, and went upstairs.

The house was empty and quiet; everyone had left.

# CHAPTER 14

My phone conversation with Mr Crowley ran through my head over and over for the next three days, to the exclusion of all else. Mom came home Christmas night crying and shouting that they'd spent the whole day looking for me, and asking where had I gone, saying she was so glad I was safe, and a thousand other things that I didn't listen to because I was too busy thinking about Mr Crowley.

The day after Christmas, Margaret came back and the three of us went out to a steakhouse, but I ignored them and my food, deep in thought. I'm sure they thought I was despondent because of Dad's Christmas present, but I'd honestly forgotten about it. All I could think about were Mr Crowley's hints and confessions, and there was no room in my head for anything else. By Wednesday Mom had stopped trying to cheer me up, though I sometimes caught her staring at me from across the room. I was grateful to finally have some peace and quiet.

Mr Crowley had all but admitted to me that he used to steal entire bodies, but that now he was only stealing pieces. It made sense in some ways. It explained why the DNA from the sludge kept showing up as the same person, because the whole body had come from Emmet Openshaw. It also explained why Crowley was so good at killing but so poor at hiding the evidence. He probably killed Jeb Jolley out of desperation, dying for lack of a good kidney, and simply didn't think ahead about what to do with the body as he'd never had to do anything with one before. As the year went on and he killed more people, he got better at it, and even started looking for unknown victims, like the lone drifter he took to Freak Lake; even now, a month later, nobody knew he was missing, nor that the Clayton Killer had claimed another victim just before Thanksgiving. Nobody knew about the one he'd killed just before Christmas either – the one I'd missed – so I assumed that would be a drifter as well. There might be others that even I didn't know about.

It also gave me a pretty good idea of why he never took more than one piece of each victim. If taking the whole body also gave him that body's appearance, he was probably worried that taking too many pieces from one corpse would start to overwhelm the appearance he was trying to maintain. His body could deal with an arm here and a kidney there, but if too much of that victim started to creep in, he could lose the Bill Crowley identity he was fighting so hard to keep.

So yes, he was getting better at killing this way, instead of the old way, but the question remained: why had he changed? And why was there a forty-year gap with no killing at all? I tried to put myself into his place – a demon, wandering the earth, killing someone and stealing their body and starting a new life. If I could do anything I wanted, why would I be here in Clayton County? If I could be as young and as strong as I wanted, why would I choose to be old – so old I was falling apart? If I could kill one person and disappear without a trace, why would I hang around, killing a dozen people and leaving more and more evidence that the cops could use to find me?

I tried to build another psychological profile, starting with the same key question: *what did the killer do that he didn't have to do?* He stayed in one place. He maintained one identity. He got old. And he killed, over and over – that had to mean something. Did he enjoy it? He didn't seem to. But if I understood how he worked, then killing this many people was definitely something he didn't have to do. He had another option. So why was he doing it?

If he didn't have to do something, that meant he wanted to do it. Why did he want to get old? Why did he want to stay in this godforsaken town in the middle of this icy nowhere? What did Clayton have that the demon couldn't find anywhere else? I couldn't figure it out on my own; I needed Dr Neblin. I had an appointment with him on Thursday, which gave me one day to plan my strategy – how to get the answers I needed without giving anything away.

Mom reminded me about my appointment over breakfast the next morning, and seemed genuinely shocked that afternoon when I actually left and rode my bike downtown. I suppose, from her point of view, it was the first active thing I'd done since running out on Christmas Day; for me, it was just a chance to talk to someone intelligent.

'How was Christmas?' asked Neblin, cocking his head to the side. He did that when he was trying to hide something – probably the fact that he'd already heard all about Christmas from Mom. Dr Neblin was a terrible liar; someday I'd have to play poker with him.

'I have a scenario for you,' I said. 'I want your opinion.'

'What kind of scenario?'

'A fake psych profile,' I said. 'I've been doing them for fun over the Christmas break, and I've got one that I'm kind of hung up on.'

'Okay,' he said, 'fire away.'

'Let's say you're a shapeshifter,' I said. 'You can change your face, and go anywhere you want, and be anyone you want to be. You can be any age, any size, any nationality, and do anything you want. Now imagine that you're in a bad situation, forced to do things you don't like. If you had this kind of freedom, why would you choose to stay?'

'So it's question of risk and reward,' he said. 'I stay me and live with hardship, or I escape the hardship at the cost of losing myself.'

'You're not yourself,' I said, and winced at how exposed I felt. I was opening myself to a lot of uncomfortable questions, especially if he thought I was obliquely referring to myself. 'You lost yourself a long time ago, and you've been a string of somebody elses for who knows how long.'

'Then it's a question of identity as well,' he said. 'If I'm somebody else, is that as good as being me? If I can't be myself any more, am I better off being nobody at all, or choosing a new self to become?'

'That's right,' I said, nodding. 'You can stay one person, in one place, doing one thing for ever and hating it, or you can be free of everything – no responsibilities, no problems, no baggage.'

He stared at me a moment. 'Is there something you want to tell me?'

'I want you to tell me what would make you stay in that situation,' I said. 'I know you think this is about me, but it's not – I can't explain. Now seriously – you've got nothing on the one side, and everything on the other. Why would you stay?'

He thought about it for a couple of minutes, tapping his pen on his pad and frowning. This was why I came to Dr Neblin. He took me seriously, no matter what I said or how crazy I sounded.

'One more question,' he said. 'Am I a sociopath?'

'What?'

'This is your puzzle,' said Neblin, 'and as we have often discussed, you have strong sociopathic tendencies. I want to know if I should be answering from a standard emotional state, or from the lack of one.'

'What's the difference?'

Dr Neblin smiled. 'There's your answer. You said that the second option, leaving and starting a string of brand new lives, had freedom – it had no "baggage". Where a sociopath sees baggage, a different personality would see emotional connections. Friends, family, loved ones – not all of us can give those up so easily. They define us, and they make us who we are; sometimes the personalities around us are what make us complete.'

Emotional connections. Loved ones.

'Kay.'

'What?'

'I . . . I said okay.'

It was Kay Crowley. Mr Crowley was really in love with her – not pretending to be, not using her for cover. He was really, truly, in love with her. I'd tried putting myself into Crowley's place and it didn't work, not because his mind was too different, but because mine was. The demon loved his wife.

'I have to go,' I said.

'You just got here.'

Crowley had done it maybe a hundred times before, maybe a thousand times, jumping from body to body, life to life. He moved to a new town and started afresh, and when his demon powers couldn't sustain a body any more he just dropped it and moved on. He'd done it in Arizona with Emmet Openshaw, and fled to Clayton County to hide and start over – but then he'd met Kay, and now it was different. Leaving this body meant leaving her, and he couldn't do it, so he was patching himself up piecemeal instead, fixing each part as it broke down instead of starting over completely.

'John?'

'Huh?'

'Is there something you want to talk about?' asked Dr Neblin.

'No, no, I . . . have to go. I have to think.'

'Call me, John,' said Neblin, standing up and pulling out a business card. 'Call me if you want to talk, about anything at all.' He wrote a second number – his home number, I assumed – on the back of the card, and handed it to me. I realized abruptly that he was worried. Lines of concern etched his face like wounds, and he was watching me anxiously.

'Thanks,' I mumbled, and left the office, picking up my coat from the waiting room and going downstairs. I got on my bike and rode home, not aimlessly, not desperately, not nervously; I was calm for the first time in weeks. I'd found the demon's weakness.

*Love.*

I spent the evening locked in my room, going over my notes and watching out of the window for Mr Crowley. Love was the chink in his armour, I knew, but I hadn't come up with a plan to exploit it yet. I crafted and discarded a dozen different ideas, desperate to find one that could stop him before he killed again, but he was already growing very sick. He'd strike soon, and I wasn't ready.

Sure enough, a little after midnight Mr Crowley staggered out to his car. He looked worse than I'd ever seen him – he was waiting as long as possible to fix himself. I wondered if he might have to replace more than one thing, and then I wondered if that was even possible. If he took too much from one person, did he become that person whether he wanted to or not? That would explain why he replaced just one organ at a time.

I opened my door quietly; Mom was still awake, watching TV. I closed it again, locked it, and went to the window. It was a long drop to the ground, but Crowley was getting away. I bundled up in my coat – and in my newest acquisition, a ski mask – and jumped.

Mr Crowley was too far gone for me to follow his lights, so I rode off as fast as I could to the Flying J, hoping he would look there for another drifter, like before. It was hard to reach by bike, so I rode to the base of the hill behind it and hiked up, avoiding the freeway and the lights. Crowley was just pulling out – alone. He hadn't found anyone yet. I tumbled back down the snowy hill and rode the few blocks to the freeway off-ramp, where I saw him come back into town and head over towards the wood plant. Maybe he'd try to get a night watchman or something; some innocent nobody in the wrong place at the wrong time. His car was swerving dangerously, and I realized he probably couldn't wait for a victim nobody would miss – he had to kill the first person he found. At one in the morning, that would be almost impossible. I followed a few blocks behind, as black as the night.

He turned a few streets early, and when I reached the corner I saw him pull up behind an idling diesel cab. The truck engine turned off, the door opened, and a man jumped down; his breath hung around him like a ghost in the freezing air. The man jogged towards the front of the truck but Crowley got out of his car and called to him. The man paused and called back; I couldn't hear what either was saying. The man pointed at a house behind him – a duplex.

My heart froze. I looked up at the street sign above me: Redwood Street.

That was Max's dad.

'No!' I screamed, but it was too late. Max's dad looked up, looked right at me, and Crowley staggered towards him, claws out, knocking him to the ground with a gleaming claw and then falling on him with animal fury. Max's dad went down in a whirlwind of blood and claws, and Crowley stood over him unsteadily for a moment before collapsing next to the body. Both men lay inert in the frozen slush. The street was as silent as a grave.

I took a tentative step forward. Crowley had pushed himself too hard – maybe he'd pushed himself past his own ability to regenerate. He hadn't even taken an organ yet. Maybe Max's dad was still alive, and I could help him. The houses were dark and still – no one had heard my scream, or the attack. I trotted slowly across to the bodies, nearly slipping on a patch of ice. Nothing moved.

As I got closer I could see that Max's dad was beyond hope – his body was in at least three pieces, all of them ragged and bloody. A pile of entrails lay steaming on the frozen asphalt. I felt the monster inside of me stirring more strongly than ever, urging me to kneel down, to feel the glistening organs. I closed my eyes and fought for control.

When I opened them again I looked at Crowley, face down and still half-demon, his elongated arms corded with inhuman muscle. His long black fingers ended in terrifying claws as white as milk. Like the exposed entrails, Crowley's body was steaming in the cold.

I wanted to kick him. I wanted to punch him and beat him and pound him into the street until there was nothing left – no demon claws, no human body, no clothes, no memory at all. My mind raged to think of all the evil he'd done, but it was more than that. I was jealous. He'd killed himself, and taken away my chance.

The steam boiled around him, and suddenly his body spasmed. I jumped back, slipping on the ice and falling onto my back. The demon's head came up abruptly, gasping for breath through a mouth too full of fangs to be real. I scrambled to my feet and backed away again. The demon pushed itself up on its arms, feebly, and turned to face me. Its dark eyelids squinted grotesquely over its wide, crystalline eyes, as if it couldn't see me clearly, and I felt my face to make sure the ski mask was still there. In this darkness, he probably couldn't tell who I was. The demon's fangs glowed faintly – a pale phosphorescent blue. It crawled towards me one faltering claw-length before collapsing again on the ice. It coughed and turned its head fitfully, searching for something, and when its gaze fell on the tattered remnants of Max's dad it forgot me and crawled towards them painfully.

I took a few quick steps around him, trying to see if I could move the body – drag it out of the demon's reach – but it was too close. I'd missed my chance. The demon was going to regenerate, and then it was going to come after me. I could only hope that it hadn't recognized me in the dark. If I could get away quickly, and stay ahead, he might never know it was me.

My house was twenty minutes away by bike during the

day, but I made it there in ten – speeding down the middle of empty streets, barrelling heedlessly through intersections, taking time only to stay out of the snow in order to leave no tracks.

I placed my bike carefully against the side of the house, trying to match its previous position as closely as I could, just in case; the house had to look exactly as it was when he left, so he wouldn't suspect me. I crept up the side steps and listened at our inner door – the TV was off, and it sounded like Mom had gone to sleep. I opened it quietly and slipped into the darkness, locking it tightly again behind me. Tearing off my gloves and ski mask, grateful for the warmth, I flopped wearily onto the couch. I was safe.

But something was wrong, and I couldn't put my finger on it.

Everything seemed quiet enough, but not too quiet – the clock in the kitchen was ticking like normal; the furnace was blowing like normal. I listened at my mom's door, rubbing my hands together in the cold, and heard her low, even breathing. Everything was fine . . .

But why was it so cold? I hadn't noticed at first, because it was so much warmer inside than outside, but I could tell now, especially here in the hallway, that it was definitely cooler than it should have been. I tried to open my door to check my room, but the handle wouldn't turn. It was locked.

Of course! I'd left by the window, not the door, and the window was still open.

Mr Crowley would be home any minute, wondering who

had been watching him, and he'd see my open window and the footprints in the snow below it. He'd get suspicious; he'd wonder if it had been closed when he left. He'd come to check, and there I'd be, alone in the dark, locked out of my room, wide awake at one in the morning. Mom would wake up and ask – in front of him – how I'd got out of my room. He'd know, and he'd kill us both.

I started to go back outside, but that would be even worse: he'd come home and see me outside, trying to climb back into the first-floor window, and know that I had followed him.

My bedroom door opened inwards, so I couldn't reach the hinges to pop them off. I thought about kicking it down, but I didn't know if I could – and anyway, Mom would hear me and wake up, and she'd never forgive me for destroying a door. I was amazed she could sleep in this cold at all. I peeked out of the living-room window. The street was clear; there was still time. What could I do?

Crowley would get suspicious if he saw me trying to hide, but what if I didn't hide at all? The street was still empty; I pulled off my coat and put on my old one – it was a different colour than the one he'd seen me in – and went back outside without my gloves or ski mask. I reached the snowbank below my window and crawled up onto it just in time. Mr Crowley's headlights appeared at the end of the street, far away. I watched them draw closer and closer, watched the car itself come into view, and just as it started to slow I ran out in front of it, waving my arms wildly in the headlights. The car screeched to a stop, and he unrolled his window.

'John, what in blazes are you doing out here?'

'Can I sleep at your house tonight?' I asked.

'What?'

'Mom and I had a fight,' I said. 'I jumped out of my window. I was going to run away, but . . . it's so cold. Can I please sleep in your house?'

He glanced across the street at my house, my window open and my curtains flapping faintly in the breeze.

'Please?' I shivered.

'I don't think that's a good idea,' he said. 'My house isn't . . . it's not safe to be out like this at night, John. There are prowlers. It's not safe for you or your mother.'

'Please don't take me back,' I said, trying to summon up tears. I couldn't. 'I don't want her to know I left.'

He thought a minute. I could tell he was healthier than before – more alert, more composed, and far more steady. You could barely tell he'd been sick. 'If I promise not to tell your mother, will you go home?'

'My bedroom door is locked from the inside. I can't get back in, and if she sees me in the living room she'll find out eventually.'

He thought a moment longer, and glanced nervously around the neighbourhood; he obviously thought his stalker was watching. 'My ladder will reach,' he said at last. 'We can put you back in that way, but you've got to promise not to run away like this again.'

'And you won't say anything to Mom?'

'I promise,' he said. 'Deal?'

'Deal.' He drove past me into his driveway, and together we pulled his extendable ladder from his shed and set it up quietly under my window. 'Can you get it put away by yourself?' I whispered.

'I'm an old man,' he whispered back, smiling, 'but I'm not helpless.'

'Thanks,' I said, and climbed up to my window. I got inside, waved at him, and he folded the ladder up and took it away. I closed the window tightly, closed my blinds and watched him from the darkness. I'd fooled him again.

Mr Crowley put the ladder away and went inside – but didn't close his door. I kept watching, intrigued, and a moment later he came back out and did something I hadn't expected. He wrote something on a piece of paper and taped it to his door. I rummaged in the dark for my binoculars, and carefully focused in on the note without budging my curtains.

YOU COULDN'T STOP ME, AND YOU NEVER WILL

It was a note to his stalker, flaunting his power and practically promising to keep killing more people, again and again. It was barely a week since the last one – how much longer till the next? He was a killer, cold-blooded and evil, no matter how much he loved his wife or helped his neighbour. He was a demon. *It* was a demon.

And it had to die.

# CHAPTER 15

The new death was all over the news the next morning. Roger Bowen, local truck driver, husband and father, was found torn in half in the street in front of his house. The killer hadn't even bothered to move the body, let alone hide it.

Mom looked like she wanted to hug me – to reassure me, or herself, that everything was going to be okay. I guess that's what mothers are supposed to do, but mine couldn't do it. I could tell by the way she watched me that she wanted to comfort me – but that she knew I didn't need to be comforted. I wasn't sad, I was thoughtful; I didn't feel bad that Max's dad was dead, just guilty that I hadn't been able to stop his killer. I wondered then if I was doing all of this because I wanted to save the good guys, or if I just wanted to kill the bad guy. And I wondered if that made a difference.

Mom asked after a while if I wanted to call Max, and I knew, objectively, that I should have, but I didn't know what to say so I didn't. Just as no one could comfort me, I couldn't comfort anyone else: that was the realm of empathy, and I would be completely useless. I suppose I could have said, 'Hey, Max, I know who killed your dad, and I'm going to kill him back,' but I'm not an idiot. Sociopath or not, I'm smart enough to know that's not how people talk to each other. Better to keep it all a secret.

As soon as the police cleared the crime scene on Saturday night there was a vigil for Max's dad – not a funeral, because the FBI forensic team were only just beginning their autopsy, but a simple gathering where we all came together and lit candles and prayed or whatever. I wanted to watch Crowley's house instead, but Mom made me go. She pulled a couple of old dinner candles from a back drawer somewhere and we drove over. I was surprised at how big the vigil was.

Max was sitting on his porch, surrounded by his sister and his mom and the whole Bowen family from out of town who'd driven in to comfort them; it seemed to me that they'd want to drive away from a town under threat from a serial killer, not into it, but what did I know? Emotional connections made you do stupid things, I guess.

Margaret joined us, and we put flowers in the street where the body had been found; there was already a big pile. Someone had started a second pile for Greg Olson, also a family man, who was still missing, but it wasn't nearly as big; many people still clung to the idea that he was guilty of something. Mrs Olson and her son were there, showing solidarity with the community, but there was a police escort hovering nearby just in case anyone started a fight.

I was cold, and I was anxious to get back to watch

Crowley's house, but most of all I was bored. All we were doing was standing around holding candles, and I didn't see the point. We weren't accomplishing anything. We weren't finding the killer, or protecting the innocent, or giving Max a new dad. We were just there, milling around, watching impotent little flames melt our candles drop by drop.

At least our Neighbourhood Watch meeting had used a fire. I could start one now, I thought. We'd be warm, we'd have light, and, well . . . we'd have a big fire. That was its own reward. I looked around for something that would burn, but Mom pulled me suddenly towards the outer edge of the vigil.

'Hello, Peg,' she said, hugging Mrs Watson. Brooke and her family had just arrived, all crying. Brooke's face was wet with teardrops, round and raised like blisters, and I had to stop myself from reaching out to touch them.

'Hello, April,' said Mrs Watson. 'It's so terrible, isn't it? It's just so . . . Brooke, honey, can you take the flowers over? Thanks.'

'John can show you where they are,' my mom said quickly, turning to face me.

I shrugged. 'Come on,' I said, and Brooke and I walked through the crowd. 'It's a good thing I'm here,' I said, half-joking and half-bothered. 'It's pretty hard to find the big pile of flowers in the middle of the street.'

'Did you know him?' Brooke asked.

'Max?'

'His dad,' she said, wiping her eyes with a glove. The

tear stained it, a patch of black moisture on the dark blue knit.

'Not very well,' I said. I did know him very well, actually – he was loud, arrogant, and shot his mouth off about anything he had even half an opinion on. I hated him. Max idolized him. He was better off without him.

We reached the pile and Brooke set down the flowers.

'Why are there two piles?' she asked.

'That one's for the missing guy, Greg Olson.'

She knelt down and pulled a flower out of her bouquet, and took a step towards the smaller pile.

'Brooke,' I said, then stopped.

'What?' Her face darkened. 'You don't think Mr Olson's the killer, do you?'

'No, I just . . . Do you think this helps? We throw some flowers in a street, and tomorrow he kills another one. We're not helping anything.'

'I think maybe we are,' said Brooke. She sniffled, and wiped her nose. Her eyes were red from crying. 'I don't know what happens when we die, or where we go, but there's gotta be something, right? A heaven, or another world. Maybe they're watching us, I don't know. Maybe they can see us.' She placed her flower on Greg Olson's pile. 'If they can, maybe it will cheer them up to know we didn't forget them.' She wrapped her arms around herself, shivering in the cold, and looked off into the darkness.

'Max remembers his dad pretty dang well,' I said, 'but that doesn't bring him back. And what about all the others? He's killed people we don't even know about – he must have. If he hid Greg Olson's body, he's probably hidden somebody else's. If remembering's important, then what happens to them? Nobody even misses them.'

Brooke's eyes teared up again. 'That's terrible.' Her face was bright red from cold, as if someone had slapped her hard on both cheeks. It made me mad to look at her, and I felt my breathing speed up.

'I didn't mean to make you sad,' I said. I stared at my candle, deep into the heart of the flame. *Remember me . . .*

Brooke took another flower from her bouquet and set it off to the side, starting a third pile on the street.

'What's that for?' I asked.

'For the others,' she said.

I thought of the drifter at the bottom of Freak Lake. Did he care that some stupid girl put a flower in the street? He was still at the bottom of the lake, and the man who put him there was still killing, and that flower wasn't going to help either situation.

I turned to walk away, but someone walked past and placed another flower on Brooke's new pile. I stopped short, staring down at the two flowers crossed on the asphalt. A moment later a third one joined them.

Everyone seemed to know what was going on, and what they were supposed to do. It was like watching a flock of birds wheeling in the sky, turning and dropping and soaring without any command – they just knew what to do, like a communal mind. What happened to the other birds, the ones who couldn't read the signals and kept going straight when the flock took a wide, communal turn?

I heard a familiar voice and looked up. Mr Crowley had arrived, with Kay alongside, and they were talking to someone just ten feet away. Crowley was crying, just like Brooke – just like everybody here but me. Heroes in stories got to fight hideous demons with eyes red as burning coals; my demon's eyes were only red from tears. I cursed him then, not because his tears were fake, but because they were real. I cursed him for showing me, with every tear and every smile and every sincere emotion he had, that I was the real freak. He was a demon who killed on a whim, who left my only friend's dad lying in pieces on a frozen road, and he still fitted in here better than I did. He was unnatural and horrible, but he belonged here, and I did not. I was so far away from the rest of the world that there was a demon between us when I tried to look back.

'Are you okay?'

'What?' I asked.

It was Brooke, looking at me strangely. 'I said, are you okay? You were grinding your teeth – you look like you're ready to kill someone.'

*Please help me,* I begged her silently. 'I'm fine.' *I'm not fine, and I* am *going to kill someone, and I don't know if I'll be able to stop*. 'I'm fine, let's go back.'

I walked back to Mom. Brooke followed, her hands shoved tightly into her pockets, her eyes darting up to my face every few steps.

'Can we go?' I asked Mom. She turned to me in surprise.

'I'd like to stay a while longer,' she said. 'I haven't talked to Mrs Bowen yet, and you haven't seen Max, and—'

'Can we please go?' I kept my eyes on the ground, but I could tell everyone was staring at me.

'We started a new flower pile,' said Brooke, breaking into the awkward tension. 'There's one for Mr Bowen, and one for Mr Olson, but we started a new one for the victims we don't know about. Just in case.'

I glanced at her, and she smiled back, weak and . . . something. How was I supposed to know? I hated her then, and myself and everyone else.

People were still staring at me, and I couldn't tell if they were staring at a human or a monster. I wasn't even sure which I was any more.

'It's okay,' said Mom, 'we can go. It was nice to see you, Peg. Margaret, please give our regards to the Bowens.'

We walked to the car and I got in quietly, rubbing my legs in the cold seat. Mom started the car and blasted the heater, but it still took a few minutes before anything warmed up.

'That was very sweet of you to start a new pile,' said Mom, halfway home.

'I don't want to talk,' I said.

I could feel myself getting worse. Dark thoughts crawled over and through me like maggots in a carcass, and it was all I could do to quell them. I wanted to kill Mr Crowley, but not anybody else; the monster was confused, and rattled my mind like the bars of a cage. It whispered and roared, begging me constantly to hunt, to kill, to feed it. It wanted more fear. It wanted to possess. It wanted Mom's head on a pole, and Margaret's, and Kay's. It wanted Brooke tied to a wall, screaming for no one but us. Over the past few weeks I'd found myself yelling at it to stop, or hurting myself to hurt it, but it was stronger than I was. I could feel my control slipping.

We rode in silence the rest of the way, and when we got home I poured out a bowl of cereal and turned on the TV. Mom turned it off.

'I think we need to talk.'

'I said I don't want to.'

'I know what you said, but this is important.'

I stood up and walked back into the kitchen. 'We don't have anything to talk about.'

'That's exactly what we have to talk about,' she said, watching me from the couch. 'Your best friend's dad was murdered – seven people have been murdered in four months – and you're obviously not dealing with it very well. You've barely said a word to me since Christmas.'

'I've barely said a word to you since fourth grade.'

'Then isn't it about time?' she asked, standing up. 'Don't you have anything to say, about Max or your dad or anything? There's a serial killer in town, for goodness sake, that's your favourite thing in the world. We couldn't get you to stop talking about them a few months ago and now you're practically mute.'

I moved out of sight behind the kitchen wall and ate another bite of cereal.

'Don't run away from me,' she said, following me into the room. 'Dr Neblin told me about your last visit—'

'Dr Neblin needs to shut up,' I said.

'He's trying to help you,' said Mom. '*I'm* trying to help you. But you won't let us in. I know you don't feel anything, but at least tell me what you're *thinking* . . .'

I hurled the cereal bowl at the wall as hard as I could, shattering it. Milk and cereal sprayed across the room.

'What the hell do you *think* I'm thinking!' I shouted. 'How'd you like to live with a mom who thinks you're a robot? Or a gargoyle? You think you can just say anything you want and it will bounce right off? "John's a psycho! Stab him in the face – he can't feel anything!" You think I can't feel? I feel everything, Mom – every stab, every hole, every shout, every whisper behind my back, and I am ready to stab you all right back if that's what it takes to get through to you!' I slammed my hand down on the counter, found another bowl and hurled it at the wall. I picked up a spoon and threw it at the fridge, then snatched a kitchen knife and prepared to throw it as well, but suddenly I noticed that Mom was rigid, her face pale and her eyes wide.

She was afraid. Not just afraid – she was afraid of *me*. She was terrified *of me*.

I felt a thrill shoot through me – a bolt of lightning, a rush of wind. I was on fire. I was floored by the power of it: pure, unfiltered emotion.

This was it. This was what I had never felt before – an emotional connection to another human being. I'd tried kindness, I'd tried love, I'd tried friendship; I'd tried talking and sharing and watching – and nothing had ever worked. Until now. Until fear. I felt her fear in every inch of my body like an electric hum, and I was alive for the first time, and I needed more right then or the craving would eat me alive.

I raised the knife. She flinched and stepped back. I felt her fear again, stronger now, in perfect sync with my body. It was a jolt of pure life – not just fear, but control. I waved the knife and the colour drained from her face; I stepped forward and she shrank back. We were connected. I was guiding her movements like a dance. I knew in that instant that this was what love must be like – two minds in tandem, two bodies in harmony, two souls in absolute unity. I yearned to step again, to dictate her reaction. I wanted to find Brooke and ignite this same blazing fear in her; I wanted to feel this shining, glorious unity.

I didn't move.

This wasn't me.

The monster was entwined around me so fully that I couldn't tell where it ended and I began, but I was still there, somewhere.

*More!* it screamed.

My wall was gone, the monster's cage destroyed, but the rubble was still there, and somehow in that instant I found that wall again. I was standing in the rubble of a life I had built meticulously for years – a life I never enjoyed, for I had cut myself off from joy, but a life that I valued, joyful or not. I valued the ideas behind it. The principles.

*You are evil*, said myself. *You are Mr Monster. You are nothing. You are me.*

I closed my eyes. The monster had named itself now – stolen its name from the Son of Sam, who'd called himself

Mr Monster in a letter to the paper. He'd begged the police to shoot him on sight so he wouldn't kill again. He couldn't stop himself.

But I could. *I am not a serial killer.*

I put down the knife.

'I'm sorry,' I said. 'I'm sorry I yelled at you. I'm sorry I scared you.'

Her fear flooded out of me, the exquisite joy of connection drained away and the link severed. I was alone again. But I was still me.

'I'm sorry,' I said again, and walked down the hall and into my room, where I locked the door.

I clutched desperately at a thin veneer of self-control, but the monster was still in there, still strong, and madder than ever. I'd beaten it, but I knew it would come out again and I didn't know if I could beat it a second time.

That was how the Son of Sam had ended his letter:

*Let me haunt you with these words: I'll be back! I'll be back!*

# CHAPTER 16

New Year's Eve passed without incident – some fireworks on TV, some fake champagne from the supermarket, and nothing. We went to bed. The sun came up. It was the same world it had always been, only older. One step closer to the end of time. Hardly worth celebrating at all.

I watched Mr Crowley almost exclusively now, peeking out of my window during the day, and peeking into his at night. One day, helping out with chores, I stole a key to the basement, and I kept it in a tiny hole in the lining of my coat. I knew their schedule to the minute, and the layout of their house to the tiniest detail. Soon they left together on a combined shopping trip – she needed groceries, he needed a new faucet for the kitchen sink – and while they were gone I slipped in through the cellar door.

There was the maze of storage in the basement, leading to the upstairs rooms that I had glimpsed but never really walked through; there was the chair where he watched TV;

there was the bed they slept in. I left a note under his pillow:

GUESS WHO?

On Friday morning, 5 January, Max's dad arrived at the mortuary, cleaned and examined and carried out of the police van in three white bags. Crowley had slashed him up and torn him in half, and I knew the FBI must have cut him up further, looking for evidence. Mom would need a photo just to put him back together again. I stood on the edge of the bathtub and watched out the bathroom window as Ron the Coroner and someone in an FBI hat transported the bags into the embalming room. Mom and Margaret came out, and the four of them chatted while they made the transfer and signed the papers. Soon the men got back into their truck and pulled away. The embalming ventilator clanked into life below me, and I shut the window.

Mom was coming up the stairs, probably looking for a snack before they got started. I retreated quickly to my room, locking the door behind me; I'd been avoiding her almost pathologically since threatening her the other night. To my surprise, her footsteps bypassed the bathroom, the laundry room, and even her own bedroom. She reached the end of the hall and knocked on my door.

'John, can I come in?'

I said nothing, and stared out of the window at Crowley's house. He was in his living room – I could see the light on, and the blue flickers on the curtain reflecting from the TV set.

'John, I have something I need to talk to you about,' said Mom again. 'A peace-offering.'

I didn't move. I heard her sigh and sit down on the floor.

'Listen, John,' she said. 'I know we've had some hard times – we've had plenty – but we're still together, right? I mean, we're the only two people in the family who've managed to stick it out. Even Margaret lives alone. I know we're not perfect, but . . . we're still a family, and we're all we've got.'

I shifted on the bed, glancing away from the window to her shadow below the door. My bed creaked as I moved, almost imperceptibly, but I knew she'd heard it. She spoke again.

'I've been talking with Dr Neblin a lot, about what you're feeling and what you need. I'd like to talk to you instead, but . . . well, we're going to try something. I know this is crazy, but . . .' Pause. 'John, I know you love helping us embalm, and I know that you haven't been the same since we banned you from it. Dr Neblin thinks that you needed it more than I realized. He says it might do you some good to help again. You were a lot more . . . in control back then, anyway, so maybe he's right and it does help. I don't know. It's the only real time we ever spend together, too, so I thought . . . Well, Mr Bowen's body is here, and we're going to get started. You're welcome to come help us if you want.'

I opened the door. She stood up quickly, and I noticed as she rose past me that her hair was streaked with a little more grey than I remembered.

'You sure?' I asked.

'No,' she said, 'but I'm willing to give it a shot.'

I nodded my head. 'Thanks.'

'There are a few rules you need to know first,' Mom said as we walked downstairs. 'Number one, you don't tell anyone about this, except maybe Dr Neblin. Especially not Max. Number two, you do exactly what we say, when we say it. Number three . . .' We reached the embalming room and stopped just outside. 'This is a very gruesome body, John. Mr Bowen was torn in half at the trunk, and most of his abdomen isn't even there. If you feel like you have to get out, for goodness sake get out. I'm trying to help you here, not scar you for life. Show me that I can trust you, John. Please.'

I nodded, and she stared at my face for a moment. Her eyes were a mixture of sadness and determination. I wondered if she could see through my eyes like windows, into the darkness inside and the monster that lurked there. She opened the door and we went in.

Roger Bowen's body was laid out on the embalming table in two pieces, with a gap of five or six inches where his top and bottom didn't quite meet. His chest was marked with a huge Y-incision – shoulder to breastbone, shoulder to breastbone, and down the centre from the breastbone to what was left of his waist. The incision was loosely laced shut, like a threadbare quilt. Margaret was on the side counter, sorting the internal organs from the autopsy bag and preparing to clean them with the trocar.

I was home again. The tools on the walls were in their right places; the embalming pump sat obediently on the counter; the formaldehyde and other chemicals stood in festive rows along the wall. I felt myself slipping into familiar patterns – cleaning, disinfecting, stitching, sealing. His face was bruised, and his jaw was broken, but we rebuilt it with putty and re-coloured him with make-up.

While we worked I thought about Crowley, and how he'd collapsed in the street after killing Max's dad. He'd pushed himself too far, waiting until the last possible moment before killing, and it made sense. Letting time pass between each kill made him harder to track, and it gave the public uproar time to die down. People grew less careful again. This time though, it had almost been too long – he'd only barely managed to replace his failing organs and regenerate. Worse than that, he'd had a witness – me – practically in his grasp, and then he'd been forced to let me get away. That seemed like a weakness I could use, but how?

There was always the fear angle – he didn't want to be discovered and now he had been, irrefutably, and in demon form. He knew now that whoever had sent him those notes wasn't bluffing – and he'd chosen to chase that person down instead of hiding the latest victim's body, which proved how desperate he'd become.

But watching him that night revealed more than fear – it had revealed something about how the demon worked, biologically. I'd already guessed that his body was falling apart, but I hadn't imagined how fragile he was. If he could get that close to death just by waiting too long, then I didn't need to kill him, just stop him from regenerating and let him die on his own. A gash through his stomach, a bullet in his shoulder: these were wounds he could heal, perhaps in seconds, but his internal organs were different for some reason. When they stopped working, *he* stopped working. All I needed was a way to make sure that they stopped working permanently.

Using a photo, Mom and I finished rebuilding Mr Bowen's face and then started on the actual embalming. The body was too damaged to embalm normally, which made our job harder and easier at the same time. On the plus side, we only had to prepare half of the body for the viewing. The upper half would be dressed and displayed, while the bottom half and the organs were tucked neatly in a pair of large plastic bags, to be shoved down into the lower half of the coffin out of sight. No matter how someone dies, it's never a good idea to look into the lower half of a coffin. Even though morticians prepare the whole body for burial, they only need to make part of it presentable. If there's any of it you can't see already, the odds are you don't want to see it at all.

The hard part, of course, was that we had to inject the embalming chemicals in three different places: one in his right shoulder, and one in each of his legs. We did our best to seal the major blood vessels before pumping in a coagulant to close up the smaller ones, and then Mom began mixing the careful cocktail of dyes and fragrances that would accompany the formaldehyde. I hooked up a drain tube, and we watched as the old blood and bile drained safely away.

Margaret looked up at the ventilator fan spinning doggedly above us. 'I hope the motor doesn't give out.'

'Let's step outside just in case,' said Mom. 'We deserve a break anyway.' It was late afternoon outside, and already below freezing, so we retreated to the mortuary chapel instead of the parking lot, and relaxed on thinly-upholstered benches while the body slowly pickled in the other room.

'Nice job, John,' said Mom. 'You're doing great.'

'You are,' said Margaret, closing her eyes and massaging her temples. 'We all are. Cases like these make me want to break down and buy a jetted tub.'

Mom and Margaret stretched and sighed; they were tired and relieved to be finished, but I was eager to do another one. This kind of work fascinated me – the meticulous details, the precise skills, the exactness required for each step. It was Dad who first showed me around. He pulled me in at seven years old and showed me the tools, recited their names, and taught me to be reverent in the presence of the dead. It was that reverence that brought my parents together in the first place, so the story went – two morticians, desperate for living company and impressed by their mutual respect for the deceased. They treated their jobs like a calling. If either of them had been half as good with live people as they were with dead ones, they'd probably still be together.

I stripped off my apron and went out to the front office. My sister Lauren was there, obviously bored. There was barely anything to do, and she was playing Minesweeper on the computer while she waited for five o'clock. It was 4.54 p.m.

'They let you help,' said Lauren, not looking up from

the monitor. The screen turned her face pale and ghostly. 'I never could get into that stuff. It's much better out here.'

'It's a lot less lively out here, ironically,' I said.

'That's right, rub it in,' said Lauren. 'You think I want to spend my whole day in here doing nothing?'

'You're twenty-three years old,' I told her. 'You can do anything you want. You don't have to hang around here.'

She clicked on the squares in her little minefield, marking certain spots with flags and testing the area around them carefully. She clicked wrong, and the screen exploded.

'You don't realize what you have here,' she said at last. 'Mom can be a hag sometimes, but . . . she loves us, you know? She loves you. Don't forget that.'

I stared out of the window; the street was growing dark already, and Mr Crowley's house squatted menacingly in the snow.

'Love's not the point,' I said at last. 'We just do what we always do, and we get by.'

Lauren turned to face me. 'Love is the only point,' she said. 'I can barely stand to be around her, but that's just because she's just trying too hard to love us, and keep us together, and pick up the slack. It took me a long time to figure that out.'

A gust of wind blew past the window, pressing on the glass and howling heavily through the gaps in the front door.

'What about Dad?' I asked.

She paused a moment. 'Mom loves you enough to cover for him, I think.' She paused. 'So do I.' It was five o'clock, and she stood up. I wondered what time it was where Dad was. 'Listen, John, why don't you come over sometime? We can play cards or watch a movie or something, huh? Sound like fun?'

'Yeah, sure,' I said. 'Sometime.'

'I'll see you, John.' She turned off the computer, pulled on her parka and walked out into the wind. Icy air blasted through the door, and she had to fight to close it behind her.

I went upstairs thinking about what she had said. Love might be a strength, but it was also a weakness. It was the demon's weakness.

And now I knew how to kill it.

I grabbed my iPod from my room, still unused since I'd tossed it aside at Christmas, and got on my bike and started driving to Radio Shack. Dad's stupid present was going to come in handy after all.

When I first started stalking Mr Crowley I'd been looking for a weakness. Now I had three, and together they formed an opportunity. I thought about it carefully while I rode, pedalling carefully through the afternoon's thin dusting of snow. It was probably going to snow again that night, a huge storm. I could use that in my plan.

The first weakness was his fear of discovery, and with it his insistence on waiting so long before he killed. He would wait and wait, putting it off until the last possible moment. I'd seen it happen, and I'd watched 'the last possible moment' grow more and more precarious. I think this went beyond fear. He avoided killing as if he hated it, as if he couldn't bear to do it until biological necessity forced his hand. The next time he killed, I was confident, he would be on the edge of death, ready to fall right in. I wouldn't even have to push him over the edge, just stop him from crawling back out.

That was where his second weakness came in: his body was degenerating faster than he could fix it. The night he killed Max's dad he'd almost died, and if he hadn't had a freshly killed victim right in front of him, he probably wouldn't have survived. If I could distract him from his hunt, and lure him away before he had a chance to kill anybody, he wouldn't be able to regenerate at all. I imagined him desperate, unable to reach a victim in time, sweating and cursing and, in the end, melting away into a boiling puddle of inky black sludge.

I pulled up at Radio Shack, propped my bike against the wall, and went in.

'My dad gave me this for Christmas, and I've already got one,' I said, pulling out the opened iPod box and setting it in front of the clerk. I didn't already have one, but for some reason I figured it would sound better if I did. I really needed this to work. 'Can I exchange it for store credit?'

The clerk picked it up and opened the side. 'It's already been opened,' he said.

'My mom did that,' I said, piling on the lies. 'She didn't know about your policy. But it's completely unused – she turned it on once, for ten seconds, and that was it. Can I still exchange it?'

'Do you have a receipt?'

'I'm afraid not,' I said. 'It was a gift.' I stood still and watched him, willing him to say yes. Finally he scanned it over his register and looked at the display.

'I'll give you partial credit for it,' he said. 'Do you want a gift card?'

'That's okay,' I said quickly. 'I'll just grab something now and bring it up.'

The clerk nodded, and I drifted back toward the GPS systems. This was going to work. I was positive I could kill Crowley this way – just distract him long enough to stop him from regenerating, and he'd die. I'd already watched his body almost kill him once, and I was certain it could do it again. And I knew the perfect way to distract him: his third weakness. Love. He'd do anything for his wife – I'd even seen him answer the phone in the middle of an attack to talk to her. If he got another call, and something on that phone convinced him his wife was in immediate danger, he'd drop whatever he was doing and run.

And with the right preparation, I could send him some very convincing evidence.

Finally I found what I was looking for: a set of paired GPS handsets, each keyed to tell you exactly where the other one was. I checked the price, took it to the front, and set it on the counter.

The clerk looked at it oddly, perhaps wondering why a teenage boy would trade a cool iPod for a boring GPS set, but shrugged and rang it up.

'Thanks,' I said, and walked back outside. I felt

disturbingly eager now that I had a plan. I wanted to rush back right then and start my attack, but I knew I had to wait. I needed some way of hiding the evidence of everything I was going to do, so the police would never link it back to me, and when the time came I had to make the threat to his wife flawlessly believable. It would be hard to pull off.

But if it worked, the demon would be dead.

# CHAPTER 17

Sunday morning I approached the demon directly, in the guise of kind-hearted John Wayne Cleaver, and asked if there were any chores I could do. It hadn't snowed in a while, though the banks were still piled high on the sides of the road, and so my normal snow-shovelling had ceased. I told him I was working on my Home-Repair merit badge, and showed him the list of repairs I needed to work on, and we spent the day roving through his house fixing leaky faucets and touching up the paint on his walls. I made sure to oil the hinges of his bedroom door – that would come in handy. He was jovial the whole time, but I watched him carefully, and I could tell he was sick. His lungs again, maybe, or his heart. It had barely been a week, but he was dying again. He'd kill again soon.

There were a handful of car-related items on the merit badge list, and though his car wasn't having any problems he was delighted to let me change the oil and practise putting on the spare tyre. It was too cold for him to stay out with me long, however, and eventually he retreated inside to sit in a warm chair and clutch his chest.

I took the opportunity to hide one of my GPS handsets in the spare tyre-well, tightly taped to keep it from rattling around. I was gambling that he'd kill tonight, because the batteries wouldn't last more than a day. I tested it when I got home, pulling out my own handset and zeroing in on the car's signal. The map wasn't incredibly detailed, but it was enough to get by. His car showed up as a flashing arrow.

Kay made a trip to the pharmacy that afternoon and I watched the flashing arrow pull into the street, drive to the centre of town, and enter the pharmacy parking lot. I saw every turn, and watched as it waited for each traffic-light and stop sign. It was awesome.

Before she came back I sneaked into their back yard and climbed up the rear wall, clinging carefully to the bricks. This was the time for the demon's nap, and I listened to ensure that he was asleep. His breathing was regular, but punctuated by gasps and wheezes. He was getting worse. I taped a note to his window and climbed down, disappearing into the carefully-shovelled walks without leaving a single footprint.

NOT LONG NOW

I collected several items for my backpack, so I'd be ready to go at a moment's notice. I needed some rope or strips of cloth for Kay, and found what I needed in the demon's own garbage can: a set of old curtains, replaced at Christmas and thrown out when the new ones were finally hung up. I took one of them and sneaked it into my back yard, tearing it into long, sturdy strips and stashing them in my pack. I don't know if you can lift a fingerprint from a curtain, but I wore gloves just in case.

The demon woke up soon after, and grew more agitated almost by the hour. I could see him hobbling back and forth past his windows, stopping now and then to grab his chest. He gripped the couch with his other hand for balance, grimacing. He wouldn't last long.

Clouds grew black and ominous in the sky, and when night fell it came as a shroud of purest darkness that blotted out the stars. When the demon could take it no longer he went shakily to his car and drove away, looking for another victim.

It was time for me to meet mine.

I was already dressed in warm black clothes, wearing the ski mask to conceal my face, and gloves to hide my fingerprints. Pulling on my backpack, I slipped quietly outside. Mom was already asleep, and I hoped everyone else on the street was asleep as well. I wanted to sneak into the demon's yard through the back, out of sight, but that way would leave footprints in the unmelted snow. It was better to run across the ploughed street and up the shovelled walk where I would leave no trace. I had always been leery of being seen or identified while sneaking around, but tonight my paranoia was multiplied a million times. There was no turning back from this; I wouldn't be able to talk my way out of the things I was planning to do tonight. I checked the street a final time when I reached our outside door, reassured myself that it was completely empty, and dashed across. At least we didn't have street lights.

Reaching the Crowleys' house, I ran around the side to the cellar door, pulling out my key. It was pitch black inside, and when I stepped in and closed the door behind me I was completely blind. Producing a small penlight from my pocket, I found my way through the boxes and shelves to the base of the stairs. Rows of glass jars winked back the glow from my tiny light, and though I knew they only contained canned beets and peaches I imagined them full of pickled organs – kidneys and hearts and bladders and brains – laid out like specials on a grocery-store shelf. When I reached the stairs I slowed down, counting each step. I had learned earlier that the sixth step squeaked loudly on the right side, and the seventh softly on the left. I avoided those spots carefully.

The stairs let out into the kitchen, which appeared stark and colourless in the moonlight. I checked the GPS unit and saw that the demon was still driving, somewhere downtown. Cruising for victims, I supposed, or on his way to the highway to find hitchhikers. Whatever he wanted, as long as he kept moving.

I walked carefully down the hallway, my penlight extinguished. I was moving half by memory now, thinking back to the repair work I had done here on Saturday. The demon had given me a full tour of the house, and as my eyes adjusted to the darkness I recognized where I was and where I needed to go. The passage from the kitchen stretched backwards into the house, and near the back door the main staircase rose to the floor above.

The house was completely silent. I checked the GPS again – the demon was still driving. I went up.

At the top of the stairs I counted the doors and approached the second one on the right. The master bedroom. I opened the door slowly, wary of a squeak, but the hinges made no noise at all. I smiled, pleased with my foresight in oiling them. The room beyond was dark, lit only by a clock radio on an antique dresser. Mrs Crowley was asleep, small and fragile. Even with a heavy quilt to bulk out her form she looked tiny, as if her lifeforce had retreated for the night and her body had folded in on itself. The bed seemed to swallow her. If not for the visible rise and fall of her breathing, I'd have doubted she was even alive.

This tiny woman was what the demon loved, so much that he was willing to do anything to stay with her. I set down my backpack, held my breath, and turned on a lamp.

She didn't wake up.

I picked over the dresser, pushing aside glasses and jewellery boxes until I found what I needed: Mrs Crowley's cellphone. I opened it, walked back to the door, faced the bed, and began taking pictures with the phone – click, save, step, click, save, step, click, save, step, closer every time. It would have a nice dramatic effect when I sent them. I bent in close for the last photo, holding the phone just above her face for an extreme close-up. The picture was ugly and invasive; it was perfect. On to phase two.

I set down the phone, its creepy photos safely stored in its memory, and walked slowly to the far side of the bed.

There I stopped and stood over her, thinking. I couldn't do this – there was no way I could ever do this. My monster had already broken loose once, threatening my mom and drinking in her fear like a life-saving elixir. If I took this last step and went through with my plan, the monster would come out again – I'd be holding the door open and inviting it out. By so doing, I would relinquish all control of my darkest instincts, and there would be nothing left to stop it from going berserk and burning down the world. I didn't dare do it.

But I had to. I knew that I had to. I'd come too far to turn back, and if I stopped now I'd be sentencing a man to death. Whoever Crowley was hunting, he'd kill, because I wouldn't be there to pull him away. And if I didn't go through with it tonight, I'd never go through with it at all, and Crowley would kill again, then again, then again and again and again until there was no one left. I had to take a stand, and I had to take it now.

Drawing in a deep breath, I slipped the case off Mr Crowley's pillow and held it over Kay's head. I hesitated, just a fraction of a moment, while the monster raged inside me and pleaded with me, begged and swore at me to do it. This was what the monster was for, right? This was why I'd let it out in the first place – to do the things I couldn't. I stared at Kay a moment longer, apologized silently, and let the monster go. My hands opened the bag and pulled it over the old woman's head.

She stirred, startled into consciousness, but she was old and woke up slowly, and I had plenty of time to tug the bag down firmly to her collarbone. She grunted something, still half-asleep, and thrashed out with an arm. Her blow was weak. I reached out and ripped the clock radio away from the wall, popping the cord out of the socket, and bashed her in the side of the head with it. Mrs Crowley choked on a scream, turning it into a half-groan, and rolled towards me out of bed. I bashed her again, the thick radio slamming hideously into the pillowcase, and when she didn't stop moving I bashed her a third time. I hadn't intended to hit her at all, but her feeble resistance was all I needed to shock me into action. I was trying to knock her out, which always looks so easy in the movies – just a quick smack and you're done – but this was prolonged and brutal, smashing the radio into her head again and again. At last she was still, sprawled grotesquely on the floor, and I stood over her gasping for breath.

I lunged for her again, eager to finish her off – hungry for the visceral impact of weight on bone, and the megalomaniac thrill of forcing a victim completely to my will. I stooped over her but grabbed the edge of the bed at the last moment, pulling myself back and forcing myself to look away.

*She's mine!*

No. My ski mask was suffocating, just like the pillowcase on Kay. I ripped off my mask and gasped for breath, fighting for control. I leaned towards Kay again and had to wrench myself away, stumbling against the wall. I felt like I was playing one of Max's video games, fumbling with unfamiliar controls and watching as my character on the screen ran helplessly in circles. The monster roared again and I punched myself in the side of the head, savouring the sharp pain in my knuckles and the dull ring in my head. I fell to my knees, breathing deeply, and a haze seemed to fall over my eyes. I ached to attack again, and the monster laughed. I couldn't stop. I raised the clock radio again.

My hand stopped in the air, knuckles white around the radio, and I thought about Dr Neblin. He could talk me out of this. I could barely think, but I knew that if I spoke to him right then it would save my life and Kay's. I didn't think about the consequences, I didn't think about the evidence I was leaving, I didn't think about the confession I was about to make – I simply curled up on the floor, pulled out the business card Neblin had given me and dialled his home number on Kay's phone.

It rang six times before he picked up. 'Hello?' His voice was tired and scratchy – I'd probably woken him up. 'Who is this?'

'I can't stop.'

Dr Neblin paused for a moment. 'Can't stop? John . . . is that you?' He was awake almost instantly, as if recognizing my voice had flipped a switch in his head.

'It's out now,' I said softly, 'and I can't put it back in. We're all gonna die.'

'John? John, where are you? Just calm down, and tell me where you are.'

'I'm on the edge, Neblin, I'm off the edge – I'm over the edge and falling into the hell on the other side.'

'Calm down, John,' he said. 'We can work through this. Just tell me where you are.'

'I'm down in the cracks of the sidewalks,' I said, 'in the dirt and the blood, and the ants are looking up and we're damning you all, Neblin. I'm down in the cracks and I can't get out.'

'Blood? Tell me what's going on, John. Have you done something wrong?'

'It wasn't me!' I pleaded, knowing that I was lying. 'It wasn't me at all, it was the monster. I didn't want to let it out, but I had to. I tried to kill one demon but I made another, and I can't stop.'

'Listen to me, John,' said Dr Neblin, more serious and intense than I had ever heard him. 'Listen to me. Are you listening?'

I squeezed my eyes shut and gritted my teeth.

'It's not John any more, it's Mr Monster.'

'No, it's not,' said Neblin. 'It's John. It's not John Wayne or Mr Monster or anybody else, it's John. You're in control. Now, are you listening to me?'

I rocked back and forth. 'Yes.'

'Good,' he said. 'Now pay very close attention. You are not a monster. You are not a demon. You are not a killer. You are a good person, with a strong will and a high moral code. Whatever you've done, you can get through it. We can make it right again. Are you still listening?'

'Yes.'

'Then say it with me,' he said. '"We can make it right again".'

'We can make it right again.' I looked over at Kay Crowley's body, crumpled on the floor with a pillowcase over her head. I felt like I should be crying, or helping her, but instead I just thought, Yes, I can make this right again. My plan will still work. This will all be worth it if I kill the demon.

'Good,' said Dr Neblin. 'Now tell me where you are.'

'I need to go,' I said, and raised myself to my knees.

'Don't hang up!' Neblin shouted. 'Please stay on the phone. You need to tell me where you are.'

'Thank you for your help,' I said, and hung up the phone. I realized the clock radio was still in my other hand and threw it aside with revulsion.

I looked at Kay. Had I killed her? I tore off her pillowcase as brusquely as I had torn off my mask, and checked her head for obvious signs of damage. It felt fine, with no blood or breaks, and she was breathing shallowly. Seeing her face was too much for me, and I turned my head. I didn't want to think of her as a person. I didn't want to think that what I had just done had been done to a living, breathing human being. It was easier without a face.

The phone rang abruptly, startling me, and I glanced at the caller ID. Dr Neblin. For the first time it occurred to me that my call to him would leave tracks – evidence on his phone, and on Mrs Crowley's, that would lead the inevitable investigators back to me. I took another deep breath. There was no stopping now. Evidence or no evidence, I needed to kill the demon.

Thought of the demon flooded me with fear, and I checked the GPS. The car was still moving; I still had time. I closed my eyes to avoid seeing Kay and pulled the pillowcase back on, more gently this time, then picked up the phone to snap more pictures. The call from Neblin stopped ringing, and moments later a small beep told me he had left a voice-mail.

My pictures now were more elaborate. I took time to arrange the body in different poses.

She was sprawled on the floor in her floral nightgown, tiny blue hospital socks on her feet and a pillowcase on her head.

She was rolled onto her back, the busted radio displayed next to her head.

She was stretched out on the floor, my shadow falling ominously across her.

I pulled the strips of ripped curtain fabric from my backpack and tied her wrists together, as tightly as I could. Her bones were thin and brittle, and I thought I could probably snap them in half if I wanted. I realized that I was already squeezing with one hand, pressing toward the breaking point, and pulled away.

*Leave her alone!*

Gently, I stretched her bound wrists above her head and tied them securely to a radiator below the window. I did the same to her ankles, tying them first to each other and then to the foot of the bed. All the while I was snapping photos, shot after shot, and keeping an eye on the GPS set.

The demon's car stopped moving.

I dropped the phone and grabbed the set with both hands, eyes glued to the dimly glowing screen. He was on the far side of town, near where Lauren lived, at the corner of an intersection. I held my breath. He started driving again and I let it out. False alarm.

I peeled back the pillowcase just far enough to see Mrs Crowley's mouth, and gagged her with another strip of curtain. She was still asleep, and still breathing evenly, but I didn't want to take any chances of her waking up and calling for help. I took another picture of her face and then pulled the pillowcase back down. I had enough photos now. The monster snarled again inside my head – a picture of her arm, lying alone in the middle of the floor, would be so effective – but I struggled to ignore it. With one eye on the GPS I repacked my bag. It was time for phase three.

And then the demon stopped again.

The street corner on the screen was unfamiliar, but both streets were named after flowers so I could guess which neighbourhood he was in – the Gardens, just this side of the train tracks that led through town to the wood plant. He was very close to where he'd killed Max's dad; it was sure to be patrolled, and he was taking a big risk. Maybe he'd been stopped by a cop. I held the GPS unit in one hand and the phone in the other, waiting. The car was motionless. It was now or never. I created a text message, attached the first photo of Kay, and dialled in Mr Crowley's number.

MY TURN

As soon as I had sent the message I created a new one,

then a third, then more, dropping the GPS unit and using both hands on the phone to keep up a rapid-fire onslaught of horror. Soon I stopped sending messages altogether, just photos, one after the other in a step-by-step catalogue of everything the demon's wife had suffered.

I paused a moment to glance at the GPS screen and cursed loudly at the motionless arrow. Why wasn't he moving? What was he doing? If I didn't catch him in time he'd kill someone, and the whole plan – everything I'd done – would be wasted. I didn't want to let him kill anyone else – not even one more person. Had I waited too long?

The phone rang again, and I almost dropped it. I looked at the caller ID and saw that it was Mr Crowley's number this time – I had his attention. I ignored the call and sent him more photos: Kay sleeping, Kay hooded and gagged, Kay tied to the radiator. A moment later the arrow on the screen jerked backwards, turned, and came barrelling back down the road. The bait had worked, but would it be enough? I watched the screen intently, hoping at any moment that the car would slow down, or careen off the side of the road – any sign that his body was finally destroying itself – but nothing changed.

The demon was healthy, the demon was mad as hell, and the demon was headed straight for me.

# CHAPTER 18

The arrow on the GPS set raced closer. I looked around at the room – at the dishevelled sheets on the bed, the scattered mess on the dresser, and the beaten body of my next-door neighbour lying bound and gagged on the floor. I couldn't clean any of it up – I would barely have time to get outside before the demon came back, let alone find a place to hide. In a few seconds I'd be dead, and Crowley would rip open my chest and pull out my heart. After what I'd done to his wife, he'd probably kill my whole family too, just out of vengeance.

(Well, everyone in the family but Dad – good luck finding him. Sometimes it pays to be estranged from your psychopathic son.)

Yet even if I had given up, the monster inside me had not. I looked up from my fatalistic thoughts to find myself gathering my things – the GPS set, the ski mask, the backpack – and heading for the bedroom door. As my intellect caught up with my instinct for self-preservation I doubled back into the room, scanning the floor for anything I might have dropped. DNA evidence didn't worry me – I had spent so much time in the house for legitimate reasons that I could probably explain anything the police found. I told myself that the phone records could also be fixed somehow, and that I could still hide who I was. As a final action I turned out the lamp and slipped onto the dark landing.

The house was pitch black, and it took a moment for my eyes to adjust to the darkness. I stumbled blindly towards the stairs, my hand on the wall, not daring to use my penlight, then felt my way carefully down, one step at a time, until halfway down I caught a glimmer of light from the window on the back door. It was brighter outside, and I could see the trees in the Crowleys' back yard glowing white in the moonlight. Reaching the ground floor, I turned towards the basement stairs, but another light was growing in the front windows, pale yellow, and the dull roar of an engine swelled rapidly to an angry scream.

Crowley was back.

I forgot about the basement and ran for the back door, desperate to be out of the house before the demon entered. The knob stuck, but I twisted hard and a little button popped out, unlocking the latch; I threw it open, hurried outside, and drew it closed behind me as quickly and as quietly as I could.

The car screeched into the driveway, and the distant trees in the back were suddenly flooded with an angry yellow glare as the car headlights reached down the side yard and out across the snow. I heard the car door open and the demon roar, and I realized too late that I'd failed to relock the back door behind me. I was still crouched next to it in fear; if he checked it, I'd be dead. I wanted to open it again and lock the knob, but the sound of the front door opening told me I was too late; the demon was in the house.

Leaping down the few concrete steps to the ground, I ran to the corner of the house. Stepping around meant facing the glare of the headlights, where it would be impossible to hide, but staying here meant he would see me when he opened the back door. I took a deep breath and ran across the headlights, diving into the shadow of the garden shed.

There was no sound behind me. The back door didn't open. I cursed myself for being so scared of something so small – of course he wouldn't notice that tiny button on the unlocked knob, not when he was racing to rescue his wife. A moment later I heard a howl from the first floor, confirming my suspicions. He'd gone straight to Kay, and I might be able to escape after all.

I crept back into the light, furtive and wary, ready to run and convinced that, if he saw me, running wouldn't make any difference. I didn't know how much time I had. He might untie Kay immediately, or he might wait until he regained his human shape; he might stay and make sure she was okay, or he might rush back outside to find the person who'd hurt her. I had no way of knowing, but I did know that my chances of getting away decreased with every second I delayed. I had to go now.

I stuck close to the house, walking softly towards the blinding headlights, shielding my eyes from as much light as possible to make it easier to adjust to the darkness beyond. When I reached Crowley's car I ran out around the far side, away from the house, and crouched by the tyre. I could peer over the hood and see the front of the house: the door hanging open, the upstairs curtains still tightly drawn. My own house was a million miles away across the street. Ice and snow surrounded it like landmines and razorwire, waiting to trip me up or show a footprint or simply delay me as I ran for the shelter of home. If I could make it into my house I'd be safe – Crowley might never suspect I'd been involved – but it was a long way, across an open street, and all it would take was a single glance through the window and it would all be over. I braced myself for the sprint . . .

. . . and that's when I saw the body in the passenger seat.

It was slumped over, below the window line, but in the dim light of the open door I could see him – a small man, half-hidden in shadow and a drab woollen coat, lying in a pool of blood.

Numb with shock, I sank down to the frozen ground. I hadn't stopped the demon from killing at all – I hadn't even slowed him down. I'd taken too long with the pictures, and with Neblin, wrestling against my darkest impulses until it didn't even matter, and by the time I distracted the demon he had already found a victim and stolen an organ. He was already regenerated, and all because I couldn't control myself.

I wanted to slam the car door, or shout, or make some kind of noise, but I didn't dare. Instead the monster inside me, smooth and insidious, crept forward to look at the corpse. In all these months of killings and embalmings, I had still never been alone with a newly dead body. I wanted to touch it while it was still warm, to look at the wound, to see what the demon had taken. It was a stupid urge, and a stupid risk, but I didn't stop; Mr Monster was too strong now.

The driver's door was open, but I was on the passenger side, away from the house, and opened that door quietly. The dashboard was beeping with that 'your lights are still on' noise, but I didn't bother turning them off. A sudden change in the ambient light or sound might alert the demon that someone was here. It was sure to come looking for me in a minute anyway, but I wanted as much time as I could. I pulled open the body's coat, looking for the huge abdominal wound.

There wasn't one.

The head was twisted grotesquely, face planted in the seat, but when I peered at it from the doorway I could see that the throat had been cut, probably by one of the demon's claws. It was the only hole. The coat was undamaged, and the flesh beneath it felt fine. The blood on the seat and floor seemed to come solely from the neck wound.

What had he taken? I peered in to look at the neck more closely; it was still attached, but the veins and throat had been sliced clean through. Nothing seemed to be missing at all.

Finally I looked at the man's face, wiping aside the blood and matted hair, and in that instant I almost cried out.

The dead man was Dr Neblin.

I staggered back, nearly falling out of the car, while the body flopped slowly back to the side, lifeless. I looked up at the Crowleys' house in shock, then back at the car.

He'd killed Dr Neblin.

My mind searched for meaning in the revelation. Was Crowley on to me? Was he already targeting people I knew? But why Neblin, when my mom was right across the street? Because he needed a male body, I supposed. But no – it was too strange. I couldn't believe that he knew I was involved – I would have seen some hint of it.

But then why Neblin?

Staring at his corpse, I remembered our phone call and felt myself grow cold. Neblin had left me a voice-mail. I pulled out the phone and dialled it up, terrified of what I knew I would hear.

'John, you shouldn't be alone right now; we need to talk. I'm coming over – I don't even know if you're at home, or somewhere else, but I can help you. Please let me help you. I'll be there in just a few minutes. See you soon.'

He had come to help me. In the middle of the night in an ice-cold January, he had left his home and gone into the empty streets to help me. Empty streets where a killer was hunting for fresh prey and finding none, until poor, defenceless Dr Neblin walked right into his sights. He was the only man in town that the demon could find.

And he'd found him because of me.

I stared at the body, thinking of all the others who'd gone before – Jeb Jolley and Dave Bird; the two cops I'd led to their death; the drifter by the lake that I didn't speak up to save; Ted Rask and Greg Olson and Emmet Openshaw and how many others I didn't even know about. They were a parade of cadavers, resting inert in my memory as if they had never been alive at all, a row of eternal corpses stretching back through history, perfectly preserved. How long had this been happening? How much longer would it go on? I felt that I was doomed to follow that row for ever, washing and embalming each new corpse like a demonic servant, hunchbacked and leering and mute. Crowley was the killer, and I was his slave.

No. I wouldn't do it. That row of corpses ended tonight.

The demon hadn't taken any of Neblin's organs yet, which meant that at any second now, he'd come barging back out of his house, desperate to regenerate. If I hid the body first, he might wither away and die. Grabbing the body by the shoulders, I pulled it upright. My gloves slid wetly across the blood from the wound, and I let go abruptly – I was covering myself with evidence. I stepped back, fighting with my paranoia. Did I dare link myself to the crime? I'd been so careful – moving quietly, hiding my tracks, planning for months to keep myself completely distanced from any of the attacks, and from any of my responses to them. I couldn't throw it all away now.

But was there any other way? Hiding the body was my one chance to kill the demon, but I couldn't do it without getting drenched in Neblin's blood. If I tried to keep the blood off myself, by dragging the body by the feet, I'd leave a trail of blood that would ruin the whole plan. I needed to pick up the body by the shoulders, keeping all the blood on my gloves and coat instead of on the ground.

A sudden howl from the house cut through the silence. I dropped back, my eyes darting first to the back door, then to the front, back and forth, wondering from which direction the demon would emerge. Mr Monster, screaming in my head, told me to run, to get out of there, to get away safely and try again next time. That was the smart thing to do – the analytical thing to do. The demon would live, but so would I. I could stop him eventually without risking anything of my own.

My eyes fell on Neblin. He wouldn't leave, I thought. Neblin had gone out of his house in the middle of the night, knowing full well that there was a serial killer on the loose, because he wanted to help me. He did what he needed to do, even though it put him in danger. I've got to stop thinking like a sociopath, I decided. Either I endanger myself, or Crowley kills again. Two months ago, even two hours ago, the choice would have been obvious: save yourself. Even now I knew, empirically, that it was the smartest thing to do. But Neblin had died trying to teach me to think like a normal human – to *feel* like a normal human. And sometimes normal, everyday humans risked their lives to help each other because of the way they felt. Emotions. Connections. Love. I didn't feel it, but I owed it to Neblin to try.

As I gripped Neblin and pulled him towards me, I could feel his slick, blood-matted head slap against my coat and cover me in incriminating DNA. There was another howl from the house, but I ignored it, heaving the doctor out of the car until his legs flopped out onto the driveway. The body was heavier than it looked; I remembered reading that dead and unconscious bodies are harder to lift than active ones, because the limp muscles don't compensate for movement and balance. It made him feel like a sack of wet cement, ungainly and impossible to carry. I kept his head and shoulders pressed tightly against my chest, my arms wrapped under his armpits and locked across his sternum. Turning my body carefully, I balanced on one foot and kicked on the door with my other, getting it nearly closed before Neblin's arm fell to one side and his body weight shifted awkwardly. I fell against the car, clinging tightly to the body and trying to hold it straight. No blood had dripped down, at least not yet.

There was a crash from somewhere inside the house, as if Crowley had fallen against something – or shattered it in a fit of rage. I nudged the car door closed and turned until I was fully facing the street, then began reversing slowly into the Crowleys' back yard. I went cautiously, step by step, relying on memory to lead me safely past the line of neatly-shovelled snow without disturbing it or leaving any traces. Step by step. I heard another crash, closer now, somewhere on the ground floor, and gritted my teeth. I was almost there.

I finally reached the shed. It was only a few feet long, but there was just enough room for me to step around the far side of it and pull the body into the narrow gap between the shed and the wood-slat fence.

The back door clattered and I held my breath. Neblin's

feet were still poking out past the front of the shed, just a few inches. This whole gap was shaded from the still-bright headlights by a wall of snow and fallow bushes, so the demon might not see them, but if he came looking – if I'd left any kind of visible trail – he'd spot them for sure.

Who was I kidding? If I'd left any kind of a trail at all, Crowley would come straight to me no matter what I did.

I held my breath for ages, listening to every sound: the low rumble of the car, the soft ding of the dashboard, the beating of my own heart. Someone took a few footsteps on the other side of the shed, arrhythmic and weak, then stepped or stumbled into the snow; the top, frozen layer crunched under its feet, once, twice, three times, followed again by normal steps back on the cement. He was unsteady and slow. This might actually work.

I listened to the footsteps drag themselves down the driveway: step-stop, step-stumble. I didn't dare to breathe, closing my eyes and willing the demon to keel over and die, to give up and be done for ever. Step-stop, step-pause, step-grunt. It moved slower than it ever had. I stayed perfectly still, afraid to move an inch, and the cold and the snow and the bitter air began to take their toll on me. I felt again the same sense of physical breakdown I'd experienced when I first discovered the demon, hiding in the snow at Freak Lake, aware of each slowed heartbeat and faltering sense. My hands and feet were on fire with pinpricks, which faded to a tingling numbness, which faded to nothing at all. My body was a spent clockwork machine, softly winding down until the last gear turned, the last spring popped, and the whole thing stopped for ever.

Balancing carefully, with no good places to put my feet in the narrow gap, I bent down and slowly, imperceptibly, pulled Neblin's feet back behind the shed. Inch by inch, not making a sound. The footsteps on the driveway continued, halting and agonized. I tucked Neblin's knees up and quietly – oh so quietly – leaned them against the shed. A black shadow passed across the headlights, filling the fence and the shed and the yard behind me with the massive shape of the demon – a bulbous head and ten scything claws, with his heavy coat and pants hanging loosely over his thin, wicked limbs. I wondered if he'd even had a chance to change back to human form, or if he'd been forced to help Kay like this. He must be very close to death.

I took one delicate step forward, placing my foot carefully, and peeked around the edge of the shed. The demon struggled to stay on his feet and staggered around the car, claws scrabbling across the paint as he leaned on the hood for support. He worked his way slowly round to the passenger's side, paused for a moment hunched nearly in half, and reached for the handle. As his hand left the car he lost his balance and fell sideways into the snow, landing heavily. My breath caught in my throat, and my heart, already straining, sped up even further. Was this it? Was it dead? With a pathetic groan the demon rose to its knees, clutched at its chest, and howled inhumanly. It was not dead yet, but it was incredibly close, and it knew it.

The demon ripped off its heavy coat and lunged forward,

falling against the car. Its huge white claws seemed to glow, and it dug them into the metal with terrifying strength to lift itself back upright. A clawed hand reached for the handle, then stopped in mid-air. It stared at the car, unmoving.

It had seen the empty seat. It knew its only hope was gone. The demon fell to its knees and cried – not a roar or a growl, but a keening, high-pitched cry.

It was the sound I would ever after associate with the word *despair*.

The demon's cry then turned to a shout, of rage or frustration I couldn't say. I watched it take a step back up the driveway, then a step towards the street, too confused to choose, then collapse once again to its knees. Using its claws, it edged forward in a crawl, and finally fell flat to the ground. I felt like I hung in that moment for hours, waiting for a twitch or a lunge or a shout, but nothing came. The entire world was frozen and motionless.

I waited another moment, long and desperate, before daring to take a step out. The demon was inert on the driveway, lifeless as the cement it was lying on. I crept out of my hiding-place, never taking my eyes off the body. Faint wisps of steam drifted up in the night air. I walked slowly towards it, squinting against the brilliant onslaught of the headlights, and stared at it.

The feeling was peculair, like a visceral thrill building rapidly to transcendence. This was not just a body, it was *my* body, my own dead body, lying perfectly still. It was like a piece of art; something that I had made with my own hands. I was filled with a powerful sense of pride, and I understood why so many serial killers left their bodies to be discovered: when you created something so beautiful, you wanted everyone to see it.

It was finally dead.

But why wasn't it falling apart, I wondered, like the spent organs had always done before? If the energy that kept him together was gone, why was he still . . . together?

A flash of light caught my eye, and my head jerked up. Someone had turned on the light in our front-room window. A second later, my mom pulled the curtains aside, looking out. She must have heard the demon, and now she was looking for an explanation. I ducked down next to the car, out of the headlights and just feet away from the dead demon. She stayed in the window a long time before moving away and letting the curtain fall back into place. I waited for the light to go off, but it stayed lit. A moment later the bathroom light came on, and I shook my head. She hadn't seen anything.

The demon twitched.

Instantly my full attention snapped back to the fallen demon, so close I could practically touch it. Its head rolled to one side, and its left arm jerked wildly. I rose up from my crouch and stepped back. The demon flailed its arm again before planting it firmly on the ground and pushing up. It raised its shoulders, the head still drooping, then kicked its leg shakily to the side. It wrestled with the leg a moment before giving up and reaching out with its other arm. It was crawling forward.

I looked up just in time to see another light go on – this time in my room. Mom had gone in to check on me, and now she knew I wasn't there.

'*Do something!*' I shouted at myself. The demon pulled itself forward the full length of its spindly arm, then reached out with the other. Somehow it had managed to regenerate itself without an external source of body parts, just like it had when it killed Max's dad. Only this time it didn't have a fresh body lying a few feet away. The nearest source of organs was me, and apparently it didn't know I was there. Instead it was crawling . . .

Towards my house.

Its claws dug into the asphalt just beyond the gutter, and it started to pull itself forward again. Its movements were slow, but deliberate and powerful. Every move it made seemed just a little stronger, just a little faster.

Another patch of light and a burst of movement: my mom had opened the side door, and she stood in its light like a beacon, her heavy overcoat draped over her nightgown. Her feet were shoved into her high-top snow boots.

'John?' Her voice was clear and loud, and had the raw edge I'd learned to recognize as worry. She'd come out to look for me.

The demon stretched another arm forward, emitting an unearthly growl as it pulled itself closer to my house – faster now than before, and more eager. It was leaving black gobs of itself stuck to the asphalt, sizzling with unnatural heat as it decomposed in seconds. Mom must have caught a glimpse of the movement, for she turned to look at it. It was nearly halfway to her now.

'Get inside!' I shouted, and bolted towards her. The demon's head jerked up, and it reached out wildly with its long arms as I went past. I ran to the side, giving it a wide berth, but it heaved itself up to its feet and lunged for me. I stumbled to the side and the demon fell, missing me by inches, and slammed back to the street howling in pain.

'John, what's going on?' my mom shouted, still staring in horror at the demon in the street. We couldn't see it clearly from here, but she saw enough to be terrified.

'Get inside!' I shouted again, dashing past her and pulling her into the doorway. My gloves left dark red stains on her coat.

'What is that?' she asked.

'It killed Neblin,' I said, yanking her back into the house. 'Come on!'

The demon was back on track, crawling straight towards us with its brutal mouth of luminescent, needle-like fangs. Mom started to slam the door, but I grabbed it and forced it back open.

'What are you doing?'

'We have to let it in,' I said, trying to push her back towards the mortuary. She wouldn't budge. 'We have to make it easy, or it might go next door.'

'We're not letting it in here!' she shrieked. It had reached our sidewalk.

'It's the only way,' I said, and shoved her back. She lost her grip on the door and tumbled against the wall, staring at me with the same horrified look she had given the demon.

It was the first time she'd taken her eyes off the demon, and her eyes moved across the blood that smeared my chest and arms. The monster inside of me reared up, remembering the knife in the kitchen, eager to dominate her again with fear, but I soothed it and unlocked the door to the mortuary. *You'll kill soon enough.*

'Where are we going?' Mom asked.

'To the back room.'

'The embalming room?'

'I just hope it can find the way.' I pulled her with me into the mortuary lobby, flicking on the lights and hurrying towards the back room. The door banged behind us but we didn't dare look. Mom screamed, and we ran for the back hall.

'Do you have the keys?' I asked Mom. She fumbled in her coat pocket and pulled out a key ring. The demon bellowed from the lobby and I bellowed back, screaming out my tension in a primal roar. It staggered around the corner just as Mom opened the lock, practically dripping now as its body began to fall apart, and we burst through the door into the room beyond.

Mom ran to the back, fumbling again with her keys, but I turned on the lights and went straight to the side of the room. Coiled in a neat pile lay our only hope – the bladed trocar, perched like a snake head on the tip of its long vacuum hose. I flipped the switch to start it, and looked up at the ventilator fan slowly sputtering to life.

'Let's hope the fan doesn't give out on us,' I said, and

threw myself against the wall right next to the open hallway. Across the room Mom opened the lock and flung the door wide, looking back at me in abject terror.

'John, it's here!'

The demon burst into the room, reaching out for her with claws like bright razors, and I swung the humming trocar with all my might straight into the demon's chest. It staggered back, eyes wider than I'd ever thought possible, and I heard the wet slurp as something – its blood, maybe, or its whole heart – tore loose from its half-decayed body and slid down the vacuum tube. The demon fell to its knees as more fluids and organs were sucked away, and I heard the familiar, sickening hiss of flesh degenerating into sludge. The vacuum tube curled and smoked with the heat.

I backed away and watched as the demon's body began to devour itself, drawing strength and vitality from every extremity to help regenerate the tissues it was losing. The demon seemed to decompose before my eyes, slow waves of disintegration travelling in from its fingers and toes, up its arms and legs, then creeping darkly across the torso.

I didn't notice Mom come to my side, but through a haze I became aware of her clutching me tightly as we watched in horror. I didn't hold her at all – I just stood and stared.

Soon the demon was barely there at all – a sagging chest and a gnarled head, staring up at us from a man-shaped puddle of smoking tar. It gasped for air, though I couldn't imagine its lungs were whole enough to draw breath. Slowly, I pulled off my ski mask and stepped forward, presenting a perfect view of my face. I expected the creature to thrash out, driven mad by rage and pain and desperate to harvest my life to save itself, but instead the demon calmed. It watched me approach, yellow eyes following me until I stood above it. I stared back.

The demon took a deep breath, its ragged lungs flapping with the exertion. 'Tyger, tyger . . .' it said, its voice a raspy whisper. 'Burning bright.' It coughed harshly, agony tearing out of every sound.

'I'm sorry,' I said. It was all I could think of to say.

It drew another wheezing breath, choking on its own decaying matter.

'I didn't want to hurt you,' I said, almost pleading with it. 'I didn't want to hurt anybody.'

Its fangs hung limp in its mouth, like wilted grass. 'Don't . . .' It said, then stopped in a fit of horrible coughing and struggled to compose itself. 'Don't tell them.'

'Don't tell who?' asked Mom.

The hideous face contorted a final time, in rage or exertion or fear, and that excruciating voice rasped out a final sentence: 'Remember me when I am gone.'

I nodded. The demon looked up at the ceiling, closed its eyes, and caved in on itself, crumbling and dissolving and flowing away into a shapeless mound of sizzling black. The demon was dead.

Outside, snow began to fall.

# CHAPTER 19

I stared at the black mess on the floor, trying to understand everything that had happened. Just a minute ago that sludge had been a demon – and just an hour before that, it had been my next-door neighbour, a kind old man who loved his wife and gave me hot chocolate.

But no, the sludge was just sludge – some physical remnant of a body that had never truly been his in the first place. The life behind it, the mind or the soul or whatever it was that made a live body live, had disappeared. It was a fire, and we were its fuel.

*Remember me when I am gone.*

'Is it dead?'

I looked up and saw my mom; I became aware of her hands clutching me tightly by the shoulders, of her body just slightly in front of mine. She'd placed herself between me and the demon. When had she done that? My mind felt tired and dark, like a storm cloud heavy with rain.

'It was a demon,' I said, pulling away from her and walking to the vacuum switch. I turned it off and the white-noise whirr died away, abandoning us to silence. The vacuum tube was twisted grotesquely, melted into a smoking pile of noxious plastic curls. They looked like the intestines of a mechanical beast. The blade of the trocar was smeared with sludge, and I pulled it carefully, with two fingers, from the mass on the floor.

'A demon?' asked Mom, stepping back. 'What . . . why? Why a demon? Why is it here?'

'It wanted to eat us,' I said. 'Sort of. It's the Clayton Killer, Mom, the thing that's been stealing body parts. It needed them to survive.'

'Is it dead?'

'I think so,' I said, dropping the trocar by the vacuum tube. 'I don't really know how it works.'

'How do you know any of this?' she asked, turning to look at me. Her eyes peered up at my face, searching for something. 'Why were you outside?'

'The same reason you were,' I said. 'I heard a noise and went outside. *It* was in the Crowleys' house, doing something – killing them, I guess. I heard screaming. Dr Neblin was in the Crowleys' car, dead, so I dragged him away where the demon couldn't find him. That's when you came out, and it crawled over here.'

She stared at my face, my blood-soaked coat, my clothes drenched in melted snow and freezing sweat. I watched as her gaze left me to travel around the room, taking in my bloody handprints on walls and counters, and the steaming, muddy ash on the floor. I could almost read her thoughts as they played across her face. I knew this woman better than I knew anyone in the world, and I could read her almost more easily than I could read myself. She was thinking about my sociopathy and my obsession with serial killers. She was thinking about the time I had threatened her with a knife, and about the way I looked at corpses, and about all the things she'd read and heard and feared ever since she'd first discovered, years ago, that I was not like other children. Perhaps she was thinking about my father, with violent tendencies of his own, and wondered how far I was going – or how far I'd already gone – down the same path. She ran through it all in her mind, over and over, sorting through the scenarios and trying to figure out what to believe. And then she did something that proved, without question, that I didn't really understand her at all.

She hugged me.

She spread her arms wide and pulled me close, holding my back with one hand and my head with the other and crying – not in sadness, but in acceptance. She cried in relief, turning softly back and forth, back and forth, covering herself in the blood from my coat and gloves and not caring at all. I put my arms around her as well, knowing she would like it.

'You're a good boy,' she said, pressing me tighter. 'You're a good boy. You've done a good thing.' I wondered how much she'd guessed, but I didn't dare to ask. I simply hugged her until she was ready to stop.

'We need to call the police,' she said, stepping back and rubbing her nose. She closed the back door and locked it. 'And we need to call an ambulance, in case he hurt the Crowleys too, like you said. They could still be alive.' She opened the side closet and pulled out the mop and bucket, then shook her head and pushed them back in. 'They'll want to see it just as it is.' She skirted the edge of the sludge carefully and headed for the hallway.

'Are you sure we should call them?' I asked. 'Will they even believe us?' I followed her down the hall to the front office, walking almost on her heels as I tried to talk her out of it. 'We can just take Mrs Crowley to the hospital ourselves – but we'll have to change first as I'm covered in blood. Won't they be suspicious?' I saw myself in jail, in court, in an institution, in an electric chair. 'What if they arrest me? What if they think I killed Neblin, and all the others? What if they read Neblin's files and think I'm a psycho and throw me in jail?'

Mom stopped, turned around, and stared directly into my eyes. '*Did* you kill Neblin?'

'Of course not.'

'Of course not,' she said. 'And you didn't kill anyone else.' She stepped back and pulled open her coat, showing me the blood on the sides and on her nightgown. 'We're both bloody,' she said, 'and we're both innocent. The cops will understand that we were trying to help, and trying to stay alive.' She let go of her coat and stooped down just slightly to bring our faces mere inches apart. 'The most important thing is that we're in this together. I will not let them take you anywhere, and I will not leave you, ever. We are a family. I will always be here for you.'

Something clicked into place, deep inside of me, and I realized that I had been waiting to hear those words for my entire life. They crushed me and freed me at the same time, fitting into my soul like a long-lost puzzle piece. The tension of the night, of the whole day, of the last five months, bled out of me like an opened vein, and I saw myself for the first time as my mother saw me – not a psycho, not a stalker, not a killer, but as a sad, lonely boy. I fell against her and realized, for the first time in seven years, that I was capable of crying.

In the few minutes before the police arrived, while Mom went into the Crowleys' house to check on them, I took Mr Crowley's cellphone from his discarded coat. Just in case, I looked through Neblin's pockets and took his as well. I didn't have time to dispose of them properly, so I hurled them over the Crowleys' back fence and into the forest beyond. There were no footprints back there, just acres of unbroken snow, so I hoped they'd stay safe until I could get rid of them more permanently. As a final thought, just in time, I remembered my GPS set and pulled the second unit out from where I'd hidden it in the Crowleys' trunk. I hurled them into the forest as well, just as the first siren grew close enough to hear.

Soon screaming sirens were followed by flashing lights and a long line of squad cars, ambulances, a Hazmat team, and even a fire truck. The neighbours watched from porches and windows, shivering in their coats and slippers as an army of uniforms spread throughout the street and secured the entire area. Neblin's body was found and photographed; Kay, still unconscious, was treated and rushed to the hospital; Mom and I were interviewed, and the mess in our mortuary was carefully studied and catalogued.

The FBI agent I'd seen on the news, Agent Forman, interviewed Mom and me in the mortuary for most of that night – first together, then one at a time while the other cleaned up. I told him, and everyone else who asked, the same story I'd told Mom – that I'd heard a noise, gone outside to check on it, and watched the killer go into the Crowleys' house. They asked if I knew where Mr Crowley was and I told them I didn't know; they asked why I had decided to move Neblin's body, and I couldn't think of a reason that didn't sound crazy so I just said that it felt like a good idea at the time. The sludge in our back room we pretty much just told the truth about: that something had chased us inside, that I had tried to fight it off with the only weapon available, and that it had melted into something black and sticky right before our eyes. I couldn't tell if they believed us or not, but eventually everyone was satisfied.

Before they left, they asked if I needed to see a grief counsellor to help me deal with the simultaneous disappearance of two men I knew relatively well, but I said that seeing a second therapist to talk about my first therapist seemed kind of unfaithful. Nobody laughed. Dr Neblin would have.

By morning the story had spread and mutated: the Clayton Killer had killed Bill Crowley while he was out driving late, and then killed Ben Neblin on his way back to Crowley's house. There the killer had started to beat and torture Kay until her neighbours – Mom and I – noticed something was wrong and interrupted him. The killer came after us but ran away when we resisted, leaving behind nothing but the ubiquitous black sludge recognizable from the previous attacks. No one believed that the attacker was some kind of disintegrating monster, so we stopped bothering to explain it that way when neighbours or reporters asked us about it.

There were just enough loose ends in the story that rumours began to fly. There were no bodies for the killer or for Crowley, so of course they might still be alive somewhere – but I knew that the long ordeal was finally over. For the first time in months, I felt peace.

I imagine that more suspicion might have fallen on me if Kay hadn't been my staunchest defender. She swore to the police that I was a good boy, and a good neighbour, and that we loved each other like family. When they found my eyelash in her bedroom she told them how I'd helped Mr Crowley with the door hinges; when they found my fingerprints on the windows of her car she told them how I'd helped to check the oil and the tyre pressure. Every question they had could be answered by the fact that I'd spent almost every day at their house for two straight months. The only truly damning evidence was on the cellphones, but so far no one had found them.

Besides all of that, I was just a kid – I don't think they ever really took me seriously as a suspect. If I'd tried to cover up what had happened that night, I'm sure I would have seemed more suspicious, but by going straight to the police with everything, we seemed to have earned a bit of trust. After a while, it was almost like it had never happened.

I expected the demon's death to bother me more – to haunt my dreams, or something – but instead I found myself focusing over and over on its last words: 'Remember me.' I wasn't sure that I wanted to. He was a vicious, evil killer, and I never wanted to think about some of those things again.

The trouble was, there were a lot of things that I didn't want to think about – things that I'd spent years not thinking about – and ignoring them had never really gotten me anywhere. I thought it was time to follow Crowley's advice, and remember. When the police finally left her alone, I went to visit Kay Crowley.

She hugged me when she answered the door; no words, no greeting, just a hug. I didn't deserve it, but I hugged her back. The monster growled, but I stared it down. It remembered this frail woman, and knew how easy she'd be to kill, but I focused all of my energy on self-control. It was far harder than I want to admit.

'Thank you for coming,' she said, her eyes streaming with tears. Her right eye was bruised black.

'I'm so sorry.'

'Don't be sorry, dear,' she said, pulling me into the house. 'You didn't do anything but help.'

I stared at her closely, studying her face, her eyes, everything. This was the angel that had tamed a demon; the soul that had trapped him and held him with a power he'd never felt before. Love. She saw the intensity of my stare and peered back.

'What's wrong, John?'

'Tell me about him,' I said.

'About Bill?'

'Yes, about Bill Crowley,' I said. 'I've lived across the street from you both my whole life, but I don't think I really knew him at all. Please tell me.'

It was her turn to study me – with eyes as deep as wells, watching me from a time long past.

'I met Bill in 1965,' she said, leading me to the living room and sitting on the sofa. 'We got married two years after that. Next May would have been our forty-year anniversary.'

I sat across from her and listened.

'We were both in our thirties,' she said, 'and in those days, in this town, being single and thirty made me an old maid. I'd resigned myself to it, I guess, but then one day Bill came in looking for a job. I was the secretary in the Water Office at the time. He was very handsome, and he had an "old soul" – he wasn't into that hippie stuff like so many people were back then. He was polite, and well-mannered, and he reminded me a little of my grandfather in the way he always wore a hat, and opened doors for the ladies, and stood up when we walked into a room. He got the job, of course, and I'd see him every morning when he came in. He was always very gracious. He was the one who started to call me Kay, you know. My real name is Katherine, and everyone called me Katie, or Miss Wood, but he said that even Katie took too long to say, and so he shortened it to Kay. He was always moving – always doing something new and running from one place to the next. He had a lust for life. I set my sights on him after just a couple of weeks.' She laughed softly, and I smiled.

Mr Crowley's past unfolded before me like a painting, rich in colour and texture, and deep with understanding of its subject. He was not a perfect man, but for a time – for a very long time – he had been a good one.

'We dated for a year before he proposed,' she continued. 'He was a very slow mover. Then one Sunday we were eating dinner at my parents' house, with all my brothers and sisters and their families, and we were all laughing and talking, and he got up and left the room.' She had a faraway look in her eyes. 'I followed him out and found him crying in the kitchen. He told me that he'd never "got it" before; I remember it so clearly, the way he said it: "I never got it before, Kay. I never got it until now". He told me he loved me more than anything in heaven or hell – he was very romantic with his words – and asked me right there to marry him.'

She sat quietly for a moment, eyes closed, remembering.

'He promised to stay by my side for ever, in sickness and in health. In his last days he was more sickness than health – you saw the way he was – but he told me again, every day: "I'll stay by your side for ever".'

I don't think my mom realized that a new person moved in with us that day, but it's been with us ever since. My monster was out for good now, and I couldn't put it away. I tried to – every day I tried to – but it doesn't work that way. If it were that easy to get rid of, it wouldn't be a monster.

Once the demon was dead I tried to rebuild the wall and put my rules back in place, but my own darker nature fought back at every turn. I told myself I wasn't allowed to think about hurting people any more, but in every unguarded moment my thoughts turned automatically towards violence. It was like my brain had a screensaver full of blood and screaming, and if I ever left it idle for too long those thoughts would pop up and take over. I started collecting hobbies that kept my mind busy – reading, cooking, logic puzzles – anything to stop that mental screensaver from coming back on. It worked for a while, but sooner or later I'd have to put them down and go to bed, and then I'd lie there alone in the dark and wrestle with my thoughts until I bit my tongue and pounded my mattress and begged for mercy.

A few years before, someone had left an embroidered sampler behind at a funeral, and Mom had hung it on our wall: *Sow a thought and reap an action, sow an action and reap a habit, sow a habit and reap a destiny.* I'd tried to start with thoughts, but that hadn't gotten me anywhere so I decided that actions were the next best thing. I made myself start complimenting people again, and forced myself to stay far away from other people's yards. I practically gave myself a pathological fear of windows, just from forcing myself not to look in them. The dark thoughts were still there, underneath, but my actions stayed clean. In other words, I was really good at pretending to be normal. If you met me on the street you'd never guess how much I wanted to kill you.

There was one rule that I never reinstated; the monster and I both chose to ignore it for different reasons. Barely a week had gone by before Mom forced me to confront it. We were eating dinner and watching *The Simpsons* again. Times like that were virtually the only occasions on which we talked.

'How's Brooke?' Mom asked, muting the TV. I kept my eyes focused on the screen.

She's great, I thought. She has a birthday coming up, and I found the complete guest list for her slumber party crumpled up in her family's garbage can. She likes horses, manga, and 80's music, and she's always just late enough for the school bus that she has to run to catch up. I know her class schedule, her GPA, her social security number, and the password to her gmail account.

'I don't know,' I said. 'She's fine, I guess; I don't see her all that often.' I knew I shouldn't be following her, but . . . well, I wanted to. I didn't want to give her up.

'You should ask her out,' said Mom.

'Ask her out?'

'You're almost sixteen,' said Mom. 'It's normal. She doesn't have cooties.'

Yeah, but I probably do.

'Did you forget the whole sociopath thing?' I asked. Mom frowned at me. 'I have no empathy, remember? How am I supposed to form a relationship with anybody?'

It was the great paradox of my rule system: if I forced

myself not to think about the people I most tended to think about, I'd avoid any bad relationships, but I'd also avoid any good ones.

'Who said anything about a relationship?' said Mom. 'You can wait till you're thirty to have a relationship if you want – it would be a lot easier on me. I'm just saying that you're a teenager, and you should be out having fun.'

I looked up at the wall. 'I'm not good with people, Mom,' I said. 'You above everyone should know that.'

Mom was silent for a moment, and I tried to imagine what she was doing – frowning, sighing, closing her eyes; thinking about the night I threatened her with a knife.

'You've been so much better,' she said at last. 'It's been a rough year, and you haven't been yourself.'

I'd been more myself in the past few months than I'd ever been in my life actually, but I wasn't about to tell her that.

'The thing you need to remember, John,' said Mom, 'is that everything comes with practice. You say you're not very good with people – well, the only way to get good is to go out and do it. Talk. Interact. You won't develop any social skills sitting here with me every night.'

I thought about Brooke, and about the thoughts of her that filled so much of my mind – some good, some very dangerous. I didn't want to give her up, but I didn't trust myself around her either. It was safer this way.

Mom did have a point, though. I glanced at her quickly – the tired face, the worn clothes – and thought how much she looked like Lauren. How much she looked like me. She understood what I was going through, not from experience but from pure, uncluttered empathy. She was my mom, and she knew me, but I barely knew her at all.

'Why don't we start with something easier,' I said, picking at my pizza. 'I'll, you know, get to know you, and then move up from there.' I looked at her again, expecting some kind of derisive comment about how talking to other people was moving up from her, but instead I saw surprise. Her eyes were wide, her mouth was tight, and there was something in the corner of her eye; I watched as it developed into a tear.

She wasn't sad. I knew my mom's moods well enough to tell that. This kind of tear was something I'd never seen before. Shock? Pain?

Joy?

'That's not fair,' I said, pointing at the tear. 'Getting emotional with me is cheating.'

Mom stifled a laugh and grabbed me in a big hug. I hugged her back, awkwardly, feeling stupid but kind of content. The monster looked down at her neck, slim and unprotected, and imagined what it would be like to snap it in half. I glowered at myself and pulled out of the hug.

'Thanks for the pizza tonight,' I said. 'It's good.' It was the only compliment I could think of.

'Why do you say that?' she asked.

'No reason.'

As the weeks turned into months the investigation continued, and Agent Forman interviewed me several times, but never as a suspect. Eventually, when no one else died, they realized that the killings had stopped altogether, and Clayton County slowly crept back towards a semblance of normal behaviour.

Still, speculation was common, and the theories grew wilder with time. Maybe it was a drifter or a thrill killer. Maybe it was a hit man harvesting organs for the black market. Maybe it was a devilish cult that used the victims in unspeakable rituals. People wanted the explanation to be as big and flashy as the killings themselves, but the truth was far more terrifying: true terror doesn't come from giant monsters but from small, innocent-looking people. People like Mr Crowley.

People like me.

You'll never see us coming.

# ACKNOWLEDGEMENTS

This book owes its existence to many people, many of whom are (to my knowledge) not serial killers.

First and foremost I must mention Brandon Sanderson, who shut me up in the car one day and told me to stop talking about serial killers and just write a book about them. That turned out to be a pretty good idea. This idea was further developed and refined by a series of writing groups and critical readers, including (but not limited to) Peter Ahlstrom, Karla Bennion, Nate Goodrich, Nate Hatfield, Alan Layton, Jeanette Layton, Drew Olds, Ben Olsen, Bryce Moore, Janci Patterson, Emily Sanderson, Ethan Skarstedt, Isaac Stewart, Eric James Stone, Sandra Tayler, and Kaylynn Zobell.

In the professional realm I must thank my US editor Moshe Feder, my UK editor Hannah Sheppard, and my absolutely incredibly wonderful agent Sara Crowe. Without their help this book would still be okay, but it wouldn't be awesome and you'd never have heard of it. If you find that it is awesome, and indeed if you find it at all, you have them to thank.

Special acknowledgement goes to my loving wife Dawn, who supported me all through the writing of this book and then didn't leave me after she'd read it. Other family members who didn't abandon me include my sister Allison, my brother Rob, my mother-in-law Martha, and my poor parents Robert and Patty. To all of you let me please reiterate that this book is not autobiographical. I promise.

My final acknowledgements are these: thank you to the Muppets for teaching me to read. Thank you to Steve Diamond, who used to be important. And thank you to Kimberly Wall, who was present when I compiled this list. I couldn't have done it without you.